Luxor
Book of Past Lives

Julie Bettendorf

To My Buddy Adrian,
Love you much!
Julie 2015

This is a work of fiction. The events and characters described herein are imaginary and are not intended to refer to specific places or living persons. The opinions expressed in this manuscript are solely the opinions of the author and do not represent the opinions or thoughts of the publisher. The author has represented and warranted full ownership and/or legal right to publish all the materials in this book.

Luxor
Book of Past Lives
All Rights Reserved.
Copyright © 2015 Julie Bettendorf
v2.0

Cover Photo: Public Domain.
Author Photo by Erin Donohue. All rights reserved - used with permission.

This book may not be reproduced, transmitted, or stored in whole or in part by any means, including graphic, electronic, or mechanical without the express written consent of the publisher except in the case of brief quotations embodied in critical articles and reviews.

Outskirts Press, Inc.
http://www.outskirtspress.com

ISBN: 978-1-4787-4947-9

Outskirts Press and the "OP" logo are trademarks belonging to Outskirts Press, Inc.

PRINTED IN THE UNITED STATES OF AMERICA

Author's Note

I love Egypt. I love everything about Egypt; its people, its otherworldly beauty, its history, and most of all, its ruins. I have a degree in archaeology, and although I do not represent myself to be an archaeologist, I have had a passion for archaeology and history since I was eight years old.

In this book, it is my hope to make a little bit of history come alive for the reader. Not necessarily the history of the famous, but the history of the everyday ancient man or woman. This is the history that is sometimes overlooked and forgotten.

This is a work of historical fiction, the background of which is as accurate for the time period as I could make it. Many sources were utilized to form the historical framework, including writings of archaeologists and historians, both past and present.

Every effort on my part was made to ensure that the setting and the ruins are described in the book as they might have appeared in 1324 BC and 1874 AD. The small details of the ruins come from historical works of early travelers to Egypt, including members of Napoleon's team of scholars, and my own personal journey to this fabulous country. The exhaustive work of current Egyptologists provided much of the framework for the historical accuracy of this book.

In the ancient Egyptian chapters, I have used the ancient Egyptian name whenever possible, such as Ipet Isut (Karnak), often in combination with the site's current Arabic name. However, in Victorian era Egypt, I have used the Arabic or the Greek name only; as in Deir-el-Medina and Bubastis, respectively.

Each chapter is designed to be a kind of "window" into the past by the addition of minute details gleaned from countless historical accounts.

Some of the characters are fictitious, and the more famous characters are, of course, drawn from history. The descriptions of the characters are a matter of conjecture on my part, but they are based on information gleaned from analysis of the mummy (Tutankhamun) and wall decoration (Ay and Horemheb).

The italicized prayers recited by Nebamun, the lead character, come from actual translated words of the pyramid texts, the Egyptian Book of the Dead. This work was known in ancient Egypt as "the Book of Coming Forth by Day." I have edited the sections, names and so forth, in order to fit the story.

Although most of these texts were written in 1240 BC, after my 1324 BC time period, I don't think the reader will object if I use a little artistic license by including them.

Finally, I have included a last chapter entitled "Epilogue in Archaeology" which provides the reader with a small glimpse of related artifacts, tombs and ruins brought to light by those valiant archaeologists I respect so much.

These discoveries and others, together with the tireless work of archaeologists, Egyptologists and researchers help to provide us with a sense of what came before. It is to these men and women who recreate the past for us that I dedicate this work of historical fiction.

I hope you enjoy this book.

Ω Ω Ω Ω Ω

Prologue

1324 B.C.

The large white ibis floated languidly on the smooth surface of the Nile, its feathers silhouetted brilliantly by the morning sun. The bird stabbed his long, slender beak down underneath his wing, to scratch an early morning irritation.

A dusky brown ox walked down to the water's edge, his ears flipping valiantly at the flies already beginning to gather for their daily feast on his blood. The lumbering animal cast out his long tongue upon the cool waters and gulped the waters greedily to quench his ever growing thirst.

The incessant drone of insects filled the air with a current of low humming sound, as if massing for some large scale assault on the citizens of Upper Egypt.

It was very early morning, and yet it seemed no one was sleeping. All life along the Nile was in an eternal race to start the day before being beaten down by the merciless sun.

Karnak Temple, the Ipet Isut, that most esteemed of places, stood out from the simple scene, its many decorated columns standing as silent sentinels over the people walking underneath them. It is the largest religious house known in the world, upon which the mound of creation began.

Every so often, a busy workman would stop and admire the brilliantly painted figures of pharaohs, plants, birds and animals carved into the columns, or cast a glance upward to take in the blue vulture goddess Nekhbet, symbol of Upper Egypt, painted with wings spread, as if to envelop the sky.

This was Thebes, known by the name of Waset, the most powerful city in Egypt, a land guided by a divine principal of balance and cosmic order called Ma'at. For the people of Egypt, both good and evil forces were at work continuously upon their lives. It was up to the gods and their divine pharaoh to ensure that good would always triumph over evil.

Egypt has become history, and has been writing its history down in hieroglyphic inscriptions for almost two thousand years. Its great pyramids at Saqqara and Giza are already over one thousand years old.

The workmen who spent their lives pulling tons of stone up mud brick ramps to build the divine pyramid forms are long dead, their bodies interred in the simple necropolis on the plateau.

Many pharaohs are gone and forgotten, with only their battles and pieces of their lives chiseled into the walls of their tombs. It is only recently that kings are known by the name meaning *Great House*, the name of *Pharaoh*.

It is the ninth year of the reign of Tutankhamun, the boy king. Ascending to the throne at the age of nine, it is said that the great god Amun himself placed his hand upon the boy's neck. He was now eighteen and held all power over the known world. While the Gods controlled the heavens and the underworld, he held control over the earth that was Egypt.

It is the second month of the great Nile flood, Akhet, the time of the inundation. Waset is preparing for the Beautiful Festival of the Opet, and the romantic scent of the lotus blossoms float in gentle currents of warm air. The sound of a woman's laughter punctuates the silence as she drops her basket of pomegranate fruit.

Ipet Isut is full of workmen busily preparing for the sacred procession from Ipet Isut to the Sanctuary of the Southern Opet and back again. The ceremonial boats are being prepared. They will be taken out of the inner sanctuary, the Holy of Holies, by the high priests, to be presented to the common people outside the sanctuary.

These ceremonial boats will hold the golden effigies of the triad of gods, Amun-Ra, the most powerful god of the sun, and his wife Mut, and their child, Khonsu, each shielded from the common gaze by their own golden shrine. The festival will be a symbol of the bond between Tutankhamun and the gods.

So important is the Opet festival, that Tutankhamun has commanded the festival to be lengthened from eleven days to twenty-seven, in honor of his alliance with Amun-Ra. The great pharaoh commissioned a vast relief decoration of the sacred boat procession on the walls of the temple of Amun-Ra to commemorate the lengthened holiday.

The gods will travel in their ceremonial boats, carried by thirty priests, from the Holy of Holies in Ipet Isut, past the ceremonial quartzite stelae commemorating Tutankhamun's restoration of the old religion of Amun. They will continue their travels down the long avenue lined with sphinxes with heads of rams, the animals most sacred to Amun.

Their final destination is the Sanctuary of the Southern Opet. This is where the gods will rest in the sanctuary for two days, in order to begin their return journey home to Ipet Isut, where they will reside for another year. Along the way, lines of citizens will soon come to the boats with offerings to Amun and his family.

The men will bring fine wines from Mesopotamia and the Aegean, and ivory from Nubia. The women will carry baskets of corn, oil, and incense from Punt to be given to the gods in celebration of the bountiful year yet to come. This is a chance for common Egyptians to commune with their gods, to ask questions of the gods, and to determine their future.

Common Egyptians will be joined in celebration by visitors from other countries, all paying homage to the Egyptian gods. Men and women from Kefti, with their curly long braided hair come with gifts of wine and olives. Those from the land of Kush bring with them tamed jaguars and monkeys. Emissaries from Retenu will bring jeweled elephants and horses.

Near to all of this color and pageantry of Ipet Isut, a plain, dusty tent stands, lonely and seemingly out of place. The entrance flap lay open and mysterious, beckoning all who may be lost to come inside. This is a busy place too, a place not of life on this earth, but of death and rebirth. The vague shadows of two men can be seen moving about inside, making preparations for an eternal journey.

$$\Omega\ \Omega\ \Omega\ \Omega\ \Omega$$

One

"Whom shall they be called?" the high priest asked, pointing to the lifeless woman and small girl lying on the embalming table. The high priest, Nebamun, rubbed his bald head with lotus oil, in preparation for the mummification rites.

He was a tall, striking man with large black eyes, black as the underworld, made even larger and blacker by a masterful application of black mesdemet powder eyeliner. His solid chin made him look fierce, but there was softness about his smile which revealed his true nature. He was a kind, just man, and he was chosen when he was a small boy to be taught the rites of Anubis.

Today, Nebamun would become Anubis, the jackal-headed god, he who is in the place of embalming, the god of mummification and guardian of the dead. He would preside over the forty day ceremony of cleansing, embalming and drying out of the bodies. After the bodies were completely desiccated, they would be wrapped completely in many lengths of soft linen made of flax fibers.

In total, it was a seventy day process, after which the dead would live life in eternity, in peace and contentment forever. It was a long process, but over the years, Nebamun had grown accustomed to it. He rubbed his head once more with oil and dried his hands with a linen cloth.

Padi, his assistant priest and friend for many years, was very short, and had to strain his neck to look up at Nebamun. His eyes were very red and he blinked incessantly. The continued exposure to natron had damaged his eyes many years ago.

Like all priests, Padi shaved himself every day to produce the smooth shiny skull representative of the profession. Today, he had cut himself with the razor, and there was a jagged cut, clotted with dried blood on the very top of his head.

"The woman is Nasra, wife of Shimra the stonecutter. You know the man, I believe," Padi said.

"Yes, indeed. I met him when I visited Ta Set Maat, the workmen's village, next to the royal necropolis," Nebamun said. "As you know, all the houses are painted white, and they have small red doors, so it was difficult to know which house was his. It took some time to find it."

"How did you finally find him?" Padi asked.

"He came out to greet me, and Padi if he weren't a stonecutter, I would think he were pharaoh himself. Such a grand bearing the man had."

"And then what?" Padi asked. "Did you see his wife? It would have been enjoyable to see her alive, I am sure." The priest relished Nebamun's stories. He rarely ventured out of the confines of his house inside the temple grounds.

"No, sadly, I did not see Nasra. As you say, it would have been agreeable to see her alive. Shimra invited me into his very small house, only two rooms, with a cellar underneath. I remember him most for his kindness, the way he invited me to share a piece of bread and cup of beer with him. He was known as a servant of the place of truth."

"He must be a good man," Padi said. "And to have such a beautiful wife, she was a blessing from the gods."

"Yes, but now he is a man who will die before his time I think, especially when he has lost his wife. I understand his health has grown poor as well. I have heard of an accident in the tombs. His foot was crushed by a block of stone."

"The man is cursed it seems; so much calamity, in one man's life," Padi said. "It does not seem as though this man will live long indeed."

"But what of the girl; I remember Shimra did speak of a daughter, but I cannot remember her name."

"This girl is she, the daughter called Amunet. Both were found in a reed patch on the Nile…drowned," Padi answered.

"Pity; when the Great Nile floods, death can often be the result, especially for the young and innocent. Those who were once alive shall journey into the afterlife. It is the same for us all." Nebamun said. "We shall proceed."

He picked up the heavy black mask and noted with satisfaction the beautiful gold work on the eyes, and edges of the ears. It seemed alive. He felt comforted by the exquisite costume, to be worn to honor the woman and her daughter.

Nebamun smiled as he placed the heavy Anubis mask over his head. He rubbed more lotus oil on his hands and arms. He enjoyed this high honor of becoming more than a mere priest; he became the god Anubis on earth.

"Is your brother, Iramen with us?" Padi asked. Padi was a lesser priest, much younger than Nebamun, but Nebamun could see he held the promise of advancing to a high priest one day. Maybe with Nebamun's help, it could happen.

"Yes, Iramen is outside; as is common, my brother is once again unhappy with his lot in life. I think he is ill from last evening," Nebamun answered.

"He is drunk from barley beer, Nebamun. You are too forgiving of your brother. It is fortunate you and not your brother were chosen by the Gods to become the great God Anubis for the ceremony. It is only natural for your brother to be envious of you, since he is the lowliest among us."

Nebamun's face grew sullen, his mouth a thin line of anger. Even with his brother's foolishness, Iramen was still very dear to him.

"Padi, you must learn your place. I am happy you are among the priests, but do not ever accuse my brother again, or you will find yourself no longer a priest, do you understand?"

"Yes, I am sorry. It will not happen again," Padi said, shifting nervously on his feet.

"Let us just begin without Iramen," Nebamun commanded. "I am certain he will be here soon."

Nebamun held the pages of bound papyrus, known as the Book of Coming Forth by Day protectively in his hands. It was the book given to him by his uncle, and passed down from his family of priests, all the way back to when it first came in to being. As he opened the ancient pages, the sweet smell of lotus wafted into the embalming tent.

"Nasra, thou and thy daughter, Amunet shall reap the eternal harvest from the fields of Iaru, and from the fields of paradise thou shall be nourished forever."

Since Nasra and her young daughter died together in the

reeds, they would both be embalmed and become mummified together. In this way, they would awaken in the afterlife, mother and daughter, together again.

Nebamun and Padi stood at opposite ends of Nasra and Amunet. The embalming table was high with the head of a lion, and tall legs each ending in a curled lion's paw. Nebamun could easily tower over the table, but it was not so easy for Padi, who had to stand on wood blocks to reach over the bodies.

"Begin Padi," Nebamun commanded.

Padi began with the mother, Nasra. She was very beautiful, with skin the color of amber. She wore a coarsely made narrow dress of what was once white linen, now muddied and brown, held up by two straps at her shoulders. Her drenched clothing clung to her thin body.

Padi cut the straps and pulled away the garments, exposing Nasra's naked skin to the dry air.

"She is quite beautiful, Nebamun." Padi said. Priests were allowed to lay with women and even marry, though both Nebamun and Padi had chosen to serve only the Gods, and not mortal flesh. But that did not prevent Padi from dreaming of it.

"Yes, she is. Remember your sacred duty, Padi," Nebamun said, as if to read the lesser priest's thoughts.

"Yes, Great One," Padi said as he removed her sandals, exposing her gracefully shaped feet. "Her sandals are of papyrus and reeds. Her family is poor."

"We perform our sacred duties for all, Padi, both the rich and the poor. We must do our very best for her, to bring joy to her family in their grief."

Nasra's wig, made of vegetable fibers, once held fast to her head by pins, now lay askew to one side, caked with dark, thick Nile mud. Padi removed it carefully, and placed it on the wet, matted pile of clothing that once covered the woman.

"Great One, shall I remove her jewelry?" Padi asked. He held up her left hand, upon which was seated a small, beautifully made ring of blue enamel, fashioned with the design of a scarab beetle."

"No, just leave the ring where it is, my friend. I am afraid the mighty scarab did not help her in this world, but he may help her in the next," Nebamun said.

"It will be as you command. She also has a circle of braided rope around her wrist. Is it to keep away evil spirits?" Padi asked.

"Yes, it is as you say," Nebamun said. "It is a tradition among the poor. Again, I am afraid it did not help her much. Just leave it where it is."

Padi nodded. "I shall begin with the daughter now."

Amunet, her daughter, was very delicate. Her skin was of a much darker color than her mother's. She wore a simple tunic of linen, tied with a thin belt of woven reeds. Padi gently cut the belt and dress and pulled it away. The girl was barefoot, her tiny toenails now caked with dark mud.

"Great One, the daughter has a matching ring with that of her mother; and she wears an identical braided bracelet." Padi said.

"Again, we shall leave them in place, Padi. Let us begin with the washing."

Padi held an alabaster vase containing purified water

mixed with natron salt. The vase was beautifully decorated with figures of Anubis, painted in black. He splashed the sacred water out onto the naked bodies of Nasra and Amunet, and then gently placed his hands on the mother's body.

Beginning with her face, Padi slowly moved his hands over the surface of her skin, washing the sockets of her closed, deep set eyes, her graceful nose, beautifully formed mouth, and delicate ears. He ran his hands down the elegant line of her neck, down to her shoulders, across her slightly upturned breasts.

Padi traced gentle circles around the firm nipples, feeling the sacred water on her cold skin. He cupped his palms over each breast, cleaning in his gentle, circular motion. He moved down her torso, placing his finger in the deep cavity of her navel, massaged down her hips, and paused between her legs.

He poured a small amount of the sacred water between her legs and moved his hand upward, carefully taking his fingers and probing her genitals.

"Padi, remember your duty. It is not your duty to defile this woman, even in your thoughts," Nebamun commanded. "Do what you need, and no more."

"Yes, great one, quite so; I am sorry, I forgot myself for a moment. She is so beautiful," Padi said.

"Yes, well, I am here to remind you. Do not apologize to me. Apologize to this woman for your impure thoughts."

Padi very quickly finished washing the legs of Nasra. He spent only a short time on the daughter. Finally, both women lay clean on the embalming table, their skin still glistening from the sacred water.

Nebamun was satisfied. Padi was a good priest, he thought. but his immoral thoughts needed to be cleansed from his mind. Only with a pure mind and heart could he become a high priest. Nebamun thought with relief how he had never been tempted by the female form, never cursed with lust. He was pure in mind and pure in heart, in service to the gods only.

Nebamun slowly turned each page of the Book of Coming Forth by Day with reverence, looking for the perfect words to accompany this sacred ritual he had performed so many times. He found a favorite passage and began to read:

"Behold, these words of power are mine, and they shall come to me from wheresoever they may be, or with whomsoever they may be, quicker than greyhounds and swifter than light, swifter than shadows.

"Nasra let a path be made for you in the Great Valley, and let you have light to guide you on your way. Those who have lain down in death rise up to see you, they breathe the air, and they look upon your face when the disk rises on the horizon. Their hearts are at peace since they behold you."

Ω Ω Ω Ω Ω

Two

1874 A.D.

The brothers Karim and Abdul Abd el Amun crouched like spiders and moved slowly down the narrow passage. They were both deeply tanned and very skinny, giving off the appearance of spindly other-worldly creatures as they painstakingly advanced through the blackness.

They carried small torches, but these were not enough to illuminate more than a few feet in front of them. They believed they were the first to enter this tomb in over three thousand years.

"Do you have the book fool?" Karim asked. "You'd better have brought the book Abdul. It took a full two months of work to buy it."

On most trips, the brothers carried with them "The Book of Buried Pearls," written in Arabic centuries ago by another treasure seeker. The book was like a treasure map, detailing the locations of countless tombs and riches beneath the sands of Egypt.

"Karim, this passageway is not in the book, so I didn't think we'd need it," Abdul said. He ran his fingers through his thick, black curly mop of hair, to soothe his own inner frustration at being so thoughtless.

"You are always the idiot brother. Suppose we don't find anything. We may want to go to another tomb. You just don't think, do you brother?' Karim asked, pointing one of his bony fingers at Abdul's forehead. Karim's black glistening eyes stared out at him in the darkness.

In fact, the brothers found this tomb themselves, without the help of the magical book, while digging a new garbage pit near their home in the village of Gourna. It was all they could do to keep the location a secret from their neighbors. Friends were no longer friends when treasure was at stake.

This wasn't a rich tomb by any means. The brothers knew they would find very few precious stones or gold; no trappings fit for kings. No, this was a communal tomb, not like the royal tombs in the valley.

This tomb had none of the fine decoration on the walls. In fact, the walls were not finished. There was none of the fine plaster, mixed with egg white to coat the limestone and make a smooth surface. Instead, these walls were still interspersed with fossilized shells and flint pieces, left there from the beginning of the world.

This was the tomb of the poor people in which the bodies of common laborers were stacked halfway to the ceiling. The dead formed their own layer of stratified humanity, with the ancient deceased forming the lowest layer, all the way up to the current residents of Gourna. The uppermost layers could have been placed in the tomb yesterday.

Today, the brothers were in search of something other than gold and jewels to sell. Karim and Abdul wanted the mummified bodies, the linen wrappings and whatever amulets or small trinkets they might find wrapped up inside the mummies. They would sell them to Rahmad, a shopkeeper and antiquities dealer in downtown Luxor. Rahmad bought everything he could get his filthy hands on, including mummies.

Rahmad knew there was a market in mummies; mummies to be ground up and pulverized into a fine beige powder. Wealthy travelers from around the world came to his small shop in Luxor, convinced the powder would cure them of disease.

"The dust; it's the dust, making me cough. I feel like I'm going to choke to death," Abdul said, coughing into his sleeve. He wiped his mouth with the dirt-caked corner of the same sleeve, and then wiped a dirty green substance from the corner of his nose.

"Damn it to hell! Will you just try and keep up? We have much to do and not a lot of time before people will be about," Karim said.

"But the sand is coming in. I can barely set a foot anywhere," Abdul said. Indeed, the sand was slowly filtering down the narrow walls of the passageway and settling underfoot.

"Stop complaining. We're almost there," Karim said.

"I hope to God, or I might just suffocate right here," Abdul replied.

Karim moved ahead faster. He could sense more air movement from up ahead, possibly from a larger room; he also wanted to put some distance between himself and his brother.

Abdul soon lost sight of his brother in the gloom. *What if I die down here?* he thought. *No one would ever know.* He had a fleeting thought of what it would be like to be entombed forever underground…all alone.

"Abdul, come quickly, you must see this," Karim said.

Abdul picked up his pace, partly from curiosity and partly from fear, still coughing from the dust caked in his nostrils. Soon he joined Karim in a large cavernous chamber. Even with the dim light of the torches, the brothers could see mummies lying all around them. The mummies were stacked one upon the other, sometimes up to chest height.

The air was a little clearer in the chamber, and the brothers could breathe a little easier. However, the air was still drenched with the scent of age…the scent of death.

"God, what's that smell?" Abdul asked, holding his sleeve to his nose. "Is that stench coming from the mummies?"

"You won't even care about the smell when you are scooping up the money we are going to make," Karim said.

"I can almost taste the mummies; the smell of them is coming into my mouth," Abdul said.

"Oh shut up, damn you. Perhaps you'd rather have stayed at home with our mother?" Karim asked.

"We could have done something other than tomb robbing, brother; something more honorable maybe? We could have been guides or something. Then we could have provided for mother, maybe?" Abdul asked.

"No, we can't. Our father was a tomb robber, and his father before him, and so on, and so on. It's in our blood. We have to do it. And as for mother, she can provide for herself, like she always has."

"I suppose so, Abdul said, nodding. The brothers began their slow circuit around the room. Not only were mummies stacked chest high, but they also were standing, leaning against the walls. Hundreds and hundreds of them, their faceless, shapeless bodies looking like eerie grey soldiers guarding the dead.

Abdul yelled loudly as a group of three standing mummies suddenly tottered forward and fell with a crash at his feet.

"We will be cursed, I'm telling you!" Abdul shouted.

"You are a fool. It is only the shifting sand beneath our feet that caused them to move. No one has walked in this chamber for thousands of years," Karim said.

Abdul seemed satisfied with his brother's explanation, and began to pick his way through the mummies, in search of the glint of gold or the sparkle of precious stones.

"Stop looking around and get moving, Abdul. You won't find any gold here, only the mummies. Let's get what we came here for."

"How do you know? In the time of the pharaohs, sometimes the royal mummies were moved to keep them from being stolen. I just might find something worthy of a pharaoh, not just these dusty, stinky mummies."

Abdul stepped between two mummies, and bent over to pick up something shining in the dark. "See, I told you, a scarab, bringer of good luck," he said, "made of lapis, I think," he said, putting the three-thousand year old stone beetle into his pocket. He stood up, and tried to move, catching his foot beneath the shoulder of one of the dead.

"He's got me. I'm going to die here, I'm telling you!" he screamed.

Karim looked at his brother with icy menace. "If you don't shut up, I'll kill you myself," Karim said. "You sound like a woman! Just stay calm and twist your foot around. Then try to pull it out. Now is no time to be scared brother."

Abdul slowly twisted his thin, gnarled foot around and pulled gently at first. He pulled his foot harder, but still couldn't move. Scared half out of his wits, he reached down and tried to move the dead body and extricate himself. He knew his brother would not hesitate to leave him alone, down in the tomb.

Abdul reached back into his pocket and took out the scarab beetle. *It would have been nice to keep this*, he thought. He placed the scarab back on the mummy and looked at it again lying there sparkling in the dark. "Maybe I can find you again later," he said to the scarab.

With one last firm pull, his foot was free; caught off balance, Abdul fell on top of a group of mummies. He felt the sickening crunch as his weight broke the fragile human remains, raising a cloud of dust in the blackness. He stood up with difficulty, wiping the dust from his face.

"You are so stupid," Karim said and began to laugh.

"What's so funny? I could have been hurt, you bastard, and I know you would not want to carry me." Abdul said.

"That's right, I wouldn't carry you; I'd just leave you down here with our dead relatives. You look just like one of them, so no one would know the difference."

Abdul's half-naked body was now covered in mummy dust, and he could smell the stench of the dead all around him. He knew his thin figure seen in the dim light must look exactly like his brother said. *He must look like he belonged here...like he was dead.*

"Come on Abdul, let's get this over with so we can make some money," Karim said.

"I *really* want to get out of here, brother."

"We can't leave until we get to work and find something to sell. You know that Abdul. So stop wasting time and get to work."

Karim crouched down and placed his hands around the head of one of the mummies. "Watch and see how it is done," he said to Abdul.

With some expertise, Karim twisted the head in a counterclockwise motion. Then he stopped and twisted the head completely around clockwise. He pulled the head forward and then backward on its mummified neck. Karim pulled hard and with one swift movement, the head came off of the neck and was free in his hands.

"Look Abdul," he said, holding up the head. "This looks just like you," he said laughing. He dropped the head unceremoniously into his linen sack. "I have become a collector of souls."

Karim continued in the same fashion with the arms and then the legs of the mummy until all of the limbs were free of the torso. He placed the mummified limbs into the sack to join the head.

"See, now that's how it's done. You start with that one over there," Karim said, pointing to a large linen-wrapped shape in the corner.

Abdul was disgusted with the prospect of dismembering the dead, but he needed the money the mummified parts would bring. He crouched next to the shape and examined it closely.

The shape was actually two mummies, wrapped together. He could make out the shape of a small child, cradled beneath the adult's left arm. He imagined in his mind that they must be related, and that this was a mother and her child; they must have died together and been wrapped up together for eternity.

"There's some writing here, Karim. Looks like hieroglyphs," Abdul noticed, pointing to the ancient message written in black on the top layer of linen.

"So what's it say? You've studied hieroglyphics, right brother?"

The brothers were poor and had never been to the one room, mud brick school in Gourna. Instead, their mother, Satre, made them work. While the other boys of Gourna were learning to read and write, the brothers Abd el Amun were perfecting their craft of robbing tombs. Abdul would have liked to read the inscription, but all he could do was stare at it.

"It was written with a reed pen I think, with some kind of dark ink. It's probably a curse," Abdul said. "I think we should leave them alone." In truth, he couldn't bear the thought of disturbing these two souls, united in death.

"That's it. That's your one mummy brother. We won't disturb that one, but no more talking of leaving things alone, right? These mummies are ours for the taking," Karim said. He didn't want to admit it, but Abdul's talk of a curse was getting under his skin. *What if it was true?* he thought. *People died suddenly all the time in Gourna. No one knew why.*

Abdul chose a mummy nearby and began using Karim's technique to separate the parts. He shivered at the cracking sound as the limbs tore away from their joints, but he hid his disgust from his ever-watchful brother.

The brothers spent most of the day down in the burial chamber, separating the ancient bones and placing the mummy pieces in their linen sacks. They were careful to include all of the wrappings they could find, so their mother could use them for lighting cooking fires. The mummy wrapping was coated with a thick, hard resin which made a nice hot flame.

Once again, the brothers assumed their spider-like posture and ascended the narrow passageway, struggling with the weight of their burdens. Their bulging sacks dragged behind them, making a deep trail in the sand.

Abdul was glad to be leaving. The mummies unnerved him, made him think only of death and how they would both die one day. Unlike the mummies, no one would take any care with their bodies, or even remember them. They would be gone forever.

He wished Karim would think of a different way to make money. Karim could always think of things to do; he was the smart one in the family. But selling the mummies made them the most money they'd ever had and gave them both some chance at a meager life.

The mummies didn't bother Karim, after all, they were dead, and the dead wouldn't need their bodies or their jewels. He didn't believe in life after death. This life was all there was and they had to make the most of it.

The brothers could come and go as they pleased and no one would ever know. They could become expert tomb robbers and live off of the ancient dead for many years.

The two brothers were quiet with their own thoughts as they advanced up toward the light. Karim dreamed of the future splendors he would uncover and the richness of his future life. Abdul's thoughts were less complex. He dreamed merely of getting as far away as possible from the both the living and the dead of Gourna.

Ω Ω Ω Ω Ω

Three

"Please begin Padi," Nebamun commanded, as he adjusted the heavy Anubis mask more securely on his shoulders.

"Yes Great One, but should we not wait longer for your brother?" Padi asked. He was hesitant to begin the arduous process of mummification without the help of Iramen. It was Padi's task to perform the special skills of head mummification and closure of the skin. *Surely, Nebamun cannot want me to disembowel them as well?"* Padi thought.

"I have heard enough of Iramen. The gods will punish him, Padi, not us. Now, proceed. We are losing precious hours of the morning." He was becoming irritated at the delay; it was going to be a sweltering day, and the longer they waited, the hotter it became.

Padi sighed and began with the mother. He looked at her face carefully. It was his duty to preserve her beauty for many years to come. He sighed again as he grasped a long, slender chisel and swiftly forced the instrument up through the left nostril of the dead woman; with satisfaction, he heard the cracking sound as the sharp point pierced the inner bones of her nose.

He picked up a small spatula which he expertly twisted back and forth within the opening and after several twists he pulled the small spatula out. Padi examined it carefully and touched the gelatinous blood clinging to it.

"Do you believe your brother is outside?" Padi asked. "Iramen should be in here with us. I will be finished with the woman soon, and we need him."

"Yes, he is getting sick outside, do you not hear him?" Nebamun asked. "I tell you Padi, he will be joining us in a moment."

Padi turned his head toward the opening of the tent. He listened and could indeed hear the sound of retching and moaning coming from somewhere outside. "Are you sure he is not too ill?" Padi asked. "I am concerned he will not be able to perform his task."

"I *know* he will be here. You must continue Padi. As I said, the morning will soon be over and we want Nasra and Amunet fully cleansed before the sun becomes too hot and they begin to rot. We must preserve their bodies fully for their soul to find them in the afterlife," Nebamun cautioned.

Padi nodded and reached for his next instrument. This was a long, delicate spiral shaped rod ending in a small spoon. He thrust the new implement into the same nostril and swiped inside the cavity created earlier. He drew out the rod and once again examined the contents.

He tapped the spoon on the edge of a brown clay bowl nearby, releasing the mixture of brain matter, blood and secretions into the vessel. Again and again he repeated the long and repetitive process, bringing out more of the dead woman's brain.

Next he used a long hook, which he inserted into the nasal cavity. He again twisted it expertly up further into the brain, moved it back and forth several times, and drew it out.

He grabbed the bowl containing the brain matter and placed it next to the dead woman's head. Turning her head to the side, he could see the steady trickle of liquid, all that was left of Nasra's brain. Padi carefully caught the liquid in the bowl, so the remains of her brain were all together again.

With a smile of satisfaction that he had done his best for Nasra, he poured palm wine into the nostril, which by now was quite large. Turning the head back and forth gently, Padi let the palm wine do its work, cleaning the inside of her skull.

He carefully wiped his instruments free of the blood and brain matter, especially the hook. He was going to need it again.

Padi reached for a thin linen strip, and using the hook, he dipped it into a bowl of heated resin, pulling it out so that the excess dripped back in to the bowl. Using the hook, he deftly forced the soaked linen up into Nasra's empty skull.

"I am finished, Nebamun. Is your brother still outside?" Padi asked.

"Just begin on the girl. I am telling you he will be here soon." By now, Nebamun was intensely irritated both with Padi's continuing questions, and his brother's inconsiderate absence. *We need to finish soon*, he thought. *It will soon be an inferno in this tent.*

Padi shrugged. It was not for him to decide, only to obey the will of Anubis, even if Anubis was really his friend Nebamun.

"What shall the daughter be called?" Nebamun asked, although he already knew her name. To say the name of dead many times ensured that the spirit would find its way back to the body.

"The girl is called Amunet, daughter of Shimra and Nasra," Padi answered.

"*Amunet, let a path be made for you in the Great Valley, and let you have light to guide you on your way. Those who have lain down in death rise up to see you, they breathe the air, and they look upon your face when the disk rises on the horizon. Their hearts are at peace since they behold you,*" Nebamun intoned.

Padi looked at the girl tentatively; she was small, much too small for the hook he used on the mother. Something else would have to be found. He glanced at Nebamun.

"Anubis, please grant me the usage of your arm ornament," he asked.

Nebamun slipped off the finely made gold coil decorating his upper arm and handed it to Padi. It was Nebamun's favorite, but it must be sacrificed in order to complete the brain removal on the girl.

To perform incomplete mummification on the pair would mean Nasra and Amunet would not be granted admittance to the afterlife, and he and Padi would not be paid for their services.

Padi uncoiled the bracelet and straightened out the metal, leaving a small hook at the end.

"This will work," he said.

Once equipped with the small hook, Padi quickly went about his business. The girl was much easier than her mother;

there was far less brain matter to be removed and within a short time, he was finished.

"You did not wait for me. I am not important enough for you, I guess," Iramen said, stumbling awkwardly into the room. He wiped a dribble of vomit from his mouth with one hand, while adjusting his loincloth with the other.

Iramen was older brother to Nebamun, which made things all the worse for him. He was shorter than his brother, much less godlike. Many called him ugly, with his hook nose and flabby skin that hung around his neck and arms.

His body was soft, his muscles unused to being challenged by activity. He was the very picture of a man who spent his evenings drinking himself to death. It seemed the only thing he had in common with Nebamun was a shaved head.

I should be Anubis, reading from the book; instead I am performing the lowest function among the embalmers, Iramen thought. It was Iramen's task to eviscerate the dead, removing the internal organs, separating them, and preparing them for later containment in canopic jars.

Evisceration was a difficult and filthy process. As a result, Iramen would often be covered in excrement and secretions. No matter how he cleansed himself, he could not rid himself of the stench. His occupation made him unpopular company. Even the lowest prostitute charged him twice as much to lay with him.

"Brother, you should not have been late," Nebamun said. "We had to start without you, or we should not be finished in time."

"Did you bring your tools, or do you need to run home

and get them Iramen?" Padi asked, barely containing his disgust for the older brother of his friend. *I cannot believe they are brothers*, he thought.

"No, I brought my sharpest scalpel, just for you Padi. What do you think I am, an incompetent fool?" Iramen stumbled against the embalming table, slightly spilling the bowls containing the brains of Nasra and Amunet.

"No, I think you are far less a man than your brother. No wonder he is Anubis, and you are left cutting the guts out of our neighbors," Padi said, gently wiping up the brain liquid and placing what he could back into the bowls.

"Quiet, both of you; your arguing is making my head hurt, and I can barely read from the book," The high priest took a deep breath and began:

"*O my divine father Osiris, I have come to embalm Nasra and Amunet, that they may not know corruption. Fashion them strongly, O lord of the funeral chest. Grant that they may enter into the land of everlastingness.*

They have never done that which thou hatest, so let their bodies not become worms, but deliver them and let them not fall into rottenness. Let life rise out of death."

"Padi let us turn the bodies," Nebamun said in a low voice after the reading.

Padi and Nebamun grasped each of the bodies in turn, and rolled them gently over, exposing the left side of the woman and the young girl side by side. Their white, naked flesh looked almost transparent in the filtered light. Nebamun traced a thin line in black ink on each body, to give instruction on where to cut.

"Iramen, please begin," he said to his brother.

Iramen began with the girl, the easier of the two. He grasped his scalpel firmly. He may have been lax at many things, but he was thorough when it came to the sharpness of his tools. He examined the razor sharp edge of the scalpel with cruel intensity and smiled with approval.

He laid one hand on the small girl, and with the other hand, he split open the skin along the line Nebamun drew for him. He cut again and again along the same line.

When he sensed that he had cut through all the uppermost tissues, he reached for his cutting instrument, identical to the scalpel, except the blade was thicker, more substantial. He continued to cut until all the skin and tissues underneath were open, exposing the internal organs to the light.

Iramen set down the cutter and reached for his forceps. The body was now awash in a sea of blood, and Iramen was having great difficulty keeping the body from slipping, and thus, ruining his work.

He used his forceps to capture each of the organs in turn, the lungs, the stomach, the liver and the intestines, which he cut with his curved scissors. He drew the organs out, placing each of them in their own separate clay vessel. Padi covered each of the organs with natron, to dry them out.

The hearts, centers of intelligence and feeling, were to stay in the bodies. Before the mother and daughter could enter into the afterlife, they would be called into the Hall of Maati, for their trial. Each of their hearts would be weighed against the feather of Maat, the goddess of right and truth, by Osiris, the Great God of the Underworld.

If the hearts were equal in weight to the feather, they could enter the afterlife. If the hearts were heavier than the feather, they would each be eaten by Ammit, the demon, the devourer of the dead, and Nasra and Amunet would be doomed in eternity. Thoth, the god of writing, would be standing by with a reed pen in his hand to record the outcome.

He turned his attention to the woman. Although she was relatively young, she was still much larger than her daughter. Iramen began to cut along the line drawn by Nebamun. He cut through the skin and each of the tissues beneath, eventually exposing the organs.

Iramen worked very slowly; he was in the midst of so much blood, from both the girl and her mother. He found it extremely difficult to hold onto the woman, and she slipped repeatedly out of his hands, as he attempted to grasp each of her organs and pull them out. Finally, he was left with only the intestines, the last organ to be removed.

Iramen took his scissors firmly and cut. A foul smell filled the air, and he drew back from the table. Iramen had cut open the intestine, and human waste was now spilling out all over the table. Instinctively, Iramen turned away, and with this movement, he lost his tentative grip on the woman. Nasra slipped, crashing undignified, onto the floor.

"There will be punishment for this desecration, Iramen," Nebamun said. Looking into Iramen's panicked, bloodshot eyes, Nebamun had little pity for his brother. "You brought this on yourself. All of your drinking, whoring…and now here you are. I, as high priest, should denounce you."

Iramen's eyes darted around the room in fear, from Padi and Nebamun, to the half dissected bodies, and back again. "Brother, can you help me? Do not speak of this to anyone, or you either, Padi. Tell me, both of you, that you will be silent," Iramen entreated, in a panicked, whiny voice.

The two men looked at each other with uneasiness. If they were to remain silent, they could be punished in the same way as Iramen if anyone found out. But, if they were to expose Iramen's desecration, his hands would be cut off, and without any means of employment, he would starve very quickly.

"It has to be both of us," Nebamun said. "It will not do for one of us to speak and the other to remain silent. I must have your word on this Padi."

"Very well; may the Gods have pity as we beg forgiveness; I will not speak of this with anyone. You have my word," Padi answered. "I only will remain silent out of my friendship with Nebamun. If you were smart, Iramen, you would begin burning incense right now to get the smell out of here."

"You will not have cause to regret it," Iramen said, as a thin smile of relief crept across his face.

The three men carefully lifted Nasra's body back onto the embalming table and did their best to clean the blood and feces from the floor, removing all traces of the desecration.

Iramen cleansed the body cavities with palm wine, wiping away all traces of the abomination he had created.

"Padi, they are prepared. Are you ready?" Nebamun asked.

"Yes, I have what I need." Padi gathered small linen packets together, some containing natron to help dehydrate the body, others held sweet smelling myrrh, and still others held sawdust to absorb the body liquids as Nasra and Amunet dried out.

He reverently placed the packets inside the open cavities

of the women's bodies and grabbed a large pick. Padi expertly stabbed along the incision lines and created uniform holes.

"Iramen, hand me those strips of cloth," Padi said, pointing to a large pile of thread-like strips of linen. "With the luck of the gods, I may be able to cover up your mess."

Padi deftly threaded the strips of cloth in and out of the holes, and pulled the strips tight, creating a nearly perfect seam along the left side of the bodies.

Nebamun once again thumbed through the pages of the Book of Coming Forth by Day until he found a marked passage and began to read:

"Nasra and Amunet, secure your head to your bones. Collect your bones, gather together your limbs, throw the sand from off your flesh. The spirit is for the Heavens, the corpse is for the Earth."

Nebamun opened the entrance flap of the embalming tent and leaned outside, immediately growing hot as he felt the scorching sun against the top of his black mask. *We are late. It is the fault of Iramen. There is no help for us now. I fear he will be the death of us,* he thought. "It is done," Nebamun said to a group of priests shuffling with impatience in the blazing heat.

Two priests entered and doused natron over each of the bowls containing the internal organs. The remaining priests came in and together, they lifted the table holding Nasra and Amunet and carried them outside into the stifling day.

With Nebamun leading the procession, followed by Padi, Iramen and the priests, the parade of death moved slowly and reverently forward on their way to the Per Nefer, the beautiful house, where the bodies would be covered in natron and left to dry for forty days.

Nebamun enjoyed this work, and realized what a great honor it was to portray Anubis. Nebamun and Iramen's uncle also played the role of Anubis, and on their uncle's deathbed many years before, he had chosen the younger brother, Nebamun, to continue the tradition. *I am certain my brother must despise me for this,* Nebamun thought to himself.

Today though, he was uneasy. He could almost trade places with the lowest of the priests. He was not sure if it was the desecration of the woman and her daughter, or that he was committing sacrilege against the gods, or just that the mask of Anubis suddenly seemed very heavy and stifling hot. The air was thick inside the mask, and it seemed as if the face of Anubis might crush his nose.

The path to the Per Nefer stretched its way around the outer walls of Ipet Isut. The walls were carved with exquisite images of past pharaohs doing battle with the enemy. Tutankhamun had not yet carved his battle images into the walls; he had not yet seen any battles.

Nebamun could see the red granite tekhenu, with their tips sheathed in a combination of silver and gold known as electrum, as an offering to the sun god Ra. These were the obelisks of Hatshepsut, the woman who dressed as a man and held power over Egypt generations before.

The woman pharaoh spared no expense on the magnificent stone sculptures which would represent her. In the papyrus archives, it was written that she spent as many bushels of gold as sacks of wheat in their construction. Now, a wall surrounded the magnificent tekhenu, placed by her successor and stepson, Tutmosis III, so that the magnificence of Hatshepsut could no longer be seen.

"Do you remember Padi, the story of when these tekhenu were raised?" Nebamun asked.

"Not entirely, Great One, please tell me," Padi answered.

"Well, as the story goes," Nebamun began, "the engineer ordered one of the workmen's young sons to be bound to the tekhenu as it was raised. He wanted the workmen to not faulter in their duties and make certain to use the utmost care when raising it. The story tells of the young boy with his arms flailing about, and the workmen jeering at him."

"Yes, yes, I remember it now," Padi agreed. "It seems the engineer cared more about his reputation, than the children of his men. Pity, but effective, for there are no cracks in our perfect tekhenu."

"Indeed, it looks as though it were raised by the gods, instead of just a ruthless engineer," Nebamun said. "It is indeed shameful of Tutmosis to hide it within a wall. He must have so hated Hatshepsut. Perhaps our pharaoh will uncover it once again one day."

"Yes, perhaps he will commence more building projects, but I have heard he is once again very ill," Padi said.

"It seems our pharaoh is quite frail," Nebamun agreed. "We can only pray for our leader to triumph over his many illnesses and infirmities."

The procession continued around the outer walls and passed a group of sculptors who looked over at the embalmers with only slight interest. They were in the midst of an argument of how best to carve the image of pharaoh into a solid granite slab. The sculptors came all the way from Memphis in Lower Egypt. Tutankhamun wanted only the best artists to carve his image that was to last for eternity.

The priests stopped briefly in the shade of a palm tree, near the Akh Menu, the most glorious of monuments, the great festival hall built by Tutmosis III. It was called "the Temple of Millions of Years," by the common people.

The Akh Menu was near the Sanctuary of the Sacred Boats, the starting point of the Opet festival. Soon, the ceremonial boats would be brought out, carrying the gods Amun, Mut, and Khonsu, to be delivered to the great temple of Amun. The gods would return to Ipet Isut when all had a chance to view them.

Today, the temple priests known as the Hem Netjer were bustling about, bathing the statues and preparing to clothe them. When the gods were finished with their dress, they would be given food and drink, to be consumed at their leisure.

The procession continued to walk through the many gateways in Ipet Isut, each erected by a different pharaoh, from a different time.

"I am sorry brother," Iramen said, suddenly coming up close behind Nebamun. "I know that you are disappointed in me. Try to remember how it was when we were young. We loved each other and would do anything to protect each other. Do you remember?"

"Yes, brother, I remember. I remember also that you were a much better brother when we were young. Now you are but a lesser man, consumed with his own desires and nothing more," Nebamun said.

The two brothers walked along in brooding, dark silence after that. Iramen's plan to make his brother feel sorry for him had failed. There was nothing left to be said.

Nebamun thought back to the time before he became

high priest, before Iramen became a vile eviscerator, hated by all. Their lives may have been different, simpler somehow. But it was too late.

They came from a long ancestry of priests and embalmers. Nebamun could remember stories of their family members from centuries ago who worked at the royal necropolis in Abydos. Their ancestors had embalmed the first pharaohs of Egypt, and buried them in long mudbrick tombs alongside an entire fleet of wooden ships, each ship encased in its own mudbrick coffin.

They passed the sacred lake, huge, still and reflective, like a giant azure mirror. Water birds, housed in the aviary next to the lake, began squawking as they walked by, their cries carried across the water on currents of hot air. The geese, sacred to Amun and raised by temple priests, began their daily cacophony of sound.

Rows of date palms and pomegranate trees lined their path, providing small life-giving amounts of shade to anyone passing underneath them. The shade was welcome, if even for a moment, as the priests struggled beneath their burden of the two dead women.

Just as Nebamun was becoming lightheaded from the heavy mask, the group of priests reached the Per Nefer. The mortuary temple stood in front of them, its soaring pillars framing the sky.

Each temple wall was etched with the god figures of Osiris, with his green face, his beautiful wife Isis, and their son Horus, the falcon god. Nekhbet, the vulture goddess was carved in to the entrance archway, with her wings spread, as if to envelop them protectively.

The priests lifted Nasra and Amunet from the embalming table and placed them on a slanted stone slab. They showered the bodies with natron. The natron crystals would help to dissolve the fat and liquefy the tissues.

As the bodies dried in the stifling desert heat, any liquid would run down channels carved on both sides of the slab, to be gathered into small bowls placed below the stone table.

With solemn faces, the priests followed each other, forming a circle around the bodies. When all was still and silent, Nebamun began:

"There is no sin in the body of Nasra. There is no sin in the body of Amunet. They have not spoken that which is not true knowingly, nor have they done anything with a false heart."

Nebamun stopped reading, and for a moment, was unable to continue. The heat and stagnant air inside the Anubis mask was unbearable. He suddenly wondered if the great god Anubis was punishing him for his brother's sin. He swallowed deeply in an attempt to moisten his parched mouth; with some difficulty, his voice cracking, he continued:

"Nasra and Amunet, grant that you may be like to those favoured ones who are in your following, and that you may be greatly favoured by the beautiful God, and beloved of the Lord of the Two Lands."

Nebamun closed the papyrus book and all of the priests bowed their heads. The group of priests picked up the bloodstained embalming table, now free of its occupants, turned around slowly, and Nebamun lead them away.

Once outside the Per Nefer, Nebamun removed the Anubis mask with a sigh of relief. His bald head, drenched in sweat, gleamed in the sunlight. He sat down on an unfinished limestone pillar and wiped his forehead with the back of his hand.

"You swear you will not tell anyone what happened today?" Iramen whispered in his ear.

Nebamun was startled.

"I did not hear you brother, so quiet were your steps. Yes, yes, I swear I will not tell even unto death. Now leave me alone."

"You know what will happen if you say anything. I will get my hands cut off and...and my head too." Iramen's face was shiny with the sweat of fear.

"Just go. And try not to drink tonight. I cannot always defend you Iramen."

Iramen walked away and joined the other priests. Nebamun sat alone, staring out at the surface of the sacred lake, its breeze slowly cooling his sweating face. *I wonder what Anubis thinks of me now,* he thought as he held the Anubis mask, gently stroking its perfectly molded surface.

He got up slowly from the hard limestone, and thought about Nasra and Amunet, taken so suddenly from their happy, busy lives. Once so beautiful and full of life, now they were hollowed out shells of flesh covered bones.

I will see you again in forty days, he thought. *I, Nebamun, will become the great God Anubis, God of mummification and guardian of the dead. I will help you on your journey into the afterlife.*

He turned around and looked at the bodies of Nasra and Amunet, lying alone in the Per Nefer, their bodies already turning brown in the midday heat.

$$\Omega\ \Omega\ \Omega\ \Omega\ \Omega$$

Four

"Yes, very valuable…very valuable, indeed; but, I make you good price because I like you," Rahmad said to a very well dressed English couple. He liked foreigners, especially the English. They always carried a lot of money.

Rahmad ran a small antiquities shop from his basement on Corniche El Nil street in central Luxor. It was the perfect location to catch unwary tourists as they disembarked from a luxury steamship a few blocks down the street.

All of Rahmad's worldly possessions were contained in a small apartment above the shop, and since he had no family, all of the money he made was his and no one else's.

The shopkeeper had no hobbies on which to spend his money, but he did like to smoke his hookah pipe upstairs in his apartment, and rub the blackened windows to get a better view of anything going on in the street.

Children joked about seeing his eyes peering out from behind the soot covered windows. He was a short, round man, and with his hooked nose shaped like a beak, and bulging hawk-like eyes, Rahmad's neighbors called him Horus, after the hawk god of the ancient Eygptians, although never to his face.

He had a fierce temper and unpleasant, selfish nature, except when he was trying to sell something to someone. He sold pieces of the ancient world for cash to any and all who ventured into his shop. He sold ancient papyrus, statuary, amulets, bowls, vessels, and small objects of little value. He carried fine objects to sell only rarely, but he counted on the gullibility of his foreign customers to not know the difference.

Right now he was intent on flattering the English couple into buying some piece of trash as a souvenir.

The Englishman, Edward Dunthorpe, and his wife, Mary, had just disembarked from the Nile Princess, one of the many luxury steamships that plied the dark Nile waters. The trip began in Aswan, the site of an ancient granite quarry about four days south.

Before winding their way up the great river, the Dunthorpes took a small detour south, to visit the temple of Philae, built during the time when the Greek Ptolemies ruled Egypt.

They disembarked to view the graceful temple of Isis, with its many columns painted in blues and greens, still vivid after two thousand years. They admired the temple walls, etched with scenes of sacred boats gliding across a ceiling of blue with accents of golden stars.

Edward and Mary saw the ancient graffiti, the Greek crosses carved into the columns by the early Coptic Christians in the sixth century. They stopped and ate a light lunch underneath the very elegant kiosk of the Roman emperor Trajan.

Their knowledgeable guide pointed to the Gate of

Hadrian, upon which the last Egyptian hieroglyphs were inscribed in 394 AD.

Further north, the Nile Princess stopped at another temple begun by the Ptolemies, that of the crocodile god, Sobek in Kom Ombo. They joined the throngs of tourists who came not just to see the temple, but to see the mummified remains of crocodiles and their babies, found in stone coffins nearby, and to gaze into the now empty basin in which these same crocodiles swam when they were alive.

Halfway up the river on their journey, stands the wonderfully preserved temple of Edfu, dedicated to Horus, the falcon god. Its first gateway or pylon is over one hundred feet tall, and is carved with a huge relief of another Ptolemy, standing fearlessly as his enemies lie helpless at his feet. Nearby stand the black granite statues of the falcon god Horus, staring mutely at all who pass inside the gateway.

It was thus after their trip up the Nile that they now found themselves in Luxor, the endpoint of their journey. They would spend a few weeks in the ancient city, and then it would be back to England, with their stories of travel triumphant.

Edward Dunthorpe had a keen appreciation of the majesty of the Egyptian temples, but it was not so with his wife, Mary. She only mildly appreciated the sites along the way, anxious as she was to find a rare shady spot to take her rest in the sweltering heat.

Neither Dunthorpe had as yet purchased any souvenirs of their trip to Egypt. Nothing was quite beautiful enough for Mary, and nothing was quite unusual enough for Edward. So far, he had only seen some old, dusty rugs, and a filthy glass hookah pipe.

Edward hoped to remedy his lack of Egyptian keepsakes by buying something in Rahmad's shop. In the depths of this Egyptian antiquities and curiosities shop, he was determined to find something perfect, and this might be his last chance.

"I think it's horrid, absolutely horrid, Edward. I don't want it in our house," Mary Dunthorpe said, blowing at an errant feather floating down from her hat.

Edward turned the small glass case around to examine all sides of the mummified hand and arm inside. There were only a few pieces of remaining linen draped around the arm, exposing a small, shriveled forearm ending in a curled hand, its fingers grasping at the air. The skin was dark, almost black, and each finger ended in a long, darkened yellow fingernail. A beautifully fashioned gold and turquoise inlay bracelet encircled the wrist.

"It might bring us some luck, Mary, and the man said he would give us a good price," Edward answered.

"Well, it certainly didn't bring its owner good luck," Mary said. "And what good is it? Certainly you don't expect me to wear that bracelet? Why, I'm certain it still smells of rotting flesh, but thank God we will never open the case to find out."

"Oh, my dear, I couldn't possibly allow you to wear the bracelet. It's only to be seen, not worn," Edward said.

"As I said, Edward, what good is it? If I can't wear it, I can't make my friends envious, now can I? You know, husband, Egyptian revival is very chic back home at the moment."

"You ladies and your Egyptian revival; can't you just enjoy the piece for its own sake? Why it must be thousands of years old."

Mary sniffed with disdain. "What is that, some kind of bird?" she asked, pointing to a graceful long necked creature silhouetted in turquoise, with tiny onyx eyes.

"That is an ibis ma'am, fashioned in turquoise from the ancient mines in the Sinai. The ancients called an ibis the god Thoth, patron of writing. We think the owner of the bracelet may have been a scribe," Rahmad answered, trying to recover what might be a lost opportunity for a sale.

"You hear that, my dear? The scribes were probably the most important Egyptians next to the pharoahs. Pity we can't take it out of the case and hold it; I'd love to get a better look at that bracelet," Edward said.

"You do that, and it will surely turn into dust, such as I have here," Rahmad said, pointing to the fine beige dust in a glass jar on the shelf, labeled "mummy."

"God in heaven; you actually grind the mummies and sell them?" Mary asked. "Unfathomable."

"Yes, yes, and a spoonful of dried mummy can be good for all kinds of illnesses," Rahmad said. "I am not a doctor, but I know this to be true."

"He's right, Mary. Before we left England, doctors were touting the benefits of ground mummy, and selling tickets to unwrapping ceremonies."

"*My god, in England?* I can imagine these heathens doing things like that, but our English people? I can't believe such a thing," Mary said incredulously.

Edward gave his wife a sideways glance. *How I wish she would be quiet,* he thought. *I don't want to insult this man. Then he won't give me a deal.* "How much do you want for the mummy arm?" Edward asked suddenly.

LUXOR

Mary's eyes grew wide with horror. "Edward, you can't mean it?"

"Well, let me see what kind of deal I can make," Rahmad said, ignoring Mary's protests. He rolled back his eyes, as if to do some mental calculation in his head. "What do think of paying me two hundred Egyptian pounds?"

"That's a thief's bargain! I'll give you one hundred pounds and not a pound more," Edward said, using his standard give-them-half-of-what-they-ask-for starting point. "Why, I could buy a good horse for that amount of money. You are a crazy person, Egyptian."

Rahmad smiled. "Mr. Englishman, you could purchase a young slave for the same amount from a man I know, but it will not provide you with even a small portion of the joy you will receive owning this bracelet."

"Disgusting, sir, the thought of owning a slave, and benefitting from the misery of others," Edward said. "Do not speak of it again."

"Very well sir, I was just using it for comparison," Rahmad said placatingly; "Now, back to the matter at hand. If you want it, you must pay me what I ask. The bracelet is gold, considered in ancient times as a divine metal. That is why so many possessions of pharaohs and gods are made out of it. This piece is from ancient Egypt, at least three thousand years old. I can keep it if you don't want to pay me."

"Maybe we can make another deal. I will pay you your two hundred pounds, or whatever, but you must give me a small sack of that dried mummy," Edward countered.

"You're not serious?" Mary asked.

"Who knows my dove, we may be able to sell some of it to our friends. In any event, I want it."

Rahmad laughed, his jagged teeth gleaming, and said "Of course, of course, you are a very smart man. This is a bargain well struck."

The shopkeeper carefully measured out a small quantity of the ground mummy powder and poured it into a rumpled cotton sack. He bunched up the top and tied it tightly with thin fibrous rope.

"There you are, fine sir and madam, gift wrapped and for your pleasure, a piece of ancient Egypt," Rahmad said as he handed the packet to Edward.

"It's been a pleasure," Edward said, extending his hand and smiling. "Egypt is a fascinating country, with so much history."

Mary was quiet. She couldn't wait to get out of the shop and out of the sight of this man who ground people into dust. She couldn't imagine selling the mummies, much less eating a dry, pulverized dead person.

"Are you feeling alright, Mary?" Edward asked. "You look a bit pale. Perhaps some mummy will make you well."

"I would rather die a thousand deaths than eat that," Mary answered with disgust.

The Dunthorpes left the shop and walked down the Corniche El Nile, Edward with one arm around his wife, and the other arm around his precious ancient cargo.

Ω Ω Ω Ω Ω

Five

When Hatshepsut was alive over one hundred years ago, the sacred barks travelled regularly every ten days from the temple of Amun at Waset, to the queen's small temple at Djanet. It was known as the Feast of the Tenth Day and was a joyous relief from the torturous, mundane lives of the common people. It was a chance for blessed release even if just for a short time.

Akhenaton the Heretic, the father of Tutankhamun, destroyed her temple and eliminated the worship of Amun. Because of this, the people of Egypt could no longer go to Djanet. Now that Tutankhamun ruled Egypt, it would still take some time to rebuild her temple and begin the feast of the tenth day once again.

Until such a day, the common people would have to be content with seeing sacred barks and the golden effigies of the gods on far fewer occasions. One of those occasions was today, for the Beautiful Festival of the Opet.

The Opet Festival began on a blistering hot day. The food merchants had lined up the night before, sleeping on the sandstone avenue of the sphinxes. They must be ready to catch the first of the hungry mob as they descend for the festival.

A crowd of swineherds stood outside the temple walls, peering inside whenever a chance afforded itself. These men were not allowed inside any temple because men who spent their lives herding pigs were certainly not pure enough for the gods.

Nebamun strode quickly around the merchants selling their swineflesh, or their fish caught in the Nile waters. Both of these things were forbidden to eat by the priests. He did take a small amount of bread offered to him by a little girl, her face besmudged by dust and sweat.

He hoped the bread would satisfy him long enough to get through the proceedings. It was going to be a long first day, and he must be at his most attentive to serve his god and his pharaoh.

Nebamun looked his best today, in a crisp, bright white tunic made of finely woven linen, edged in a border of thin gold thread. Over this he wore the skin of a young leopard, the forepaws of which formed his sleeves. He could hear murmurs of adoration as he walked through the crowd. Today, his head was bare, in humble adoration of the gods, and he could feel the already piercing heat cooking his skull.

He found Padi, just underneath the tekhenu, the obelisk of Hatshepsut, looking up at its shining tip of electrum with admiration. His friend had also worn his best today, a long white linen sheath of fabric, held up by thick straps of red leather on his shoulders. Despite the richness of the ensemble, it only served to make Padi look even shorter and far less noble.

"You look wonderful my friend," Nebamun said with a warm smile. "Come let us get organized. It will be a long and happy day, praise Amun."

"Praise Amun, and his family of gods," Padi agreed.

The two priests made their way through the meandering, jostling crowd. They were to meet their pharaoh and his party at the Akh Menu, the Most Glorious of Monuments. From there the group would proceed into the sanctuary to perform the Opet rites.

"Just look at all of the babies, Great One," Padi said. "It seems to have been a bountiful year for many families."

Nebamun had not noticed before, but now it seemed what Padi said was true. The high priest could not remember such a time when there were so many young women, carrying each of their babies in a shawl slung on their backs, with smiles of joy on their faces.

"Those could have been our babies, Padi," Nebamun said thoughtfully. "Do you have any regrets about becoming a priest?"

"No, Great One; it has been my greatest joy to serve you. What about you, my friend, do you wish you were in another trade, like that of the lowly fisherman, or perhaps a stonecutter, your lungs would be black now."

Nebamun smiled. "Perhaps not, but I do think about it on occasion. How my life could have been different. Then perhaps my brother would not have hated me so much, and we could have been friends."

Just then, one of the women stopped. She thrust her naked baby forward into Nebamun's face.

"Blessings Great One?" she cried. "Will you bless my baby boy so that he may live on in happiness and prosperity on this most perfect of days?"

Nebamun looked closely at the naked child, now crying

in distress. Something was wrong with the baby, but he could not tell what it was. The boy seemed inattentive somehow, and then he realized that despite the boy's large, beautiful brown eyes, the child was blind.

"Blessings on you child, may the gods provide you sight once more on this most perfect of days," Nebamun intoned.

The woman smiled and without another word, she ran to join her companions, the now blessed baby bouncing on her back.

They continued on through the steadily thinning crowd. The common people could only go so far on the sacred grounds of Ipet Isut. The Akh Menu and Sanctuary were reserved for the priests and pharaoh alone.

Ipet Isut was designed such that the rays of sun god Ra should shine fully upon the entrance to the temple. Further into the temple, the light would gradually change to only half illumination, as if proceeding from the living world, into that of the underworld.

Nebamun and Padi stepped inside the Akh Menu, grateful for the cool darkness within. The temple monument was built by Tutmosis III over one hundred years before. In an effort to outshine Hatshepsut, his predecessor and stepmother, his many achievements were carved upon its walls.

There were magnificent carvings of many different types of plants, animals, birds and flowers brought back from his journeys to Syria and East Africa. The columns within the Akh Menu were painted a brilliant red, to resemble the wood of tent poles used during festivals.

The pharaoh, Tutankhamun, was already there, attired in an apron of rich, multicolored leather, designed with impressions of lions' heads. The border of the magnificent garment was a row of royal snakes, gilded in gold. Today he wore the pshent double crown of white and red, the symbol of a united upper and lower Egypt.

He looked briefly at the two priests and bowed slightly in recognition. He was joined by members of his royal entourage, including priests Nebamun had never seen before. These were young men, young as Pharoah, even.

They proceeded into the small rectangular room known as the Sanctuary, or the Holy of Holies, where the sacred bark of Amun was stored. Tutankhamun would greet the gods face to face, and Nebamun and Padi would witness his divinity.

The opulent gilded surface of the sacred bark of Amun shone out even in the dim light of the sanctuary. Its bow and stern were decorated with golden rams' heads, the animals most sacred to Amun. Six of the stronger priests picked up the sacred bark and carried it high in the air.

Nebamun and Padi followed Tutankhamun through the columned hall, its walls decorated with reliefs of conquered slaves, along with the plants and animals native to conquered countries.

The gateway doors of Ipet Isut were all open today, the immense golden gilded wooden doors beckoning all to come in. The procession continued through the two gateways, and travelled south to arrive at the temple of Khonsu, son of Amun Ra.

Here, the original group was joined by the priests of the temple of Khonsu, carrying the god's sacred bark, also beautifully gilded in gold, but adorned with the heads of falcons.

The two groups moved slowly to the last temple, that of Mut, wife of Amun Ra, and mother to Khonsu. The final group of her temple priests joined in, carrying the bark of the goddess, just as magnificent as the others, with bow and stern each in the shape of a woman.

Once outside the sanctuary, the crowd was free to admire and adore the gods who had come out to see them. Waset citizens continued to pour through the gateway, as red and gold banners floated gently in the subtle wind. They thronged into the colonnade and massed in the inner courtyard.

The final huge procession moved out into the avenue of sphinxes, on the way to the temple of Amun Ra, the final resting place. But they were not alone.

A line of musicians playing ivory double pipes walked down the avenue. This was followed by another line of musicians playing the sistrum, and others playing small hand held drums.

These musicians were followed by beautiful young women dancing a fluid graceful movement to the music. The women were naked to the waist; their only covering was a tiny short black skirt.

In one continuous motion the willowy figured women bent over backwards, their long, black wigs sweeping the ground. They did a quick backflip and they were upright again. Over and over these women repeated their acrobatics, all in preparation for what came next in the procession.

A great white bull, known as the Apis Bull and sacred to Min, the god of male fertility, was led on a thin tether, all the while being fed lettuce leaves to ensure its ability to sire many offspring.

The divine bull would be raised according to the highest standards of health; indeed, no water from the Nile would enter into the bull, for fear of the fattening properties of the river water. Only water from the sacred lake was good enough for the Apis.

This Apis Bull, along with its predecessors, would be allowed to live for twenty-five years. Then, amid solemn ceremony, it would be killed, before it became old and weak thereby bringing misfortune to Egypt. The divine creature would be mourned for sixty days, and then embalmed and interred in its own stone coffin near Memphis. A new Apis Bull would be found and installed for another twenty five year reign.

The procession continued on until it reached a temple designed by Senenmut, the architect of Hatshepsut. It was made of red quartzite and shown out brilliantly under the rays of the morning sun.

This was the largest of six temples along the festival route, a place where the pharaoh and priests could stop and rest. It was a place to make offerings to the gods and pray for a bountiful year to come.

The procession stopped here and placed the three sacred barks inside the temple. Pharoah and several of his priests, including Nebamun and Padi went inside also, grateful for the cool rest.

"Our progress is good, Great One," Padi said.

"Yes indeed my friend," Nebamun agreed. "We are already to the red temple and it is only the second day of the festival. If we continue at this rate, we will be at the Sanctuary of the Southern Opet within the next two days."

"Are we in a hurry, Great One?" Padi asked.

"As much as I love the festival of Opet, I am always happy to return home to Waset. It is where I belong." Nebamun answered.

After a few hours of rest, the procession picked up and moved on, proceeding south along the avenue of the sphinxes, each ram-headed figure staring down at them as they passed.

They rested several hours later at the temple of Senusret, an ancient place, built over five hundred years before the time of Tutankhamun.

The temple was built from the finest white limestone, and the entire surface of each block was covered with the most detailed carving in all of Egypt, each image meticulously rendered in stone.

Once again, the procession moved on, arriving at each of the four remaining smaller temples on the route to the Sanctuary of the Southern Opet; each time placing the three sacred barks inside and gaining a few hours rest from the merciless sun.

In time, the procession entered the gateway to the Southern Sanctuary, walking past the bright lapis blue and emerald green banners welcoming them in the gentle wind. There were very few common people within the walls of the sanctuary. It was a much more solemn place and lacked the vibrant throngs of people that were at Ipet Isut.

They stopped in front of the triple shrine of Amun Ra, Mut and Khonsu, and Tutankhamun went inside alone. He knelt to each of the gods in turn, offering prayers to the triad of gods thanking them for the life they had in Egypt, and the eternal life that comes after death.

From the triple shrine, the procession entered into the semi-darkness of a long columned room, begun by

Amunhotep III, Tutankhamun's grandfather. Nebamun saw a slight smile of pride on the face of his pharaoh, knowing that Tutankhamun had completed the room his grandfather began so many years ago.

The walls of the room were decorated with scenes from the same festival they were participating in today, commemorating the Beautiful Festival of the Opet.

They entered into the Sun Court, where a select group of high ranking officials and prominent citizens joined them to admire the gods, before the pharaoh and his high priests moved into the Chamber of the Divine King.

In this chamber, Tutankhamun gloried in his own purification and union with the divine Amun Ra. The pharaoh on earth had been joined to the gods.

The group then proceeded to the Central Bark Sanctuary, where the ordinary bulls were sacrificed to the gods, while the divine white Apis bull looked on with disinterest. He had already seen many of his companion bulls fall down in death, in honor of the gods over the years, and would see many more to come.

Finally, after several days' journey, they arrived at the very far end of the temple, to the Sanctuary of the Southern Opet. After many prayers and sacred rites they were at the halfway point in the festival.

The barks would remain in the Sanctuary, unseen by anyone except pharaoh and his select group of priests. When the gods had rested and were ready, they would be brought out once again to make their way back to Ipet Isut, to be admired by thousands of adoring citizens.

Ω Ω Ω Ω Ω

Six

Karim and Abdul reached Rahmad's shop just as the English couple walked out into the sunlight. The Abd el Amun brothers noticed their fine clothing, how the man was dressed in his crisp, clean white linen shirt, and how it gleamed in the sunlight; how he strutted down the street, his head topped with a tan fedora. They noticed the woman too, with her haughty expression of superiority, veiled in the shade of a lace parasol, to protect her from the Egyptian sun.

The curious stares of the two brothers were met with not even a glimmer of greeting. The Dunthorpes looked past the two young men, with all the indifference born of generations of carefully bred aristocrats. It was as if the two brothers were bothersome gnats to be swatted aside, or worse, as if they didn't exist at all.

"What do you think they bought?" Abdul whispered.

"I don't have any idea, but I'm sure they could afford anything they wanted. No doubt they are rich," Karim answered with a sneer.

"All English people are rich," Abdul said with authority.

"They've never had to scrape like we have, brother," Karim answered. "Did you see how clean they are? I would like to be that clean someday instead of scratching in the dirt and sand just to live."

Abdul said nothing. He could tell his brother was getting into one of his moods of envying all those around him and it was best to keep quiet and let him get over it. *Envy never does anybody any good,* he thought.

They opened the door to Rahmad's shop, and went inside, their entrance announced by the sharp ringing of a small metallic bell. Rahmad immediately appeared.

"Oh, it's you!" Rahmad said with disappointment, thinking the English couple had returned for another purchase. "Have you come to sell me some worthless trash again?"

"You'll be glad we came in today, I promise you," Karim said. "Just wait until you see what we have for you, Rahmad."

Abdul was distracted by a very beautiful small copper statue of Isis, and he reached out his hand to touch it, when Rahmad intervened.

"Don't touch that!" Rahmad said, striking Abdul's outstretched arm. "You can't just come in here and touch whatever you like. Some of these pieces are very old and very valuable, unlike the garbage you carry in your bags," Rahmad said, glancing at the brother's dusty, tattered sacks.

"I told you, we have something special for you, and we will make you a good price," Karim said.

"I'll show you special," Rahmad said. "Just don't touch anything."

He drew back a dirty cloth curtain and motioned for the brothers to walk through the doorway. Inside were row upon row of small blue glass statues, each inscribed with columns of hieroglyphs etched in black.

"These are shabti figures. Shabti means "the answerer," and they are made of what's called faience, a kind of molded glass," Rahmad explained. These little beauties were placed in the tombs to do the work of the dead. If the gods needed the fields plowed, or the sand carried, the shabti would perform the task asked of its owner. See how each of the faces is different? Faces were sometimes carved to resemble their owners."

"Are they worth much?" Karim asked, taking one in his hand.

"It's always about money with you! I told you not to touch anything, and here you are, with your grubby fingers on a three thousand year old shabti. If you break anything, I will make you work for me for free until you die, so don't touch anything."

Karim carefully handed the shabti back to Rahmad. He didn't want to work for this bastard, for free or otherwise. "What does the inscription mean?"

Rahmad held the shabti lovingly in his hands. "The shabti answers to the gods, *'I will do it. I am here when thou callest.'*"

"That's nice, but how much are they worth?" Karim asked again.

"I can get a fair price for them, to the right buyer…like those English people; some foreigner with a lot of money who doesn't know what things might be worth. Come let me show you what else I have, so you will know what I am interested in buying from you."

Rahmad showed the Abd el Amun brothers around the back room of his shop, where there were many statues of Hathor, the cow goddess and favorite goddess of women. There were small figures of the hippopotamus goddess Taweret, guardian of women in childbirth, and of the god Bes, guardian of the household.

Rahmad picked up one of the statues very carefully and held it out for the brothers to see.

"See this? This is Osiris, the husband of Isis you saw earlier. Do you know the ancients believed Osiris was almost three times as tall as we are?"

"That is very interesting, but of little use, Rahmad," Karim said.

"I cannot help that you have no interest in your ancestry. But I can tell you, I have over five hundred figures, some of blue glass, some turquoise, some copper, but only one Isis and Osiris. Tell me, do you know the story of Isis and Osiris?" Rahmad asked.

"No, and we don't have time for any of your stories, Rahmad," Karim said rudely.

"I want to know the story," Abdul said. "We have plenty of time, brother."

Rahmad looked at Abdul with an increased appreciation.

"You see that, Karim? You could learn something from your brother."

"My brother Abdul does not know when to keep his mouth shut," Karim said. "Go ahead and tell us Rahmad, but do it quickly."

"The story goes like this," Rahmad began. "Osiris is king of Egypt and Isis, his wife, is queen. He is murdered and cut into pieces by his brother Set. His body parts are scattered to every region of Egypt."

"That's all very interesting, but can we get on with it?" Karim interrupted impatiently.

"I'm not finished," Rahmad said. "Isis, his wife, gathers up the body parts and binds them together with fabric. This is the story of the first embalming. Osiris was the original mummy, you might say."

"I really like that story, about so much love a wife gives to her husband," Abdul said. "Maybe I can find a loving wife someday."

"Luxor will drop into the Nile before you find a woman to put up with you, brother," Karim said. "You will probably live with me forever."

Abdul frowned, and Rahmad decided to change the subject before they got into a fight right inside his shop. That would surely turn away the customers.

"Most of the shabti figures were given to me by a great man I know," Rahmad said proudly.

"Great man, hah! Probably just a grave robber like us," Karim said. "Do you want to see what we have for you or not?"

"If you must show me, I will take a look," Rahmad said, his feelings hurt for a moment.

Karim drew out a mummified head, its skin black and tightly stretched, with thin wisps of henna dyed hair still clinging to the leathery scalp. He held it up for Rahmad to inspect it. It seemed to Abdul, in comparison to the beautifully made copper and blue glass statues, he and his brother carried bags of death and filth.

"What am I to do with that?" Rahmad asked.

"You can grind it up and sell the powder to the English,

or you can sell the head just as it is," Karim said. "I think you are just trying to buy things cheap from us."

"I will give you a fair price," Rahmad said, looking offended. He reached into his pocket and pulled out a few grimy coins; "what else do you have for me?"

Karim was encouraged. He opened his linen sack and nodded to Abdul, who also opened his. Rahmad drew closer to Abdul's linen sack and stuck his hand inside. He pawed around the contents, moving pieces out of the way, until he could feel the bottom of the bag. Rahmad held up the bag, as if to weigh the contents. Abdul felt sick that the dead were treated in such a way.

I'm going to stop selling bodies as soon as I am able, he vowed to himself; *even if it takes me forever.*

Karim handed his bag to Rahmad, who lifted it slightly. Karim's bag was bulging with mummified body parts, and was much heavier than the bag offered by Abdul. Rahmad decided Karim must be much greedier than his brother and probably would want more money.

I can pay one brother fairly, and cheat the other, he thought. *Today will be a good day.*

"I will pay you ten pounds" he said to Karim; "But for you I will pay only five," he said, pointing to Abdul. "Think on it quickly now, before I change my mind and decide not to buy your trash."

"We will take it," Karim said, before Abdul could say anything. "We will take the offer, with the promise that you will buy more from us. But we must save some wrappings for our mother's cooking fire."

"Yes, yes," Rahmad said impatiently. "But next time you

come, bring something besides just mummy parts. Perhaps something shiny, to tempt the English, you know."

He reached again into his pocket and pulled out several coins, covered with oil and dirt. Rahmad paused, reluctant to part with his money, especially to these grave robbers. He sighed and counted out ten pounds to Karim and another five to Abdul.

"We will return soon Rahmad, so keep your coins handy," Karim said as the brothers stepped out into the sweltering sunlight.

The brothers walked slowly along the Luxor waterfront, grateful for the slight breeze coming off of the water. They passed steamboats moored in readiness for the onslaught of tourists, and carriages pulled by emaciated horses, their ribs outlined against their brown bodies.

They passed by a small food market, with tables overflowing with enormous Nile perch, their eyes bulging and clouded over in death, some already growing putrid in the heat. Underneath the tables were large clay vessels containing live eels, swimming around in large masses at the top of each clay container.

On other tables there were baskets of onions, garlic, barley and fava beans, all ready for purchase by a hungry customer. The smells of the food market all congealed in the stifling heat to form a stench which hung like a thick layer in the air.

"God, it stinks here," Abdul said as he held his nose. "I can hardly stand the smell. You know how I hate fish, brother."

"What did you say, Abdul? Doesn't matter," Karim said

before his brother could answer. "I know just what I will buy with this money," Karim said, as he counted out the money in his hands. "You should have demanded more money brother."

But Abdul was satisfied with his payment, and very glad to leave the antiquities shop and quit the company of greedy Rahmad.

He imagined Rahmad bent over a grinding wheel late at night, grinding…grinding…until a once living body was ground into a pile of dust. The ancient ones of Egypt now enclosed in jars, ready to be sold as medicaments.

Abdul shivered in spite of the heat.

Ω Ω Ω Ω Ω

Seven

"How many were sacrificed?" Nebamun asked, looking down at the dead cats, soaking in a large clay barrel of natron-salted water.

"At this count, about five hundred, I believe. We received many of them from Renostris, the priest of Bast," Padi answered. We searched most of the valley to find the rest of them."

"It must have taken Renostris some time to kill them all." Nebamun said. He grew cold as he thought about the priest Renostris, a fat, sweaty old man. He remembered his eyes most of all, black as the night, and painted with black mesdemet powder to look like cat's eyes, slanted toward his temples. Like all priests, he was completely bald, with a skull shaped exactly like an egg. Nebamun was quite sure he was the ugliest man he had ever seen.

Renostris' sole task in life was to tend to Tutankhamun's garden of Bast, dedicated to the cat goddess, a favorite place of pharaoh to enjoy some solitude and prayer. Bast, the goddess of protection against disease and evil spirits, was very dear to pharaoh.

Tutankhamun came to the garden often, walking arm-in-arm with his wife, Ankhesenamun. She would gather papyrus and lotus blossoms and present them to her young husband. He would smile and invite her to try and conquer him on his beautiful ivory senet board, or play her a battle charge on his silver trumpet. He was destined to never play the battle charge for real. He was far too sickly to go into battle himself.

Renostris was very proud of the attentions paid to him by the pharaoh, and was happy to do whatever pharaoh commanded. Renostris said prayers himself for his king, praying for Bast to help with Tutankhamun's malaria, which continually caused him headaches and high fevers. He prayed for his king to have relief from his deformed foot, which caused pharaoh to walk with a cane.

The one redeeming quality Renostris had was a great love and loyalty to the boy king. Nebamun understood such a love, for it was Tutankhamun who saved them from the heresies committed by Tutankhamun's father, Amenophis IV.

Amenophis IV took away the old gods for seventeen years, and replaced them with the one god Aten, the sun disk. He changed his own name to Akhenaten, and built a new capital dedicated to his new god. He called this new city Akhetaten.

Akhenaton had temporarily taken away the wealth and the power of Eygpt's pantheon of Gods and priests, and for this he was severely punished. He and his queen were now dead, and every monument bearing his name was either defaced or torn down, and the bricks reused for monuments to the new pharaoh, Tutankhamun.

The young son even buried blocks from the temple of his father underneath a gateway in Ipet Isut, as if to bury the man's memory forever.

But now the old gods had returned, and Nebamun was

relieved to have all as it once was. Waset had almost returned to peace and serenity.

The garden of Bastet itself was a stunning circular enclosure filled with bright yellow mimosa and sparkling white lotus flowers. The garden was arrayed around many small ponds, each with an abundance of fish darting through the water, to delight and entertain the cats, servants of Bast.

During their short lives, the cats enjoyed every pleasure fit for the servants of a goddess; succulent pieces of duck meat, seasoned with only the finest licorice root and mint. Once every seven days, the cats were given live quarry, usually unfortunate small mice, bred to be food.

Renostris enjoyed watching a cat play with a mouse, batting it around, and then feigning disinterest. With false hope, the mouse would try to escape, only to be picked up by the cat's sharp teeth, and beaten senseless against a rock.

During the springtime of each year, the time of Peret, Renostris was in charge of providing the gift to the goddess for her festival. Many cats were slaughtered, along with their kittens. He and his lesser priests were dispassionate, adept at killing. Taking each cat in turn, holding it by the neck, and swiftly twisting until the creature's neck cracked.

Nebamun remembered the face of the priest. It was a face devoid of feeling as he ended the life of the animals he had cared for since birth, and then cast them into a pile to be mummified. Nebamun was certain Bast would not approve of her servants being handled in such a manner.

"Of all the celebrations to the gods, the feast of Bast is my least favorite. I am grateful I am in charge of their immortality, and not their death," Nebamun said.

"So, my brother with the soft heart, remember you are serving Bast," Iramen said with a slight smile. "I am certain Bast will be grateful."

Nebamun looked at his brother curiously. He found it difficult to tell what was in Iramen's mind when he spoke. He loved his brother, but he found it difficult to trust him. There was always an undercurrent of jealousy in Iramen's speech, always some secret meaning. Nebamun knew there were often hidden motivations in anything Iramen did.

"Come brother, I am pleased you are here. Padi and I will need your help today. We must prepare the gift to Bast," Nebamun said reluctantly. He spread his arms wide and began the short prayer preceeding the embalming ceremony:

"You have crossed over now, into the spirit realm. May you walk with Bast, and I will see you again someday. Bast, we give you back your children, noble, regal, honorable cats. Watch over them, and guide them on their to the spirit world. May they be blessed in your name, and hunt ever after beside you.

Iramen looked down at cats, their bodies softening in the natron. He was irritated that they should have to stand in the blazing sun for such a lowly creature. It was just a cat, after all.

He reached down and roughly picked up one floating at the top of the barrel. He held it by the whiskers and smiled grimly as its head hung limply to one side. He petted its black fur, as if it was still alive.

"Beautiful thing," he said. "No more mice to chase for you, little one. Maybe in the afterlife you will play your games again."

He brought out one of his Ethiopian stones, a smaller one than he usually used, custom fit for a smaller body, and cruelly sharp. He smiled as he turned the cat over, its belly jutting upward, its eyes looking at him sightlessly. He moved swiftly, making a jagged incision along the animal's underside. Nebamun shuddered at his brother's insensitivity towards the creature's fragile body.

"This one's fur is making it difficult to cut cleanly. I hope they are not all like this, or we could be at work long after the festival of Bast," Iramen said.

He reached two fingers inside the animal and drew out the bloody organs, shook the cat twice to make certain all contents were removed, and handed the carcass to Padi. Again, Nebamun struggled to hide his disgust.

"Be gentle, brother. Remember these are the servants of the goddess," Nebamun said.

"We have no time for gentle. There are far too many cats for the three of us," Iramen said. For once, even Padi agreed with him.

"Nebamun, perhaps your brother is right," Padi conceded. "We could benefit from some help."

"Yes, yes, quite right; we should assemble some other priests to help us. Please tell them to come quickly Padi," Nebamun agreed.

Priests of all ranks were called in to serve Bast. The many bald heads and white linen clad figures assembled in a large group, shuffling uncertainly, wondering why they were called out of their daily routine. Soon, nearly twenty priests of all ranks stood in the embalming tent.

Nebamun lead them in prayer:

"*Bast, lady of Per Bast, may you grant all life and power, all health, and joy of heart.*"

"Iramen, show these priests what they are to do," Nebamun instructed, pointing to a group of five young men.

"Yes, great one," Iramen said, bowing ceremoniously as he picked a dark grey cat out of the clay barrel. *I must give my brother reverence in front of these lesser priests*, he thought.

He made his customary incision along the underside, pulling out each of the organs efficiently and casting them into a reed basket. Unlike people, the animals organs were not kept, but instead were thrown into large baskets and left to dry in the sun, for use during planting.

Padi then took the cat and gathered a small group of priests for a demonstration. He placed the dark grey form on the stone slab in front of him. Then, after dipping his fingers in cedar oil, he carefully washed out the body cavity. He stuffed the body with sand and handed the limp corpse to the priest next to him down the line.

Heru, one of the lesser priests, took the cat and laid it down gently. He pulled the edges of the incision together and sewed up the opening with a razor thin strip of linen. He pulled on the seam carefully, and after making certain the seam would hold together, he passed the cat down the line.

Mahu, brother of Heru, took the cat, placed it in a sitting position and wrapped it in linen, tightly criss-crossing the strips of cloth across its head, neck and body.

The cat was moved further down to a young lesser priest named Ani, who along with four companions, were charged with wrapping the cat completely, placing layer upon layer of linen strips, one on top of the other, until the cat was completely covered with a thickness of cloth.

The face painters were close to the end of the line. These men were in charge of making the small bundles of cloth look like cats once again. These men were highly skilled artists, usually reserved for recreating human faces on the bodies of the deceased, but today they painted slanted cat eyes, whiskers, and the small enigmatic smile of the servant of Bast.

"Wonderful," Nebamun said, looking at one of the cat faces smiling up at him. "It looks alive. I am grateful for your fine work today," he said to the artist, who bowed slightly to acknowledge the compliment.

Nebamun handed the wrapped and painted parcel to one of the men who were in charge of the final step in the process, coating the corpse of the cat with resin. These men took large reed brushes and spread the thick paste-like resin over the linens. With a thorough coating of resin, the sacred animal was protected against the hot, dry climate.

The resin painter placed the small animal outside the tent, to dry in the sun. It would remain so for another forty days, and at the end of this period, the small cat would be ready for the festival. Its body would be protected until the day it would be resurrected to serve in the afterlife.

Thus the process of preparing the cats continued throughout the rest of this day, and into the next, each man performing his task in turn.

At the end of the embalming, each cat would take its place as a gift to the goddess, and be handed out to a citizen of Waset. Men and women alike would take their small parcel and board large boats for their pilgrimage down the great river, to an ancient destination on the Nile Delta.

The floating celebration would make its way along, singing and shouting at the townspeople on the bank as they floated by.

After stopping at many towns along the way, and after much celebration and drink, the trip would end in the sacred city of Per Bast, beloved city of the goddess. The many newly mummified cats would be placed in the mudbrick necropolis, alongside thousands upon thousands of their more ancient counterparts, all in service to the goddess.

Ω Ω Ω Ω Ω

Eight

"Mother, see what money we have made," Karim yelled out. His voice fell flat against the walls of their small whitewashed home.

In spite of the midday heat, the house was cool and dark, thanks in part to some small open holes high in the walls, next to the ceiling. These were designed to let in the cool night breezes, but not the hot sun of the day.

Karim and Abdul lived in the small village of Gourna, at the foot of the Theban hills, along with their mother Satre. It was a desolate place, where people scraped by doing whatever they could to make their lives bearable. The villagers would look out across the Nile at the bustling city of Luxor and dream of a better world.

It was the house of a poor person, of which there were many such houses in Gourna. There were only a few villagers with any money, and they let it be known by the size of their houses.

The houses of the better off were more than one story, and were often surrounded by gardens of palm trees. There was often a pool, with ducks and lotus flowers floating on the ripples of water, a stark contrast to the brothers' barren home, surrounded only by the dry, scorched earth.

It was a typical house, all one level, with only two rooms. The three of them slept all in the same room, on beds made of the same dried mud as their house. There was a thin layer of straw mattress, covered in dirty linen, the only thing separating their bodies from the hard surface of mud while they slept.

A poor house in Gourna could be distinguished by the brownish red clay pigeon house on the roof. The family could add to their meager meals by raising pigeons and then slaughtering and eating them whenever their supply of meat ran low.

The Abd el Amun house was one of the few without a pigeon house, and whether from poverty or sheer laziness, the family had never possessed one. Their house did not smell of bird shit and so they were able to sleep on the roof in summer. In this way, the family could take advantage of any cool night breeze that might drift toward their house in the night.

Inside or outside, at night Karim and Abdul listened to their mother Satre's deep, resonant snoring, and her occasional talking in her sleep. She seemed to carry on entire conversations with someone, and at times she sounded very angry at her invisible companion.

The brothers had no idea who she talked to, but they suspected it might be her husband, their father, who deserted the family years ago. He was a tomb robber from a long line of tomb robbers, going back to the time of the pharaohs.

According to Satre, their father's ancestors started out as craftsmen, living in Deir-El-Medina, the town of the tomb builders. They started as honorable stonecutters, but soon found they could make considerably more money robbing the tombs of all treasure which lay inside.

Because they were part of the initial building of the tombs, they knew in advance where the treasure would be kept. It was an easy matter to go in after the burial and take what they could carry.

The brothers were fascinated by the stories their mother told them when they were boys, of treasure hunting back in ancient times. They especially liked the part about one ancestor who was caught plundering a tomb. He was punished by having his nose and ears cut off, and then being buried alive.

"Let me see," an excited voice called from outside. "Money is always good news. Come, let me see what you have brought me."

The brothers walked through the cool rooms of the house, pushing aside the simple wooden table and three chairs, and found themselves once again out in the midafternoon heat.

"God, it's hot. Mother, why are you out here? You must be mad," Karim said with a look of disdain. He was ashamed of his mother, always had been ever since he could remember.

The fat, red-faced woman who was their mother bent over a large clay pot, her arms extended, working and kneading the barley seed flour used for making beer. She gasped with the exertion, as large drops of sweat ran down her heaving cleavage.

"Someone has to make the beer, and I know I can't count on you boys to do it," she answered, barely able to get out the words. "You're never around when I need you for anything."

"That's because we have more important things to do

than women's work. Stop a moment and see what we have brought for you," Karim said as he held out some small coins in the palm of his hand. It looked like a princely sum when Rahmad first gave it to them, but now it looked barely enough to feed one of them, but it had to feed three.

Karim failed to mention he kept a few coins out for himself, to spend on gaming and village prostitutes.

"Not much to speak of," Satre said, her eyes narrowing. "I knew I shouldn't trust you to deal with money matters," she said, turning toward Abdul. "How much do you have?"

"I have only this, mother," Abdul said, holding out his few coins for her inspection. "You are welcome to all of it, for whatever you choose," Abdul said.

"Well of course! I couldn't leave any money in your care, now could I?"

Without another word, Satre grabbed the coins with her puffy, arthritic fingers and slid them neatly into her open pocket. Karim smiled with satisfaction as he patted the hidden coins he saved in the pockets of his tunic. *His brother was foolish to give her all of his money; they had done all of the work besides,* he thought.

"Do you have anything else?" she asked, looking greedily at them.

"We brought back some wrappings for you. They should make a nice fire for the bread oven," Karim said smiling, handing her his sack, now much lighter than before.

She reached inside and pulled out a wad of dark brown rags, stiff with resin.

"These will do just fine, the darker the cloth, the hotter the fire," she said as she threw them on the ground. "Do you have anything for me too, Abdul?" she asked, looking at Abdul with distrust.

"I hate burning these, mother," Abdul said, handing her his cloth sack; "almost as much as I hate the shopkeeper grinding the bones down to dust. These people were alive once, like we are now."

"Don't be even more foolish than you already are, Abdul. They are dead now. Why shouldn't we use them as we can, to make our lives better. If we don't use them, someone else will," Satre said.

That was true. All of the poor families of Gourna would be more than happy to have the rags and whatever else they could find to heat their cooking fires.

"Now, both of you, don't just stand there, help me, will you?" Satre asked. "If you two want beer, get down here and help me make some.

The brothers joined her reluctantly and the three kneeled under a palmetto branch in the only sliver of shade around the house.

They sat in silence as they formed small, dense loaves of bread from the barley flour mixture. Later, the loaves would be cooked, and then smashed into containers of water mixed with date juice. The delicious liquid would then be filtered into a large clay barrel, providing drink for the three of them and whomever they could sell the beer to.

"On one of your trips, I'm coming with you," Satre said suddenly.

"What are you talking about, where?" Karim asked.

"When you go into the tombs, I want to come with you."

"Why?" Abdul asked.

"Fool. Why do you think?" Satre said.

"I don't know. Why would you want to come with us mother? It's dirty and dark, and, it smells," Abdul said, scowling.

"Well, of course it smells, my son the idiot! But, I think you two are cheating me. I want to find out just how much you bring back in a day, and I might go sell to the shopkeeper too."

Karim did not like the direction of Satre's thoughts. The last thing he wanted was for his greedy mother to meet Rahmad. *After she gets through with him, he may not buy from us ever again,* he thought.

"It's too dark in the tombs, mother, and the passages are too narrow for you to crawl through," Karim said carefully.

"Oh, so now I'm too fat! I'm going with you, and there's nothing you can do about it. I don't trust you boys with what you are doing, and I want to see for myself. Who knows, I may even find a bracelet to keep for myself," Satre said, extending her bare, sweaty, swollen arm admiringly.

"Mother, it is unsafe for you," Karim said in a voice he attempted to keep calm. "Why will you not listen to reason, and yes, you are too fat to enter the tombs without risking everything. You could end our trips for good, and then what would we do?"

"I am going, and that, my son, is that," Satre said with a triumphant flourish of her hand. "Now, you two get out there and finish grinding that barley into flour." She pointed to a heavy sack of barley, lying next to two millstones, baking in the sun.

The two brothers looked at her through squinted eyes filled with resignation. There was nothing they could do about it now, and the more they spoke, the worse their lives became. Now, they would have to sit out under the scorching midday sun and grind until their fingers bled. One small idea crept suddenly into Karim's mind. He wished his mother would die.

Karim and Abdul each poured a bit of the barley into their respective millstones, picked up their pestles and began to grind the full grains into fine powder. Satre and her sons grew silent once again, as they focused on their work of making bread and beer, the two main forms of sustenance to keep their family alive for another few days.

They were so focused in fact, they paid little attention to the common millstones they were using; millstones that were hewn from temple blocks cast aside long ago.

If Karim would have looked closely, he would have seen the small figure of Akhenaton, carved in elegant relief, the original colors long since destroyed, and the carving weathered by time.

There was Akhenaton, father of Tutankhamun, in all of his battle gear, holding the heads of his captives, ready to smite them with his upheld sword.

Abdul, for his part, used a millstone hewn from a different block of limestone, from a different sculptor. Instead of death and triumph, this millstone was carved with small animals. A pair of oxen, ducks, and goats marched across the stone surface, surrounded by a graceful design of interlaced palm trees.

The brothers could have seen the last vestiges of Akhenaton, from his temples destroyed centuries earlier, if only they had looked.

Ω Ω Ω Ω Ω

Nine

"Whom shall he be called?" Nebamun asked, looking down at the dead, strangely clothed man withering in the sun. He was wrapped in what was once white sheep's wool. Now it had turned a dirty grey color and was crawling with insects trying to make a nest in the thickly curled hair.

"He is called Zannanza, a prince of the Hittites. It is said he was attempting to marry an Egyptian of royal blood, to keep himself alive," Padi said.

"He should not have delayed in finding himself a wife," Nebamun said, bending over to examine the Hittite more closely.

The Hittite prince was young, stocky and powerfully muscled, with a face that was square shaped and stoutly formed. The face ended in a chin with the beginnings of a sparsely growing pointed black beard. His expression, even in death, looked unmistakably regal, a mixture of disdain and arrogance. His once dark brown eyes were now clouded over, and stared sightlessly out at Nebamun.

Multiple golden loops dangled from large holes in the man's ears, and gold and silver rings, each inlaid with precious stones adorned the Hittite's fingers. He carried some semblance of a gold crown on top of his head, although now it was flattened down to the man's head.

Nebamun knelt beside the prince, and grasped the damaged crown. It did not come off easily. In the desert heat, the crown had become scalding hot, almost as if it had melted to the man's skull. When Nebamun finally loosened the crown enough to pull it off, a slice of dark skin and a few strands of black curly hair came with it.

"This must have caused his death I believe," Nebamun said, gently touching an immense bruise on the man's head. "His skull is soft underneath, crushed."

"Yes, it is almost certain he was murdered. He could not have fought many battles. His face is unscarred, and he is young, middle twenties, I think," Padi agreed.

"Yes, he is young. Far too young to have met his death by execution," Nebamun said. "It is certain he has no family here, no one to mourn him, a sad ending, indeed."

"What shall be done with him?" Padi asked.

"We shall place him in one of the caves above Ta Set Maat, the town of the tomb builders. He must be placed apart from our people. It is unfortunate, but he must spend eternity alone," Nebamun answered.

"What of his clothing, his sheepskin?" Padi asked.

"We must leave him covered with it. As you know, sheepskin is not pure, as this Hittite is not pure, so we must leave him in like manner. Iramen, we will have no need of you today."

"Why?" Iramen asked. He wanted to participate in this most unusual burial.

"Hittites and other foreigners are not to be fully embalmed; their organs are not to be placed in canopic jars, but are to be left in the body, by order of Tutankhamun."

"Well, easy day for me then, brother," Iramen said, grateful not to have to work any longer in the scalding heat. "Perhaps I will get drunk instead."

"Yes, easy for you, brother, but, I insist you remain for the reading at least," Nebamun said, opening the Book of Going Out into the Day.

"This animal is not worthy of a reading," Iramen snarled. "We should let him just rot out here in the sun, without blessing, with no entrance into the afterlife." Iramen spat out the words, "He is not one of us."

"Silence; I will not have you desecrate the dead. All people deserve a blessing, and this man was a prince, fool! His Hittite gods will torment us if we do not show him honor. The Hittites have over one thousand gods, did you know that? So think carefully before you speak," Nebamun warned.

"Surely Nebamun, our Egyptian gods are more powerful. We have little to fear from foreign gods, perhaps Iramen is right," Padi said, trying to calm the situation. He did not want to stand out in the hot sun and listen to arguments.

"Padi, do not tell me you agree with the sacrilege my brother speaks. You of all people need understand. We must treat all with dignity, lest we find ourselves unworthy when we face Osiris at the end of our time."

"Yes, you are right, Nebamun," Padi said. "Is your brother not right, Iramen?"

"Yes, I suppose he is. After all, he is the great god Anubis on earth, even if he is just my brother," Iramen answered, his voice dripping in sarcasm.

"Silence, both of you; let us get this done quickly, so we can all finish our day in peace. Quiet, while I find a reading for this man," Nebamun said.

The reading for the Hittite would need to be different, but it was not going to be so easy finding a passage for his burial. He was not Egyptian, and since he died before he was able to marry an Egyptian, he remained a foreign person. But, he was still a prince, and royalty deserved some form of tribute. Nebamun turned many pages, and after finally deciding on an appropriate passage, he began to read:

"Haste on the way to me; your heart is with you. I sit down at the head of the great ones who are chiefs of their abodes. The wardens of the members of Osiris shall not hold you captive, though they keep ward over souls, and set a seal on the shadow which is dead. The way is open to your soul and shadow. Heaven shall not shut you in."

Padi and Iramen placed the Hittite prince on a litter and Iramen threw the sheepskin on top of him, covering his face.

"Brother, do not insult this man. I have warned you of the Hittite gods and their justice," Nebamun commanded. "Padi, please take care of this man properly."

Padi nodded and removed the sheepskin. He replaced it carefully on top of the dead man, leaving his face exposed. Padi scratched and swatted at the teeming swarm of tiny beetles which had moved onto his arms in a matter of seconds.

"See, there, that is what happens when you give a foreigner more dignity than he deserves," Iramen said, pointing to the large welts appearing on Padi's red arms.

"Be silent or be gone from this place, brother," Nebamun commanded, trying to remain calm. "Do you not feel anything for this man, taken in the prime of his life?"

"I feel nothing. He is but the wrong man, in the wrong place, at the wrong time. We owe him nothing," Iramen answered grimly.

"As Anubis, I owe him the best I can do for him. He was a royal person and he deserves his dignity preserved in death as in life."

"He deserves nothing," Iramen said stubbornly.

Nebamun looked at his brother as if he had never really seen him before. *How could he have become so vile?* He thought.

Nebamun looked down once more at the young prince. *He looks smaller somehow, tragic and vulnerable*, Nebamun thought. He replaced the thin crown back on the Hittite's head.

"Great one, he was found with this shield, lance, battle dagger, and his chariot. Who shall have this man's possessions?" Padi asked.

"This man's possessions shall be placed with him, so that he may have use of them in the afterlife. To be buried among strangers in a land not his own, they will provide little enough comfort for him." Nebamun replied.

"Surely not; if you will not take them Nebamun, I will take something for myself. Perhaps this dagger," Iramen said, picking up a finely made sickle shaped bronze dagger, the hilt of which was encrusted with large, brilliant red stones.

"No! I shall not pillage the dead," Nebamun said, "And you shall not either Iramen. Put down the dagger. Come, let us carry Prince Zannanza to the caves and let the desert do its work. He will dry in the desert heat. He will lie in the darkness, alone, with only his few belongings for company."

Iramen said nothing as lesser priests picked up the litter, and Nebamun and Padi began the procession. They would travel across the Nile by boat, up the west bank to the cliffs above Ta Set Maat, the town of the tomb builders.

Iramen was grateful he did not have to attend them and make the climb in the blazing sun. Soon, he would be sitting in the shade of a date palm, with a goatskin flask of beer in his hand. Perhaps later, he would enjoy one of the few of the Waset prostitutes who would lay with him.

He was certain he could find the cave again, and he knew he would be back to collect a few things. He had no fear of the one thousand Hittite gods; there was nothing this Hittite's gods could do to him. This was Egypt, and he did not believe in the power of the gods too much anyway.

Ω Ω Ω Ω Ω

Ten

"Don't you just love animal mummies?" Rahmad asked, as he handed Edward a small, rectangular shaped bundle. "It's an ibis, a large white water bird. The god of writing, Thoth, was an ibis in ancient times."

He was happy to have the Dunthorpes back again, and was going to make the most out of the opportunity to sell them something.

"Yes, I know about Thoth, god of the scribes. But this could be anything," Edward said, knocking on the hardened surface of the bundle. "I've heard about how people were cheated, even back in ancient times. They would put bones from anything, even their half-eaten meals, inside these wrappings and no one would ever know."

"I can assure you sir, this is an ibis mummy, but even so, I cannot allow you to unwrap it."

"I have no need of an ibis mummy," Edward replied, as he handed the bundle back to Rahmad

"I think they're disgusting, the poor things." Mary said. "Edward, don't you dare buy any of these."

"I'll buy what I like, thank you my dear. Certainly there must be something here that has caught your eye."

"I'll make you good price once again, because I like you. You are my favorite people among the English," Rahmad said.

"We are your favorite fools among the English, you mean," Mary said.

"Mary, look at this. Didn't you say you wanted a little kitty around the house?" Edward said, holding up a small, wrapped, bundle. He looked at the delicate pointed ears, slanted eyes, whiskers, and the small enigmatic smile. "Wonderful," he said.

"That is a servant of the cat goddess Bast. It was found along with hundreds of others at Bubastis, or what the ancients called Per Bast," Rahmad said. "It's beautiful isn't it, almost lifelike."

"I still feel sorry for the poor thing. No doubt it didn't die of old age," Mary said.

"Yes, that is true," Rahmad explained. "It was most certainly killed for sacred reasons. Cats held a very special place in ancient Egypt. Back when the Romans were in Egypt, a Roman citizen accidentally killed one, and he in turn was set upon and murdered by a crowd of Egyptians."

"Well, serves the man right. Killing a poor little creature, absurd, if you ask me," Mary said.

"Well Mary what do you think about this?" Edward asked, running his hand along the tightly wrapped linen encasing the body of a very large mummified crocodile. "I know it's a little large, but can't you just see it sitting out in our garden back home?"

"That, my dear English friends, is the servant of the crocodile god Sobek. Found along with her young at the sacred temple of Sobek at Kom Ombo," Rahmad explained.

"Look Mary, aren't they cute?" Edward asked, holding up one of the tiny dried crocodiles, about ten inches long.

"Sad, that's all I can say," Mary answered. "It is sad to treat god's creatures in such a way."

"So, have you tried a bit of the dried mummy powder I sold to you before?" Rahmad asked, changing the subject.

"Yes, yes, and I do think I feel more energetic, more virile," Edward said, casting a sideways glance at his wife.

Mary rolled her eyes. "You couldn't pay me to eat that."

"Let me show you something else, made from our friends the mummies. See this?" Rahmad asked, holding up a thin sheet of parchment.

"You make *paper* out of the poor things?" Mary asked incredulously.

"Yes, indeed, as long as the wrappings don't have that much dark resin on them, we can make paper, looks like our papyrus. But, if there is quite a bit of resin, the paper turns out brown, only good for packing meat," Rahmad explained. "Sometimes the mummies were wrapped in hundreds of yards of cloth, giving us a lot of paper to sell."

"My Lord, but that is disgusting," Mary said; "Makes one believe in cremation."

"Yes, indeed madam, but we are not the only ones who make paper out of the mummies," Rahmad said, smiling.

"What are you talking about?" Mary asked. "Who else but Egyptians would think of such a thing?"

"There is a man, an American, I've been told," Rahmad explained. "He is, as we speak, importing mummies for his paper mill."

"You are joking,"Mary said.

"No Madam, I most certainly am not. It seems there is now an outbreak of cholera, traced to the brown paper sold to a butcher. The butcher's wrapping paper came from this man's paper mill, and now his paper mill is under suspicion. I am afraid the American will no longer be a customer," Rahmad said with a wink.

"That's fascinating, Rahmad, but I think I'm just going to buy the little kitty cat mummy with the sweet face. What do you think Mary?"

"If you must, maybe I can put her out in the garden, instead of the crocodile, or, she might make a good doorstop."

"So, Rahmad, I'll take the kitty, and some more powdered mummy, you know, like the deal we had before," Edward said.

"Edward, you can't be serious. What did you do with the other mummy powder?"

"I mixed it with water, and drank it, as instructed. Well, sometimes I mixed it with Scotch too. You know what Mary? It does make me feel better, stronger even."

"Yes, yes. The mummy powder I sell is from many different mummies, maybe even some pharaohs," Rahmad said.

"You hear that Mary? I might even have some pharaoh in me right now."

"For you sir, I make special deal. I sell you the cat with the smiling face, the powdered mummy, and I give you a special present, because I like you," Rahmad said.

He went back behind the counter and retrieved the top copy of a book, from a pile of identical books. Rahmad dusted off the thick layer of dirt on its cover, and presented it to the Englishman. The book was bound with a cover of hard black paper, embossed with gold lettering. A group of Egyptian figures marched across the front, carrying a funeral ship.

"Is this the Book of the Dead?" Edward asked; "the famous Book of the Dead? I've read much about this, but it doesn't seem quite as impressive as I thought."

"This, my friend, was known in ancient times as the Book of Coming Forth by Day, that is, the book of going into the afterlife. This of course, is just a copy. The original book was written on scrolls of papyrus, about twenty four hundred years before your Christ was born."

"What's in it?" Mary asked. "If we read it, we won't be cursed or anything, will we?"

"Don't be silly, Mary. There are no such things as curses," Edward said. "Don't be afraid of just a simple paper book."

"Yes, yes, do not be afraid, Madam," Rahmad said soothingly. "Why, we would all be cursed if there really was such a thing. It contains magic spells for entering into the afterlife, what the ancients called the Duat."

"Magic spells? Curses, you mean," Mary said, unconvinced. "As a Christian, such things are blasphemous."

"Don't worry, my dear. I am here to protect you," Edward answered. "Besides, it's a gift. How could we refuse a gift from our new Egyptian friend, Rahmad?"

"Quite so; so you will take my little cat mummy home with you, a little more of the dried mummy powder, and my special gift. Is there anything else you would like?" Rahmad asked hopefully.

"Well, if you should happen upon a human mummy, you know; the whole thing. Something unusual, I would be very interested, indeed," Edward said.

"*Edward, how could you?* Mary asked, with a look of horror on her face. What could we possibly do with an entire mummy? Surely, you don't want to bring the thing home with us?"

"It's not a thing, Mary. Remember it used to be a walking, talking human just like us. I thought it would be fun for our friends. You know, we could have a dinner party and a mummy showing all in one evening."

"God help us. I never should have married you, Edward. You're some kind of ancient history fanatic, not at all a practical pursuit."

"But you did marry me, and here we are, in Egypt, and I want a mummy," Edward announced defiantly.

"I do not wish you to argue, especially in my shop. For now, it's just the cat, book, and mummy powder, so don't worry Madam," Rahmad said.

"Fine; Edward, can we get out of here please? I have had enough buying of souvenirs for now, thank you very much," Mary said.

"Yes, my dear," Edward replied, as he tucked the cat mummy under his arm. "Goodbye for now, Rahmad."

"Goodbye, goodbye," Rahmad said with a satisfied smile.

"Rahmad, I hope this is goodbye forever," Mary said. "I hope to never come into your shop again."

"As you wish, Madam," Rahmad answered. He leaned in and whispered in his ear, so that only Edward could hear, "I will do what I can to find you that mummy."

Ω Ω Ω Ω Ω

Eleven

"Nebamun, they are ready for us," Padi said, gesturing down to the bodies of Nasra and Amunet lying on the slanted stone slab. The channels of the slab were caked with a thin film of dried fat, ending in a large dried pool of body fluids on the ground.

By now, in the shade of the Per Nefer, the bodies were completely dried out, their dessicated flesh looking like withered fruit. The brown skin of the mother and daughter was shriveled tightly over their bones, and they lay there together, waiting for their trip to eternity.

"Very well, remove the packaging and wash the bodies please. But, Padi, my friend, do not touch the body of the mother as you did before. Just do what you must and no more, understand?"

"Yes, Great One, you need have no fear of that. She no longer looks like a woman to me, only the dried remains of who she was before."

"Very well, begin please," Nebamun commanded.

"Great One, it seems their rings are missing. The braided bracelets are still around their wrists, but the blue glass rings are gone," Padi said. "You remember, they each had a scarab beetle insignia."

"Yes, yes, I remember," Nebamun said. "Are you quite certain they did not fall off? As the body dries, the fingers become much smaller, narrower, and the rings could have fallen to the ground."

Padi dutifully checked underneath the dried corpses and the pools of fat and fluids, even the drainage channels in the stone, but he could find no jewelry.

"I am afraid they are not here, Great One." Padi said. "Do you have any idea who may have taken them?"

"Why do you think someone has taken them?" Nebamun asked. "I am certain you have someone in mind, Padi. Speak now. Who has stolen the rings?"

"Your brother," Padi said simply.

"*Iramen?* That cannot be possible. Do you remember what I said about accusing my brother?" Nebamun asked. "Why should he do such a thing?"

"Yes, I remember. You said I might not remain a priest, but it is my sacred duty to tell you this no matter what may happen to me."

"Speak then," Nebamun commanded.

"Great One, I saw him trying to trade them to a prostitute for her services, but he did not see me. I saw the woman accept them in payment." Padi said. "I could not be certain until I returned and examined the bodies. But now that I see no rings, I am certain. Your brother took them. Of that, I have no doubt."

"That is the final sacrilege," Nebamun said. "I cannot believe my brother would steal from these two innocents. It is time he must pay for his crimes. I will have him arrested when we return home today."

"You should at least wait until after the Feast of Sobek," Padi said.

"Why do you say that my friend?" Nebamun asked. "Surely he should face justice as soon as possible, do you not think so?"

"As high priest, you preside over the Feast of Sobek," Padi explained. "You should do so with a calm heart and not be upset by your brother. This matter can wait for a few days at least."

"As is often the case, you are right Padi. This matter can wait until after the feast," Nebamun said. "I must admit, I am relieved not to have to deal with my brother's transgressions, with the ceremony being held in two days time. It is just too much."

"I am happy you have reached your decision. I think it is most wise," Padi said, flattered at the compliment.

"So, with that settled, let us begin, so that we may soon finish before midday."

Padi nodded. He expertly cut open the incision and removed the packets inside the bodies, first Nasra, and then Amunet. Despite having been changed several times during the forty days, these packets were dark brown, damp with oil and body secretions. He washed the body cavities with palm wine.

"Do you have the onions and myrrh?" Nebamun asked.

"Yes, I have them, and the sawdust packages. Shall I place them now?"

"Yes, Padi, place them and stitch the bodies please."

As commanded, Padi placed an onion in each eye socket of Nasra and Amunet, to give more life to their faces. He placed myrrh and linen wrapped sawdust packages inside the dead women to better fill out their bodies and make them look more as they did in life.

"Nebamun, I have a suggestion," Padi said.

"Yes, go on, my friend. What is your suggestion?" Nebamun asked.

"Well, I suggest I stuff Nasra's breasts with linen, to give them more shape."

Nebamun looked at Padi with curiosity, unsure whether he could trust the priest not to touch the woman in an unseemly manner. After the admission about his brother, Nebamun decided he must trust his friend to do what is correct.

"Yes, you are quite right, proceed please," Nebamun commanded.

Padi rolled up the softest linen he could find, until he had two round shapes of medium size in his hand. He pushed them through the incision and moved them up into the space where Nasra's breast tissue had been. He pulled the skin taught over the linen, so that Nasra's nipples protruded beneath two full, voluptuous mounds.

"That should do nicely," Padi said. "But there is one more thing, Great One.

"I have heard that other embalmers have begun stuffing the women's birth canal with linen, to close it up and prevent evil from entering the body," Padi said. "They have begun to do this for all women, not just the royal ones."

"If it is as you say, we must do all we can for them. It is the least we can do after their bodies have been robbed of all their small treasures. Begin please Padi; but remember what I told you about only touching what is necessary, and no more. Do you understand?"

"Yes, Great One," Padi said. "I will do as you command me, in all things."

Padi gently spread the withered legs of Nasra enough to slightly open what was left of her vagina. He gathered small pieces of linen and dipped them in hot resin, and then pushed them up into the crevice with a spiral rod. For added protection, Padi scooped up some melted wax and lightly placed it over Nasra's vagina, covering the dark pubic hair with a sticky mass.

"I am satisfied Great One," Padi said.

"I am satisfied also, my friend," Nebamun said. "You have conquered the carnal lust which I know burns within you. You are a good man. Now, do the same for Amunet, please."

Padi smiled appreciatively and spread the young girl's legs apart. She was much more pliable than her mother, and Padi was quickly finished sealing her vagina with molten linen and wax.

He expertly stitched the torso incisions closed with a length of tiny linen thread. Padi then covered the incisions with wax plates, each embossed with the wadjet, the eye of Horus, to keep evil spirits from entering the body. As a final step before wrapping them for eternity, he anointed each of the bodies with cedar oil, and closed up the ears, nose and mouth with beeswax.

"It is done, Great One, the bodies are sealed completely."

Nebamun placed a roll of papyrus under Nasra's arm. On the papyrus were written all of the spells and verses which he had used for Nasra and Amunet. The messages of joy and rebirth would follow them into their life after death.

"Padi, begin the wrapping, please."

"Nebamun, what shall become of your brother?" Padi asked suddenly. He was momentarily sorry he had spoken of the misdeeds of Iramen. The revelations had made his friend the high priest, very sad. But, it had to be done. Iramen had committed a grave sacrilege, punishable by death, and Nebamun knew this.

"He may be executed," Nebamun said, as if reading Padi's thoughts. "My hope is that he will be banished from Waset, perhaps all of Egypt may not see him again. Most likely he will take his vile ways with him and just move to another village."

"Will you be content, my friend?" Padi asked. "I hope that you do not miss your brother, for you are his family."

"I no longer know my brother. I have no thoughts on where he might go. I must not think of him, Padi. I will grow sad, and we have much work to do."

"That is so. I will speak no more of Iramen," Padi said with a comforting smile. "We can perform the wrapping, just the two of us."

"Good. Let us begin," Nebamun commanded. "We shall use cheaper cloth for the underlayers, those closest to the skin. And we shall use the finer linen on the uppermost layers."

"Why, Great One?" Padi asked.

"We do this to save the husband from unnecessary expense. The uppermost layers are all anyone will see. Now, shall we start with the mother?"

Padi nodded, pleased with Nebamun's wise decision. He began by placing a long strip of linen underneath Nasra's head and wrapping it closely against her skull. When her face and the back of her head were completely covered over several times, he twisted the cloth across her chest.

He started on the fingers, wrapping each of them separately and then joining them together, covering each of her hands several times with linen. Padi then wrapped each of Nasra's arms completely up to her shoulders.

He moved down to the feet, wrapping each toe individually, and then joining them together with a cloth wrapped several times around each foot. He added a length of linen and proceeded to work the wrappings around the entire length of each leg.

Once the head, arms and legs were wrapped, it was time for her torso. Nebamun began by placing a large scarab beetle, beautifully carved in green jasper, next to her heart to protect it. He pronounced in a solemn voice:

"O my heart of my mother! O my heart of my mother! O my heart of my different forms. Do not stand up as a witness against Nasra. Do not tell lies about Nasra in the presence of the Great god. Do not create opposition against her, or tip the scales against her in the presence of the Keeper of the Balance! You are the soul which is in her body. Go forth to the happy place whereto we speed."

Padi used a broad width of cloth to wrap the abdomen in several layers and cover the torso completely. He paused as Nebamun dipped a sharpened reed in a small pot of black ink and wrote "Nasra, wife of Shimra" on this first layer of linen.

Padi wrapped Nasra's body with a second and third layer of wide linen, pausing each time for Nebamun to inscribe

"Nasra, wife of Shimra" on each of the layers. It was important to write her name often so that her soul, her Ba, would recognize her in the afterlife. In this way, her soul would return to her.

Padi secured each of her arms and legs firmly against her body with a fourth layer of linen so that she became one single bundle of cloth. He secured these last layers with thick strips of cloth placed lengthwise along her body and across her head and legs.

He gathered together the four alabaster canopic jars, each representing the sons of Horus, which would hold the organs of the dead woman. They would be joined together with her body in the afterlife. Nasra's organs were now little more than small brown pieces, looking much like dried dates. He anointed each of them with perfumed oil and wrapped them separately, each in their own small bundle of linen.

Padi placed her stomach in the canopic jar with the head of the jackal Dwamutef, the baboon god Hapy received the lungs, the intestines belonged to the falcon god Qebehsenuef, and the human headed canopic jar of Imstey received the liver.

Nebamun sealed each of the canopic jars with wax to make certain they were safe for the journey into the afterlife.

"Nasra is complete. Padi, you may begin with the daughter now."

Padi nodded and began wrapping Amunet in the same way as her mother, pausing just long enough for Nebamun to place a small heart scarab, also of green jasper, next to Amunet's heart and pronounce the sacred text from the Book of Coming Forth by Day:

"O her heart of her mother! O her heart of her mother! O her heart of her different ages. Do not stand up as a witness against Amunet. Do not tell lies about Amunet in the presence of the Great God. Do not create opposition against her, or tip the scales against her in the presence of the Keeper of the Balance! You are the soul which is in her body. Go forth to the happy place whereto we speed."

Padi wrapped the young girl's torso, and Nebamun inscribed "Amunet, daughter of Nasra and Shimra" on each of the layers of linen. Her body was much smaller than the mother and they completed the wrapping of her corpse quickly. Padi wrapped each of her tiny organs in small packets of linen, and Nebamun placed them each in their sacred canopic jar.

"It is time to wrap them together, Padi," Nebamun commanded.

Padi nodded. Nebamun held Amunet's head, and Padi held her feet, and together they moved the small girl next to her mother. Amunet's head was resting just underneath her dead mother's arm. They would protect each other in eternity.

Padi encased their bodies in large swaths of linen, wrapping their bodies securely together, and then binding them firmly with strips running from their heads down to their feet.

Nebamun quoted the final message from memory and in a solemn voice he pronounced:

"You shall not decay. You shall not rot. You shall not putrify. You shall have your being. You shall live. You shall flourish. Your bodies shall not become a ruin or be destroyed on this earth. You shall wake up in peace."

"The pen and ink please, Padi," Nebamun asked. "Perhaps one day you will again allow me to try and teach you to read and write. It would save us both much time."

"Yes, Great One," Padi replied. "But I am not as wise as you, not so quick to learn. That is why you are high priest, and I serve you."

"You can learn, my friend," Nebamun said. "Just remember that the lines of writing may be read in either direction, depending upon which way the characters are facing. If the characters face to the left, the line must be read left to right. If the characters face to the right, the line must be read right to left."

"It is all very upsetting to me. I cannot think," Padi replied. "And then there are the different colors for everything. My mind is in chaos thinking about it."

"That is easy also, my friend. Objects made of wood are painted yellow, and those of bronze are painted green," Nebamun instructed. "It is the custom to use blue to paint building plans and circles, squares, and shapes like them. The baskets and pots containing our food are usually red. Does that help you?"

"No, I am afraid it does not. I am just a fool, I think," Padi replied. "And then there are so many characters, each meaning something different. I cannot remember them all."

"There are some more important than others. For example, the vulture," Nebamun began again. "Meaning mother, because the bird loves her children so much, she feeds them with her own blood."

"Such an ugly creature, but I suppose it does have some good qualities," Padi conceded.

"Yes, and the bee," Nebamun continued. "We must not forget the bee, meaning our ruler, the head of our people."

"Yes, but why the bee?"

"Because our ruler must respond to the needs of a government, much the same as the bee responds to the needs of the hive."

"I suppose that makes sense," Padi said, nodding.

"Do not forget that most important of characters, the jackal. When drawn by himself, means only a scribe, but when the same animal is drawn on a pedestal, he refers to us, the priests. We oversee all things sacred much like a faithful dog oversees his house."

"I am beginning to understand, but there is so much to know," Padi said. "My mind cannot hold all of it inside."

"Well, perhaps you will learn one day, when I am dead and you are writing an inscription for my corpse. Now, shall we get back to work?"

Padi nodded and passed the sharpened reed and pot of black ink to Nebamun, who smoothed down the layers of linen wrapping, making a smooth canvas for the final inscription. He wrote:

"Come for our souls! The sacred barque will be joyful and the great god will proceed in peace when you allow our souls to ascend. May it see our corpses, may it rest on our mummies, which will never be destroyed or perish."

"A perfect inscription, Great One," Padi said, after Nebamun read it to him.

"Yes, I believe it is. Let us hope that Nasra and Amunet find the life in the underworld that they were denied on earth. What else can we hope for a mother and daughter, both taken too young?"

"Great One, it is sad, is it not? I can only wonder what Shimra, the stonecutter is feeling," Padi said. "How empty his life must be without their laughter filling his house."

"Yes, but now he will honor them with a procession of family and friends. They will be carried down to their tomb and placed among all the things they hold dear, with Anubis and Osiris to comfort them forever," Nebamun said.

"Yes, I am happy we wrapped them together one encircling the other," Padi said. "It is good they will be together at least."

"Let us hope you and I will have such honors," Nebamun said. "I would have liked to be wrapped in the arms of someone dear to me, but fate called for me to be the servant of Anubis, and for that I am grateful."

"Indeed," Padi said, "and I am grateful to be a priest, and to be your friend, Nebamun."

"And I, yours, my friend," Nebamun answered. "Padi, I believe we are finished for today. I shall see you tomorrow for the funeral procession."

"Tomorrow, then. We will send these women into the afterlife with all speed," Padi said.

As Padi walked away from the Per Nefer, he expected at any moment to hear the footsteps of Nebamun behind him, but he heard only his own sandals crunching against the sand.

He turned around, but Nebamun hadn't moved. Nebamun was still standing in the shade of the Per Nefer, still staring down at the large, shapeless bundle of linen.

Ω Ω Ω Ω Ω

Twelve

"What are you trying to sell me now?" Rahmad asked, as he placed a thick, gold bracelet in the design of two pacing lions on his arm.

"That's beautiful! How much is it worth?" Abdul asked.

"More than you will ever make. This is Sekhmet, goddess of war. Appropriate I should sell it to the English I think. All they do is make war and destroy things. They think they are helping us. What arrogance!"

He held his arm up for the brothers to admire what they could never have. "I'm going to sell this for a lot of money, or, I may just keep it for myself." He smiled, exposing a set of jagged teeth, the color of brown earth. A small piece of half-eaten bread clung to an open space between his two front incisors.

"We have something very special for you today. We found it just this morning," Karim said. He placed a large canvas bag on top of Rahmad's filthy glass countertop. Abdul placed the small cedar box he was carrying next to it.

"Careful, don't break anything. Let's carry it to the table. I'll take a look, but no promises. If I don't like, I won't buy," Rahmad said with a warning look.

Abdul opened the box and set out the four alabaster canopic jars onto the countertop. Other than being covered with dust, they were in perfect condition. The etched alabaster still retained its polish after centuries of being buried.

Karim carefully pulled the canvas bag down, while Abdul pulled out an ancient mummy, still perfectly wrapped. Strips of linen, hardened with centuries-old resin encased the slim form.

Larger linen strips criss-crossed the body, further defining the delicate curves of what looked like a woman. A small, linen-covered bump poked out from between her legs.

"We think it's a baby; a baby and its mother. The mother probably died giving birth to it," Karim said.

"There is only one way to know. Let's unwrap it," Rahmad said. "It will take a small chisel to get through this hard resin."

"But you will ruin it, and then it will not be worth nearly so much. You're trying to cheat us," Karim said.

"How do I know you're not trying to cheat me, unless I can see what's underneath, could be a pile of sawdust for all I know," Rahmad said. "Unwrap it, or I won't pay you anything for it and you can go. It makes no difference to me."

"Yes, I suppose. But you'd better pay us what it is worth," Karim threatened.

"Let's see what is inside this jar first," Abdul said. "That will be fun."

Before Rahmad could stop him, Abdul opened the human-headed jar and tapped its contents into his hand.

"Looks like a dried date," Abdul said. He poked at the

small brown thing, shriveled and wrinkled lying in his equally wrinkled palm.

"More like a turd, brother," Karim said laughing. "You have found an ancient turd. Congratulations. I will let you keep what it is worth."

"That is the embalmed liver. Did you find the jars close to this mummy?" Rahmad asked. "If you did, then these jars contain the mummified liver, intestines, lungs and stomach of this woman, or whoever it is. Now, shall we get down to business and unwrap it then?'

The brothers nodded their agreement and with a broad smile, Rahmad produced a chisel. He began to chip away at the smooth, dark surface of the mummy. Small pieces of hardened resin fell to the floor like shards of glass.

"Sweep those up," Rahmad commanded, handing Abdul a straw broom. "I can grind up those pieces and sell them too."

Rahmad began to sweat. Cutting through the hard resin was more difficult than he thought.

"Karim, give me that handsaw over there," he said, pointing to a small multi-toothed blade sitting on the dusty back counter.

He began to saw through the hard casing, as Karim looked on anxiously. He cut more quickly now, through the larger strips of softer inner cloth. The strips fell to the floor, and Abdul gathered them up and put them in the pile of chippings for Rahmad. The cloth could be sold too.

Rahmad made a small cut through one of the inner linen strips and began to remove the wrappings from the mummy. The linen strips circled the body in many layers, yards upon yards of cloth. As the linens gradually fell away, small, beautifully carved objects tumbled out.

"Amulets. I love amulets," Rahmad said, rubbing his hands together.

"Look at this; it means maybe we'll have good luck," Abdul said, holding up a small scarab beetle formed out of brilliant blue turquoise.

"Don't touch it. If I decide to pay you, I don't want your filthy hands on anything I can sell later," Rahmad said.

"Yes, but you haven't bought anything yet, so my brother can hold anything he wants. We found it, remember?" Karim said.

Abdul smiled appreciatively. His brother never defended him before, only criticized and belittled him. Maybe his luck was really about to change. He wanted the small scarab beetle, wanted it very badly.

More amulets peeked out from under the wrappings.

"This is the eye of Horus," Rahmad said authoritatively. "It was called the wedjat in ancient times, used to protect good health and guard against evil. In ancient times, sailors used to paint this on the prow of their ships to gain safe passage on the sea."

"I know this one," Abdul said triumphantly, as he held up a loop shaped object cut from green jasper. "It's the ankh, symbol of eternal life."

"Everyone knows that, fool, but Rahmad, what is this one?" Karim asked as he picked up a small amulet made out of ivory.

"It's called the Djed pillar," Rahmad answered. It represents the backbone of Osiris, and symbolizes stability. There was a spell associated with it that would allow its owner to sit up and have use of his spine. Now if you have no more questions, can I finish this?"

"I'm just asking. No harm in asking, sorry," Karim answered sarcastically.

Rahmad delved further down into the wrappings, ripping faster and faster at the fragile linen coverings. He stopped only to remove the stray amulets that tumbled out; the soul Ba, a bird figure with a human head, Taweret, the hippopotamus goddess of expectant mothers, and more scarab beetles, although less beautiful than the one coveted by Abdul.

One amulet, a strange dwarflike man with his tongue hanging out, carved in dark blue lapis, caught Rahmad's attention.

"That's Bes, the god of childbirth. Between this amulet and that of Taweret, that must mean there is a baby in here," he said, rubbing his hands excitedly.

He removed the last linens covering the woman, and she lay there, naked for the three men to gaze upon. She still had her long strands of hair, which lay in stiff curls around her throat, but they had now turned red from embalming chemicals.

Her head was crowned with a leather band, placed there thousands of years ago by a loving family member. Her skin was unlike that of most mummies Rahmad had seen. This one looked fuller somehow, not shriveled and dried up.

"She looks almost like she could get up and walk away," Abdul said.

"Well, she can't. She's been packed with sawdust, Rahmad answered, "to give more form to her body."

"What's that covering her face?" Karim asked pointing to the thin yellow film spread over the woman's forehead, down to her chin.

"Yellow ochre," Rahmad answered. "Later mummies were painted like this one, yellow ochre for women, and red ochre for men."

"What makes you such an expert?' Karim asked suspiciously. "You seem to know a lot for a shopkeeper. You're probably a tomb robber just like us, aren't you?"

"Many people have come through my little shop, from all over the world they come," Rahmad said. "They call themselves archaeologists, but they really only want to steal from Egypt. They only want to rob the tombs, just like you two. But I have learned a lot from them."

"Let's get on with the baby," Karim said impatiently. "Enough with the history lesson; I want to see what the baby looks like."

"Yes, yes, let's see what we have in this small bundle. Finally, now we will know," Rahmad said, after removing the last bit of linen to expose the small bulging object between the woman's legs.

It was indeed shaped like a small infant. The delicate figure was wrapped securely with its own set of linens, but these were not encased in the hard resin of the mother, but were soft and pliable.

"Do you think it was a boy or a girl?" Abdul asked. "I wonder what its name might have been."

"What does it matter? They are both worth the same to us."

Karim was back to his old self. Biting, sarcastic, Abdul

thought. *Yes I really want to keep the scarab and bring my good luck back.*

"A royal baby, then at least; A prince or princess," Abdul went on.

There was only a small amount of resin sticking to the linens covering the baby, and they fell away quickly until only one small layer of wrapping remained.

"Now, finally we will see," Rahmad said, again rubbing his hands together. He carefully pulled away the final layer of linen and exposed the ancient corpse inside.

"*My god, what is that?*" Karim asked his face contorted in a scowl of disappointment.

A small, dead monkey looked up at the three men with sightless eyes. The tiny face was wrinkled and distorted, with small tufts of hair still springing out from its skull. Its pitiful, spindly arms and legs were squeezed into its body and held there by a small piece of rope. Its wax covered mouth was frozen open in a scream of agony.

Ω Ω Ω Ω Ω

Thirteen

"Has Shimra, the stonecutter, paid for a sarcophagus for them?" Nebamun asked. "Surely, he can afford even a simple one."

"No, there is no sarcophagus made for Nasra and Amunet, Great One," Padi answered. "It seems the husband has very little to trade, and the bread loaves he did have, he used to pay us, for the embalming. He wishes them to be buried very simply, with no coffin, and in a communal tomb, with all the others."

"Poor man; It is his sacred duty to provide the best he can for them. He must be sad for his wife and daughter, that he cannot do more for them."

"Yes, Great One, perhaps one day the gods will honor him in his death," Padi answered.

"I know that Osiris will grant a bountiful existence for Nasra and Amunet in the afterlife. That is all we can hope for," Nebamun said sadly.

He placed the heavy mask of Anubis on his head, and motioned for four junior priests to lift the litter containing the bodies of the mother and daughter, embalmed together.

With Nebamun as Anubis, leading the procession, Padi

stepped in behind him, carrying a wooden box with the canopic jars. The four junior priests came forward with the litter containing the bodies, followed by more junior priests who were to help carry Nasra and Amunet's earthly belongings.

They left the shade of the Per Nefer, out into the blazing sun. The sand was a brilliant white in the radiant heat. Once again, they made their way down the rows of palm and pomegranate trees and around the outer walls of Ipet Isut.

The procession passed the Sacred Lake, its surface slightly rippled by a slight breeze. Nebamun wished he could feel the air around him, but he could not; the Anubis mask was too tight.

The songbirds of the aviary began their music, only to be drowned out by the throaty sounds of the sacred geese of Amun.

Once again they passed the incomplete statue of Tutankhamun. The sculptors were not at work in the heat of the day, but a funeral procession knew no such boundaries of time.

They marched along, a cloud of dust forming behind them. The citizens of Waset looked at them with vague curiosity, wondering who might lie beneath the mummy wrappings. At the outskirts of Waset, they came to the narrow street which had been home to Nasra and Amunet.

The street looked deserted at first. But then, one at a time, people opened their doors and came out to line the street as the funeral procession passed. A few women, wearing cones of perfume on their heads, resembled Nasra, and Nebamun took them to be the dead woman's sisters. Most of the people along the street were just curious neighbors.

Weepers, women mourners paid for by Shimra, beat and scratched their bare breasts and smeared their faces with dirt. They looked up at the sky and stretched their arms wide; with wailing cries they lamented the loss of the two people they had never met.

Some members of Nasra's family carried an offering of food or drink to be placed in the tomb and used by Nasra and Amunet in the afterlife. Others carried everyday objects, favorite things used by Nasra in life; a chair made of reeds plaited together, a favorite senet game, and a delicate clay container for the dead woman's cosmetics. The younger family members carried smaller items for Amunet; a favorite doll made from linen cloth, and a toy box carved of wood.

But what of the husband, Nebamun thought. *Where is he?*

As they neared the end of the street, a man limped out, and Nebamun could hardly recognize the man he had met years before. Shimra was much different, years spent cutting stone had aged him. The once youthful body was now bent over at an angle, such that it was difficult for Shimra to look anyone in the face.

He had the painful, eternally red eyes of a stonecutter, and he had a deep, persistent cough, as he tried in vain to catch his breath. The most obvious of his infirmities was that Shimra's right foot was gone, crushed by a fallen block of stone.

In its place was a foot shaped prosthesis, made of leather and wood. It looked in every way like a foot, but it did not bend, so Shimra dragged it on the ground and leaned very heavily on a walking stick. It was by this means that he shuffled slowly through the crowd and joined the procession. He paid no attention to the pitying murmurs of his neighbors, but walked straight ahead.

Nebamun would have liked to acknowledge Shimra, but as high priest during a procession, he was forbidden to give even the slightest wave. Instead, Nebamun could only watch as Shimra joined the procession, carrying a small linen bundle, the stonecutter's arms etched with deep scratches from decades of cutting sharp limestone.

As the procession wound its way through the maze of streets, more and more people gathered to bid farewell to the dead. By the time they arrived at the docks next to the Nile, a large crowd had gathered. It seemed to Nebamun as if many in Waset knew this family.

At the docks, two large funeral boats were decorated and ready for their arrival. The boats were made of cedar wood, held together by ropes of grass. The planks creaked and moaned as if in agony as the party climbed aboard.

One boat carried the members of the procession, and the dead with their belongings. Relatives and friends of the family attending the tomb ceremony filled the other.

They were bound for the necropolis at Qurna, on the edge of the plains of Waset, where Nasra and Amunet would spend eternity.

"There are many gathered for them, Nebamun," Padi said. "Shimra must be pleased that so many are here to bid them farewell."

"Yes, Padi, but many are here just for the celebrations and the food," Nebamun answered. "I am certain there are also some in the crowd who are here to note where they are buried. They will return later to rob them of anything of value."

"Surely not. They are going into a communal tomb, where the burials are modest. Perhaps they will be left alone," Padi said hopefully.

"Perhaps," Nebamun said, "although it is unlikely. No one is spared from the greed of the tomb robbers." He looked out over the glassy surface of the Nile, watching the reflection of the funeral boat in the water.

I do not like when he becomes like this, Padi thought. *It will be a very long day indeed if he is not of glad heart.*

"What is wrong, my friend. Can I help to cheer you?" Padi asked.

"Padi, my friend, it is only that some days I grow weary of spending so much of my life in the company of the dead. I would like to be among the living."

"Yes, my friend, but you are the Great One, the incarnation of Anubis on earth." Padi reminded him. "You are the guardian of the dead."

"Yes, but look at us. We are both without family. I might have enjoyed a wife, children, but I have only a brother, who is soon to be banished, forbidden to return on pain of death."

"Where do you think your brother will go?" Padi asked.

"I do not know. It is my hope he will go far from here, where he will not be found; somewhere with an abundance of drink and whores to satisfy his needs. I do want him to be happy," Nebamun answered. "Padi, we have a long day today. I would like to be alone now, please."

He really is not like himself, Padi thought. "Yes, Great One, please ask if you need anything, and I will come."

"You are a good friend to me, Padi. I am sorry if I am difficult today. It is not my intention. Forgive me, my friend."

Padi smiled. "You are forgiven. Now, enjoy the day, do you not think the Nile is especially beautiful? Truly, the great river is a gift from the gods."

Nebamun looked out across the Nile, its dark green waters curling in small waves. He could see in the distance the immense seated statues of Tutankhamun's grandfather Amenhotep III, guarding the entrance to the pharoah's mortuary temple.

He marveled at the size of the figures, constructed from sandstone quarried many days journey from Waset and hauled over land on sledges pulled by oxen and men.

Nebamun thought about the immense scarab beetle statues of Khepri, God of the dawning sun, carved in red granite, sitting atop a stone block on the grounds of the mortuary temple. He remembered when he was a small boy how groups of small children ran around the beetle.

He smiled as he remembered how Iramen and he would join the group, running around the scarab seven times for good luck in life. He and Iramen were dear to each other as the gods in those days.

He could see the edge of the desert and the dim outline of the royal necropolis and its many tombs cut into the rock.

The distant outline of the workmens' village stood out as a dark, muddy brown blur against the golden sand. His imagination conjured up images of the workmen and their families bustling about, taking care of whatever tasks they could perform in the desolate wasteland.

The women would be making lamp wicks of twisted flax fibers, to be sold to the workmen who toiled in the dark tombs. The men would be taking advantage of a moment of peace, drinking beer and sitting in the cool interior of their small windowless houses.

He could imagine the sound of light laughter floating across the water, and the delicious smell of bread roasting in the mud ovens.

It must be nice to be happy, and live simple lives, Nebamun thought. *I should have married and had children, but now it is too late.*

The boats reached the West Bank of the Nile and there was another crowd awaiting them as they disembarked. People of all ages crowded the riverbank, watching in fascination as the burial procession began again.

It was a short walk to the communal tomb, but it was entirely uphill, and soon the junior priests carrying the mummies were laboring under the weight of their burden. The procession stopped several times for the men to catch their breath.

One by one, members of the crowd began to drop off, believing that it was probably not worth their trouble to continue up the steep slope in the middle of the day. Finally, all that remained were the members of the procession, the family, and the weepers, still beating their chests and smearing their faces with dirt. Their cries echoed in the desolate canyon.

They continued up the narrow dirt path, further and further up the slope, toward the dark hole above them. Small pieces of rubble and sand fell away as their feet trudged upward. Finally, they reached the entrance to the communal tomb. The procession crowded together and Nebamun spoke:

"Do not say any bad thing against Nasra and Amunet before Osiris, the great god of the dead." "I am the soul of Ra, who guides gods to the Netherworld when they go forth. The souls on earth will do what they desire, and the souls of Nasra and Amunet will go forth at his desire."

Nebamun walked into the dark passage, followed by Padi carrying the canopic jars, and the priests carrying the mummies of Nasra and Amunet. The last to enter were the family members, lead by Shimra, whose bent back was soiled with large swaths of sweat. The weepers, with their dirt smeared faces and filthy hair, did not enter the tomb. Their task was completed until the next customer paid to have them cry for the dead.

The procession continued down a long corridor, and into a small offering chamber, where carved wooden Ka figures of Nasra and Amunet stared out at them in the darkness. Family members placed small loaves of bread and figs next to the Ka figures near the entrance to the next room.

These figures were the exact likenesses of the dead women. Their function was to consume the offerings made by the family. The dead person's Ka would then be able to provide these offerings for them in the next life.

Nebamun and his party entered the larger room. This was an immense room with smooth walls. It smelled of dust and linen, with the faint smell of beeswax and myrrh. Mummies were stacked, one upon another, and lining the walls. But, this was a new communal tomb, so there was enough room remaining to stack mummies for years.

"Hold Nasra and Amunet, so that we may help them to live once again," Nebamun commanded.

As was the custom, the nearest relative, Shimra, held one side of the mummies and Padi held the other. Together, the two men lifted the embalmed bodies and held them upright, so that they would face their audience of mourners.

It was time for the opening of the mouth ceremony, a dedication to Ptah, the creator god, a time to bring the five senses back to life. At the end of the ceremony, Nasra and Amunet would be able to see, hear, smell, breathe and eat once again in the afterlife.

Nebamun produced a setep, the wood adze used to make the dead live again. He spoke in a commanding voice:

"Nasra and Amunet, the form of your faces shall not disappear. Your heads shall not be separated from your necks. Your tongues shall not be removed. Your hair shall not be cut. Your eyebrows shall not be shaved away. No evil defect shall assail thee. Mighty Ptah, he who created the world through the wishes of his heart, open their mouths so that they may breathe and eat."

Nebamun recited the words as he touched their mouths with the setep. He touched their noses and said, *"Open their noses so that they may smell once again."* Finally, he touched their eyes and spoke, *"Mighty Ptah, open their eyes so that they may see."*

Shimra and Padi gently lowered the mummies onto the floor, and Nebamun opened a papyrus containing the special instructions for going out into the day. He spoke once again, commanding the attention of all who mourned for the mother and daughter:

"Hail, O ye who make perfect souls to enter into the House of Osiris, make ye the well-instructed soul of the mother Nasra, and her daughter, Amunet, whose words are true, to enter in and to be

with you in the House of Osiris. Their ears shall not become deaf. Let them hear even as ye hear; let them have sight even as ye have sight; let them stand up even as ye stand up; let them take their seats even as ye take your seats."

Padi burned an incense cone in front of the mummies, and the cloud of smoke floated over the heads of the funeral procession and out into the eternal blackness.

Awaken Nasra and Amunet! Nebamun commanded. *May you be alert as living ones, rejuvenated every day, healthy in millions of occasions of god sleep, while the gods protect you, protection being around you everyday."*

Ω Ω Ω Ω Ω

Fourteen

It was after midnight when the three members of the Abd el Amun family left their simple home. The light from the moon played upon the sand, creating eerie ghostlike figures swirling in their path.

"It's hot...I didn't think it would be so hot, especially at this hour," Satre said.

"What did you think it would be like mother... floating in the Nile? Perhaps you should go back," Karim said.

"I wouldn't think of it. It's just very hot, that's all."

The two brothers walked on each side of their mother, trying to hold on to her fat, swaggering arms as she flailed about. She moved like an ancient tortoise clawing her way across the sand and gravel.

"Mother, please, I don't think you are going to be able to climb down into the tomb," Abdul pleaded.

"Of course I can. I will be able to do whatever the task requires; now no more talk of me going back, do you hear me?"

The brothers grew silent with resignation. Their mother was with them now, no matter what happened.

They made their way behind the village, across the bleak landscape, and up to the hills behind Gourna. There were many dark holes in the cliffs, hewn by hand from the limestone, looking like tiny puncture wounds on the face of the desert.

"Looks like many people have been here before us," Satre said. "Are you sure we are going to find anything?"

"Of course, we will find something," Karim said with a look of sarcasm. "Already you are starting in, never any good things to say, only bad."

"I only meant we might want to go somewhere else," Satre said. "This looks like it's been picked over pretty well."

"Mother might be right," Abdul chimed in. "We might want to go somewhere a little more out of the way. This is pretty close to Gourna."

"Well, it's too late, we are here," Karim said, as they arrived in front of a small, dark opening in the cliffs. "Are you ready mother?"

"Yes, yes, but are you sure this is the tomb?" Satre asked, as she looked down at the opening, unimposing and unimpressive, barely large enough for a dog.

"Yes, this is exactly where the book says it is supposed to be. What's the matter mother, are you afraid?" Karim asked.

Satre's eyes were wide and staring, and the look of fear was plain on her face.

"I can do this, I tell you. It's just that I didn't think the opening would be so small."

"Don't worry, it widens out further down the passage. We can dig it out a little for you," Abdul offered helpfully.

Karim frowned. This was all taking too much time. The daylight would come quickly.

"Let's get moving then," Karim said as he cupped his

hands and scooped a small clod of dirt and sand. He threw it to one side, and scooped another as Abdul joined in. Occasionally even Satre bent down and threw small pieces of limestone out of the way.

After laboring for over an hour, the hole was now nearly triple in size, and a pathway leading downward was clearly visible in the darkness.

"Is it big enough for you to fit through now mother?" Karim asked, the corners of his mouth curled in a slight sneer of disdain.

"Yes, I think so. Let me try." Satre gingerly placed one foot inside the hole, and then the other. She eagerly squeezed her legs through, and then jiggled and waggled until her waist was also within the opening.

"I'm inside," she said gleefully as she squeezed her upper body and then her head through the opening. "See, I told you I could do this!"

"Move down, mother," Karim commanded. "We need more space for us all to get inside."

Satre shuffled further down the passageway, followed by Karim and finally Abdul, who was carrying the torch.

"I can't see anything, Abdul, hand me the light. And then you two follow close behind me. We need to stay as close together as we can," Karim said.

The torchlight danced on the smooth walls of the tomb as the three made their way downward. The passageway was long, narrow, and steep. The way down was slippery, and more than once Satre slipped and fell down on her short fat legs. Abdul grabbed her flabby arms and helped her up each time.

"Thank you my son," she managed to grunt reluctantly. "I know now that I should not have come. It is harder than I imagined."

"I told you! You are right for once, mother," Karim said. "You should not have come, but there is nothing to be done about it now, so you must just be quiet and manage as best you can."

"Very well, my son who knows everything; I will be quiet, but don't get any ideas about leaving me behind down here," Satre warned.

"You are reading my mind, mother," Karim said, as they reached the bottom of the path.

The ground levelled out and they knew they were inside the burial chamber. The strong, pitch-like smell of resin hit their nostrils, and as they moved, a thick cloud of dust and sand filled the air.

"I can't breathe. God, it stinks down here," Satre complained, holding her arm up to her nose. "I don't think I can stand it! I need to go back up."

"Oh no, there's no going back up, mother. You won't be able to see without my torch, and I am not going to give it to you," Karim said. "Now, get busy."

They moved about in a tight circle with the torch light illuminating just a few feet in front of them. The chamber was big, with mummies stacked one on top of the other, almost all the way up to the top of the high ceiling.

Pieces of clay offering vessels lay littered across the dusty floor, and yards and yards of linen wrappings were strewn about everywhere.

"How can we find anything of value down here, with all

this mess," Satre asked. "I can't see anything, just a bunch of dirty, old wrappings. I can bring them home for our fires, I suppose."

"Oh don't waste your time with those," Karim said. "We will find something worth taking, I promise. You just have to have patience, mother."

Karim moved away in the darkness. His mother irritated him with her continual complaining. *It was not as if she has such a bad life. After all, it is he and Abdul who do most of the work. I do not know what she has to complain about,* he thought.

Just then, Karim saw something in the dim light. It was another mummy, but this one was encased in something. He moved closer to it. He could just make out the linens tightly wrapped around the body, and the body lying in what looked like a long, wooden object.

"It's a mummy in a boat," he yelled. His voice boomed across the cavernous tomb. "Come, you must help me, we must take this with us."

Satre and Abdul moved alongside Karim, inspecting the boat and the mummy inside.

"Looks kind of plain to me," Satre said. "Not very interesting at all. Let's look for something else."

"Mother, this is something Rahmad would buy from us," Abdul said. "I agree with Karim. Let's take it with us."

"The surface of the boat is decorated," Karim said. "Just look at the hieroglyphs, painted all along the sides. I like it."

"But, just look at the mummy," Satre continued. "It has a big hole in its head, and an even bigger one in its chest. If there was any gold jewelry, it is now gone, melted down and sold most likely."

"Yes, that is true," Karim admitted. "But let's take it anyway. We haven't found anything else, and it's getting late."

"Karim, come see this!" Abdul said excitedly. "This might be just what we are looking for." Abdul had grown tired of the incessant arguing of Karim and his mother, and he had moved away to one of the furthest corners of the chamber. His voice echoed back to them in the darkness.

"What is it? I can barely see you, Abdul. I don't want to come all the way over there only to find out it is just some piece of trash," Karim warned.

"Oh, don't worry. It's a coffin, Karim, and I'm sure it's worth a lot of money!"

Karim and Satre hurried over to the far corner where they could see Abdul, bent over something long and shiny lying on the floor.

"Look, it's beautiful," Satre exclaimed. "It must be worth a fortune!"

The coffin, made of cypress wood, lay there, as it had for three thousand years. Its surface had aged into a beautiful amber color, and they could see the lifelike features of the face of the coffin's owner.

The face was that of a man, peacefully smiling out into in the eternal darkness. His open eyes were heavily outlined in black and he had a long, pointed black beard carved into the wood.

The ancient craftsmen had carved him with a wig, represented by long, alternating stripes of black and the natural color of the wood. He wore a crown of lotus flowers on his head.

His body was elegantly carved in one sinuous line,

encased almost completely in an exquisitely carved shroud. The only part of his body visible was a pair of hands, carved by the ancient artisans, in an attitude of calm death.

Except for the face and hands, the entire surface of the coffin was covered with design; god figures, ancient symbols and hieroglyphs. The wings of the vulture goddess Nekhbet, painted in brilliant blue, lay across his waist, as if to protect the dead man.

The many Gods of Egypt, some in human form, some as animals, marched across the top of the coffin. All were clothed in a spectacle of color, and the ankh, symbol of eternal life, was painted in every extra space on the coffin's surface.

"Abdul, I think you are right this time," Karim agreed. "This will be worth a fortune. We are not going to need the mummy in the boat after all."

$$\Omega\ \Omega\ \Omega\ \Omega\ \Omega$$

Fifteen

The fat, white goat bleated plaintively, struggling against the tether holding him in place. He stood on the stone platform, his body freshly cleansed and anointed with oil. He moved his head back and forth, his ears twitching from the flies gathering around him. There was no pity for the goat among the crowd of onlookers, who cheered and raised their hands to the sky.

Vendors selling refreshments made their way through the maze of people. Onlookers traded their deben tokens to the vendors, in exchange for delicacies including honey cakes and a special bread hollowed out and filled with roasted vegetables. For those not interested in food, there was always beer carried around in clay pitchers and goatskin bags.

Small children ran about and played with little toy wooden crocodiles specially made to commemorate the feast, laughing as they made the beasts mouths fly open and shut again with a wave of their hands.

Older children tossed a painted clay ball to each other, high over the heads of the crowd. Occasionally the ball would go astray and hit one of the thousands of glistening sweaty heads in the crowd. The recipient of the errant ball would sometimes keep the ball for himself in order to prevent being hit again. More often, the victim would erupt with good natured laughter. It simply would not do to be sad on such a day.

The crowd could look forward to dancing later. The young men would hold two young women in their powerful arms, and swing them around in a fast moving circle. Hand held drums and tambourines would beat out a joyful tune and the women would laugh playfully. The men would smile, enjoying the feeling of the women's bodies crowded next to them.

There would be gambling too, placing a small object underneath a series of four cups, and the unwary traveler would have to guess which cup housed the object, or lose his fortune. Many men would be relieved of their possessions by the more skilled of the gamblers. All around, there was the sound of happy laughter as the gambler's luck rose and fell throughout the afternoon.

It was the first month of the season of Peret, the Egyptian spring. It was a time to celebrate the crocodile god during the Feast of Sobek, god of protection to the pharaoh, Tutankhamun. Nebamun as one of the high priests claimed the honor of tending to Sobek. Today, he did not wear the black jackal mask of Anubis; instead, he was able to show himself as he really was, tall, handsome and with a commanding presence.

He cleansed himself three times this morning, and took longer than usual to shave himself. His dark skin glistened with the lotus scented oil he slathered on in several layers. Today, it was his sacred duty to look perfect for the Feast of Sobek. He would be admired by everyone.

Nebamun cared nothing for the admiration. He dressed himself only for the gods, and only for his sacred duty as high priest. He was the perfect priest, selfless in every respect.

Iramen was in the crowd too. He was a stark contrast to his brother, much shorter, with his clothing thrown together and dirty. Today, as in most days, he smelled of beer. He held a goatskin flask of beer in his hands even now, as he made his way through the crowd.

Iramen watched with envy as his brother took a central place next to the goat. *That could have been me, should have been me, not Nebamun*, he thought. *Someday, all will be right, and I will have the life I deserve. But I am certain I must first crawl out from under my brother's shadow.*

The boisterous crowd grew silent as two bulbous glistening eyes suddenly appeared above the dark surface of the water. The eyes were the only evidence of the huge creature lurking beneath the Sacred Lake.

Although Sobek was a god who took the form of a crocodile, the earthly incarnation of Sobek was a very real, immense, scaly beast kept in the Sacred Lake at Ipet Isut. This sacred crocodile enjoyed a daily feast of roasted duck and honey cakes, fed to him by a loving group of caretakers. Only the best food would be served to Sobek.

On sacred celebration days like today, Sobek would enjoy a fresh meal, served to him in front of a crowd of onlookers, who cheered at his every movement. Today, he would enjoy a hapless white goat.

The goat could see the eyes in the water, moving steadily towards him. He struggled more frantically now against his tether, and the bleating became more insistent, turning into a plaintive song of dread.

A temple priestess dressed in an almost transparent white tunic bent down over the goat and placed a wreath of brilliant red flowers around the neck of the poor creature. She caressed and stroked its neck and whispered gently in a vain attempt to calm it. The goat struggled all the more, trying to free itself from its tether, its eyes looking beseechingly out at the crowd.

Sobek's dark green body slithered relentlessly toward the edge of the Sacred Lake. His powerful tail sliced through the water with eerie determination. Families in the crowd held their children a little closer and the older children watched the spectacle in fearful fascination.

Sobek flipped over onto his back, exposing his pale grey underbelly. He had been trained to perform in front of adoring crowds and it appeared as though he enjoyed the praises of the onlookers as he flipped back over again. His great bulk displaced a large wave of water which fell over the heads of the enamored people standing at the waters edge. They shook off the drenching with good natured enthusiasm. This was a happy day.

The huge, magnificent creature reached the submerged front step and began to laboriously climb out of the lake, his leathery, wet back glinting and twitching in the sunlight. His ponderous body moved ever forward, step after step until he was standing directly in front of Nebamun.

The high priest laid his large, powerful hands on the snout of the crocodile, and the crocodile suddenly relaxed.

"Behold the Crocodile God–who dwells amid his terrors...the Crocodile-god who seizes his prey like a ravening beast. He is the great fish...the lord to whom bowings and prostrations are made."

Nebamun spoke in a commanding voice so that even the furthest in the crowd could hear. The crocodile Sobek shook his body with delight. The gold bracelets surrounding each of his feet jingled with each movement of the swaying tail. Sobek was adorned with a fortune in gold and precious stone ornaments.

I should have such wealth, Iramen thought. *Instead, it is wasted on this ugly creature. Surely, one so ugly could not be a god.*

Iramen stopped believing in the crocodile god as anything more than a crude animal after he had disemboweled one that had died. He remembered with disgust the day Sobek's predecessor gave his last breath.

The previous incarnation of Sobek was nearly eighty years old when he died, having outlived his caretaker by at least twenty years. His immense scaly body was carried to the mummification tent by six men, who sweated and grunted with the weight of him.

The men laid Sobek on his side and Iramen cut his immense body open with a massive Ethiopian stone blade. Sobek's guts flew out forcefully, splaying all over Iramen's arms. He continued to cut and pull at the entrails, and one by one the huge reptile's organs came out.

He remembered the smell as meal items from hours before came hurtling out onto the table. Two putrid Nile perch came out, along with a half-digested grey mass of barley cake. He remembered the skeleton of an unfortunate duck, probably surprised while peacefully paddling around on the Sacred Lake, a few feathers and tendons still clinging to its pile of bones.

Iramen washed the inside of the crocodile carefully, pulling out any last remains of internal organs. He took a small amount of palm wine and rubbed it inside the open cavity; then with the help of five additional men, Iramen picked up the animal and laid him outside in the sun to dry.

Iramen was only involved with removing the internal organs; a different team would return in forty days and complete the mummification. They would stuff the animal with linens and wrap it carefully in several layers of linen strips, coated with resin. The body of Sobek would be placed in a sacred stone sarcophagus to be interred into the tomb of Sobek, to join many other crocodiles in the afterlife.

I should go to Elephantine, he thought. *Then I could kill and eat these ugly monsters, instead of praying to them. Maybe one day I will go elsewhere, and find my fortune.*

Iramen looked up just in time to see Sobek open his massive jaws and clamp down on the head of the terrified goat. With calm determination, Sobek began to drag the goat under the water, claiming what was his by divine right.

The goat kicked bravely, but its sharp hooves were no match for the raw power of the crocodile. The bleating sounds grew softer, less urgent, and soon all sound and movement from the goat stopped. The crowd grew silent once again as Sobek dragged the lifeless white shape down the stone steps and into the sacred lake.

The animal floated on the surface of the water for a few moments, its fur spreading out listlessly. A large, oily red smear floated upward and onto the surface of the water. Nebamun raised his hand as Sobek flipped the goat around and began to devour it. He proclaimed in a loud voice:

"Sobek, thou who art green of plume, watchful of face, raised of brow, the raging one who came forth from the shank and tail of the great one. Your face belongs to righteousness. Your mouth encloses the magic which is in it. Your teeth are a knife. Thou art the Lord of the Water and thou shall endure forever."

The clouded water seethed in turmoil as the crocodile turned over and over, the half-eaten goat still in its jaws. Sounds of bones crunching filled the air, and the crowd cheered happily. After three large protracted gulps, the goat was gone.

With one last flip of his tail, as if to take a bow for a performance well done, Sobek slipped back under the dark waters of the lake. After a few moments, he raised his eyes once more above the water, to take a last look at his adoring audience.

$$\Omega\ \Omega\ \Omega\ \Omega\ \Omega$$

Sixteen

"Let me take a closer look at this," Rahmad said, trying to hide his excitement as he looked at the coffin. "Let's see if you've brought me something of value, or if it's just garbage like everything else you bring in here."

"Don't try to cheat us, Rahmad," Satre warned him. "My sons have told me all about you. I want you to know, I am wise to your tricks, unlike my boys."

"I wouldn't do such a thing. Why, I've only been fair and good to your boys. I can't help it if they never bring me anything of value, just mummy parts."

"Well, times have changed. I will be coming with them from now on. What do you think of that?" Satre asked. "I want you to go through me from now on, when you want to purchase something."

Rahmad shrugged. "As you wish, madam, but remember this, I do not have to buy from you at all. So you had best be respectful to me, or you will find yourself out on the street. Now, are you interested in selling this to me or not?"

"Yes, most assuredly we do want to sell it to you," Karim said. "Don't listen to my mother. You deal with me understand, just as we have been doing."

Satre opened her mouth to speak, but then thought the better of it. She closed her mouth, her lips forming a thin, stubborn line across her face.

Rahmad was relieved. *Karim will be easier to cheat than his mother. She is like Nekhbet, the vulture,* he thought. *She looks at me as though I was a tiny mouse she could grab and eat.*

"So what do you think about it?" Abdul asked hopefully. "I think it is beautiful, the nicest thing we've ever found. Do you think the person might have been important?"

"Yes, possibly. Indeed, a fine example of cartonnage, very well made," Rahmad agreed. "The amount of detail, it isn't usually done for common people; and the way the face was painted, it almost looks alive. These hands folded across his chest look as if they could just reach up and touch me."

"I thought so too," Abdul agreed. "I wonder who the person might have been, what his life must have been like and how he might have died. I wish he could speak to us."

"He is long dead, idiot," Karim said impatiently. "Can we get on with how much you will pay us for it?"

"Your brother is only asking questions. You should ask such questions, Karim. Perhaps you would become smarter, instead of remaining the poisonous snake that you are. I can see who you get your traits from," Rahmad said smiling and looking at Satre.

"I was only trying to make certain my boys did not get cheated by you," Satre said defensively. "I was only looking out for them."

"Oh yes, I am sure of that," Rahmad said. "I am certain you are the perfect mother."

"Rahmad, what is this cartonnage you talked about?"

Abdul asked, anxious to change the subject. He looked apprehensively at Satre, but she stood by, silently enraged.

"The ancients used very fine linen, mixed with a thick paste, which they then molded over the top of a human shape," Rahmad explained. "They could then paint an exact copy of the features of the dead person. This would help them be recognized in the afterlife."

I like this brother Abdul, Rahmad thought. *He has a good heart, and he is interested in knowing of things. But the other two, Karim and the mother, are two of a kind. Both are ignorant and selfish. What a pity I cannot just deal with Abdul. I could do a good business with him.*

Rahmad marveled at the figures of the gods, painted as if they were walking across one entire side of the coffin. He ran his sweaty grease stained fingers along the smooth lines of the coffin, noting each of the intricately painted figures.

"This one here, this is Anubis," Rahmad said, pointing to the black figure with the head of a jackal. "And this green one here, this is Osiris. This one, this must be the dead man himself," he said, pointing to a man in the center, dressed in white, surrounded by the gods.

"The design here, on the side, do you see this boat?" Abdul asked, pointing to a long slender boat rendered in black paint.

"Yes, that symbolizes the journey into eternity," Rahmad said with authority. "Yes, truly, a beautifully made coffin. The coffin was known as a neb-ankh, meaning possessor of life, in ancient times."

"So fine, enough with the history lesson, Rahmad," Karim said impatiently. "What will you give us for it?"

"Well, I am not through looking at it," Rahmad answered. "The design on the front of the coffin, truly spectacular. You see, the forehead, how the lotus flowers are painted there. You can almost smell them."

"Wonderful," Karim said, his voice dripping with sarcasm.

"And you see, this goddess here, with the wings?" Rahmad asked, pointing to a beautifully detailed figure of a woman, her wings outspread across the top of the coffin. "That is the goddess Nut. She is the sky, ready to receive this person into the afterlife."

"Just pay us for it, Rahmad," Karim said, beginning to get angry.

"I will in a moment. But first, the three of you come help me lift the lid. I can't tell you anything unless I take a look at what's inside."

With two people on each side of the coffin, the ancient wooden lid came off easily, and they placed it to one side. Rahmad peered in.

"Such designs, I've not seen one with so many patterns! Here is the Djed pillar, backbone of Osiris and the symbol of stability," he said, pointing to the large spine shaped form painted inside. "And here, Anubis the jackal seems to be everywhere. Here is the Ba, the symbol of the soul, with a bird's body and the dead man's face for a head. Wonderful."

"I'm so happy you like it Rahmad, now, how much? I want so much to be done with this," Karim said.

"The coffin is indeed beautiful, but where is the mummy of its owner?" Rahmad asked. "Do you have the mummy for me to see?"

"We didn't open it," Abdul answered before anyone else

could speak. "We didn't know it was empty. We just carried it out without opening it."

"Well, now that's a pity. It's not worth very much without the mummy inside of it," Rahmad said. "You should know that, my boys."

"It is just as my sons told me. You *are* trying to cheat us." Satre had suddenly regained her voice, and she stared at Rahmad malevolently. "Do you want the coffin or not? If not, we will find another buyer."

"You should have kept your mouth shut," Rahmad warned. "I was going to buy it from you, but now I have decided against it. You can take your treasure back to wherever you stole it from. You can always see if someone else will buy it from you, but they will tell you the same as I. Now go, the three of you, get out and don't come back."

"Mother, I could kill you for this!" Karim screamed at her. "What are we going to do with this now?"

"As I said, we can find another buyer," Satre answered. "But let's get moving. I don't want to be carrying this thing around Luxor all afternoon."

"We can always take it back to where it came from," Abdul offered. "Maybe it is an omen that we should take it back."

Karim and Satre stared at Abdul uncomprehendingly, as if they didn't know who he was.

"You are a crazy man, brother," Karim said. "Of course, we will not take it back."

"I would rather burn it for firewood than take it back. You are so foolish, almost as if you are not my son," Satre chimed in.

"Maybe the boy is right," Rahmad said. "Maybe you

should take it back. But, in any case, get out of my shop and take your coffin with you."

The family of Abd el Amun left Rahmad's shop, carrying the wondrous ancient casket with them down Corniche El Nil street. They lumbered slowly forward, toward the many booths selling fish and bread. The sun began baking their heads almost immediately.

The smell of the food made Abdul begin to think about what they might have for dinner. But, they would have to sell what they carried in order to buy dinner this night.

Satre knew she was right in speaking up. *After all, Rahmad was trying to cheat us,* she thought. *It is good that I came with my boys, now we can sell it to another buyer for even more money.*

But Karim knew the coffin would be difficult to sell to someone else. The brothers had no working relationship with anyone but Rahmad. They had been selling to him for years without any problems.

The family stopped at three antiquities shops near the water, but these proprietors were known for their trickery to foreign tourists. Satre haggled with the first two shop owners, convinced that she would be able to sell the coffin for a small fortune.

Karim and Abdul stood by and watched their mother try to squeeze more money out of the men. In the end, Satre only managed to convince the men not to buy from her at all.

In the third shop, the family was lucky. It was the shop of carpenters who created beautiful boxes out of ancient pieces, for tourists to buy.

The carpenters purchased the coffin for only one hundred Egyptian pounds, a fraction of what it was worth. They began their work immediately.

Abdul wiped away a tear as he watched the men cut up the coffin into small pieces, to be used in constructing their boxes. He did not know why he was sad; maybe it was because with the destruction of the ancient coffin, the person's memory was destroyed as well.

Karim for his part had no such sad thoughts. He missed the money they could have made if his mother had kept her mouth shut. As much as he distrusted Rahmad, at least the shopkeeper would have paid them more money. *If only mother hadn't come with us, we'd be fine,* he thought. *I wish she would die.*

Ω Ω Ω Ω Ω

Seventeen

"Whom shall he be called?" Nebamun asked.

"This is Sinuhe, he committed great sin, and was buried alive," Padi answered. "They found him buried at the foot of a pillar at Ipet Isut."

"What was this great sin, that he should receive such severe punishment?" Nebamun asked, feeling pity for the man.

"He robbed a tomb belonging to one of Tutankhamun's scribes," Padi answered.

"Do you know which scribe?" Nebamun asked.

"The scribe's name was Sakhmet, I believe," Padi replied. "Why do you ask, Great One?"

Nebamun had known Sakhmet when the scribe was alive. He was an ugly, misshapen man, his back bent over like a bow, his face frozen in a malevolent snarl.

Sakhmet was well into his middle years, and yet he preferred the company of very young, very beautiful women, and with the status of a scribe, he could command much in Egypt. Sakhmet was responsible for recording taxes, but as a scribe, he was exempt from paying any himself. This made him a very rich man.

"He was a most terrible man, Padi, and he deserved

robbery and much worse," Nebamun answered. "It was rumored he paid families for their daughters. I can tell you for certain, Padi, I know of one such daughter."

"Tell me about this," Padi entreated. "I would know this story."

"This girl's family was very poor, but the daughter was beautiful, dark and mysterious looking, even as a young girl," Nebamun began. "Sakhmet paid the father an amount he could not refuse, and Sakhmet took the daughter away. No one ever saw the daughter alive again, but the daughter did end up on my embalming table. I remember her very well."

Sakhmet had paid Nebamun and his men a large amount of money to cover the damage he had done to the girl. Her face was battered almost beyond recognition, with dark bluish-black bruises covering what used to be her youthful eyes. Nebamun remembered the slap marks on her face; he could even pick out the rough shape of Sakhmet's hand on her skin.

Worst of all was the damage to her body, her torso, and between her legs. The blood lay in thick clots between her legs and buttocks. The evidence was clear that Sakhmet must have raped the small girl, over and over again, and beat her severely when she resisted.

But there was nothing Nebamun and his men could do but try to hide the damage from her family and others. Sakhmet was a powerful scribe and no one, not even the high priest Nebamun, dare make him angry.

Sakhmet was rich, as were most scribes, but he was richer than most. Along with the many rolls of papyrus and reed writing pens which were buried with scribes, it was rumored that his tomb in the Valley of the Nobles was full of gold jewelry and furnishings.

He had a side business of demanding bribes in exchange for praise to the pharaoh, since he was part of Tutankhamun's inner circle.

Woe unto the man who could not pay Sakhmet the price he asked, for Sakhmet would make up lies about him. With his power, he could exact pitiless revenge upon anyone he chose.

The citizens of Waset were greatly relieved at the death of Sakhmet. There were very few tears shed over Sakhmet's corpse.

"Do you think this Sinuhe could have been ruined by Sakhmet?" Padi asked. "He might have decided to get back what was coming to him by stealing from the dead scribe."

"It's possible, but I prefer to think he did it as revenge for a daughter taken away in her young years," Nebamun said. "It's possible he might even be a relative of the dead girl I spoke about earlier."

Nebamun bent down and touched the dead man's face. Sinuhe was not yet thirty, but he had the deep set wrinkles of a man who led a very hard, poor life on the streets.

His eyes were closed into small, wincing slits, and below the eyes, there was an ugly mass of flesh which used to be his nose. Nebamun noticed the man's ears were also missing. Below the remains of the nose, Sinuhe's mouth was an open gaping hole. His lips stretched tight around his jagged teeth, frozen in the act of screaming for his life.

He could picture the man as he lay in the darkness; his mouth filling with sand after each ear piercing wail. No one would answer his call in the darkness, and now here he lay.

Nebamun turned the man over. He couldn't bear the thought of looking at the open mouth, with the corners of his lips downturned in a silent expression of agony.

"Thief or no, he still deserves the sacred rites. This man can be redeemed by the Gods. I will read for him," Nebamun said, opening the Book of Coming Forth by Day, he read:

"Sinuhe, collect your bones, gather together your limbs. Throw the sand from off your flesh. Come forth pure by day after your death, and perform every transformation your soul desireth to make."

"Please begin Padi," Nebamun said. "I wish for you to enter through the back of Sinuhe's head."

"As you wish, Great One. I must first remove the uppermost bone in his spine in order to gain the access I require," Padi said.

"Will this damage him? I prefer to not disfigure him any more than he has already suffered."

"Do not worry on that account, Great One," Padi said reassuringly as he made a small incision on the left side of Sinuhe's neck. Padi used strong metal pincers to try and grasp the uppermost vertebral bone, but it was slippery work.

Blood and spinal fluid oozed from Sinuhe's spine and out on to the table.

"Just try with your hands, Padi," Nebamun said. "Let us get the task completed."

Padi nodded and inserted his hand into the neck opening. When he could feel the hard surface of bone, he made several quick wrenching motions with his hand. He continued until the veins in his hands began to protrude and throb with the exertion. Finally, with a cracking sound, the bone gave way and Padi pulled it out.

"Well done, my friend. Wipe your hand and let us continue," Nebamun said.

Padi nodded and picked out a thick spiral chisel and began to carve a hole at the base of the man's skull. Pieces of bone and blood flew onto Padi's forearms and slowly dribbled down to the floor. Eventually, a circular opening appeared at the base of Sinuhe's skull.

Padi felt the soft, gelatinous mass that was the dead man's brain. He picked out his spatula and chopped at the mass, cutting it into smaller pieces until the brain was mostly liquid.

Then, he took his spoon and twirled it expertly between his fingers. Carefully, he reached inside the opening and drew out the brain contents one scoop at a time, placing each scoop into a small bowl. As a last step, he poured palm wine into Sinuhe's skull, jostled the skull back and forth, and poured the cleansing wine back out into the bowl.

"Nebamun, I will be finished soon," Padi said, as he took some small pieces of linen coated with Natron and palm oil, and wadded them up into a ball. He carefully stuffed them inside the dead man's head.

"Let's turn him over," Nebamun ordered. He turned away as they flipped Sinuhe onto his back. He was trying not to look at the man's mouth…at the fear and horror on the man's face.

He wasn't certain when death began to bother him, but he knew he couldn't let it be known to anyone. He must keep his revulsion hidden, or else he would no longer be Anubis, the guardian of the dead. He might not even be a high priest, and then what would become of him?

"We must have an eviscerator, Great One. None of the other priests want to do it, and if we send to Memphis for one, this man could rot by the time he gets here."

"I will do it," Nebamun said, "but you must help me Padi."

"Surely, you cannot do it, Great One. If our neighbors find out you have become an eviscerator, they will have nothing to do with you," Padi said.

"Well, let's hope they don't find out then. Let's just do the work and be done with it, Nebamun said.

They turned Sinuhe onto his left side and Nebamun drew a black line and cut him open. Between the two men, they scooped out his entrails, and placed the liver, lungs and kidneys in small bowls. They carefully washed Sinuhe with palm wine, placed myrrh and sawdust packets inside his body and sewed him up.

"Because he committed sin, he is not going to the Per Nefer. He is to remain here. Let us move him outside the tent, for his drying out. Since you have no further need of Anubis, you and the priests can finish with Sinuhe. I am going home." Nebamun said.

"As you wish. Perhaps we will have a new eviscerator tomorrow," Padi said hopefully. He was sorry for Nebamun and how sad he had become without his brother in his life. He was sorry he had talked badly about Iramen, but he just couldn't help himself. And now, because of his drunken brother, Nebamun and Padi were forced to do the vile work themselves.

"Perhaps we will, perhaps not," Nebamun said. "I do miss Iramen, in spite of his vile ways. But, I do not know my brother anymore. He has become a stranger to me. I can only hope he finds a peaceful life somewhere."

Nebamun stepped out into the brilliant sunlight and intense, sweltering heat, leaving Padi and the priests to finish their work. *I am happy to be finished today*, Nebamun thought. He instinctively waited and scanned the horizon in search of Iramen, but there were no footsteps in the sand. All was still, and there was no sign of his brother.

Ω Ω Ω Ω Ω

Eighteen

"It was your fault, mother," Karim said. "Rahmad will never let us into his shop again, after you opened your big mouth. Lucky we found someone to buy it at all."

"Well, perhaps I should not have accused him of trying to cheat us," Satre conceded. "But I had no idea there were so few buyers in Luxor, and that we would end up selling it so cheaply, but we did sell it, right?"

"If you can call it that. We didn't really sell it. More like we gave it away," Karim said. "Rahmad is a stubborn man, and I am not sure he will ever do business with us again, thanks to you."

"Yes, but we did sell it. I thought for a moment we might have to use it for firewood, but we found those carpenters who bought it from us," Satre answered.

"Yes, and they have destroyed it. It was beautiful, and now it is nothing," Abdul said. "Mother, you should not have come with us. You brought us bad luck, and that's why we could not sell the coffin. We would have found it and sold it to Rahmad if it weren't for you."

"*Even you, Abdul?* Where is the love and gratitude for the woman who gave birth to you?" Satre demanded.

"See there? Even Abdul does not want you with us." Karim said. "You gave birth to us, but that does not mean we cannot leave you at home easily enough, mother."

"I will make you a bargain, my ungrateful sons," Satre said. "I will not go with you to Rahmad's shop ever again, and I am certain he will buy from you, if I am not there."

"And so, what is the other part of the bargain, mother?" Karim asked. "You want something else, don't you? You might as well say it."

Satre shuffled her feet and looked down at the ground. "I want to go with you again to the tombs. Just one more time, please, and then I will leave you two alone. I swear it."

"*No!* You have no business going down into the tombs, mother," Karim yelled. "It is too difficult and dangerous for you to go, and besides, you slow us down. We can find and bring back many more things if we don't have to worry about you."

"Karim is right," Abdul said. "You really should listen to him. You should not go with us again."

"I am going," Satre said defiantly. "I just want to find something that I can keep for myself. You know Karim, a piece of ancient jewelry or something worn by a royal lady."

"No, you cannot go," Karim said. "I am not looking after you again. I have enough to worry about with Abdul. I would do much better if I was alone. I have to take my brother, but I don't have to take you too."

Satre said nothing and looked down at the ground. She brushed her hand against her face, wiping away a false tear. A small sound escaped her lips, like the sob of a dying woman.

"Let her go, Karim," Abdul said, taken in by the ruse.

"She's our mother, and she deserves to find some treasure for herself."

And that was how the conversation went, leading up to the three members of the Abd el Amun family finding themselves once again at a tomb, its white limestone entrance gleaming in the twilight.

The brothers had never been to this tomb before, and Satre was nervous as she peered into the large, black opening. It was a steep vertical shaft, going down into the depths of the earth.

"I can't see anything. How are we going to get down there?" she asked.

"With this rope," Karim said, as he held out a long, thick braided cord. "I will tie one end to this rock, and let the rope down into the opening. We climb down the rope. Easy."

"I'm not a monkey, Karim," Satre said sarcastically. "It may be easy for you, but not so easy for me."

"Once again, I told you to stay home, but you don't ever listen," Karim said. He looped the rope twice around a stone block nearby, pulling it taught. He tied a large knot and pulled on it, testing it for strength. "I'm telling you, it's easy; I've made it safe for you. You just have to try."

"Yes, mother, it looks easy enough," Abdul agreed. "I'm sure you can do it. We will be right behind you. You'll see how easy it is."

"Fine. You two had better be right about this."

Satre placed her two pudgy, swollen hands on the thick rope, her knuckles whitening as she gripped it tightly. She slowly lowered herself hand over hand down into the opening.

"See, I told you I could do---"

Her voice broke off in mid-sentence, her eyes wide with surprise as her hands slipped off of the rope and she plunged down through the hole and into the deep blackness of the tomb.

Satre's plaintive wail echoed out from the darkness for a few seconds and then came the sickening sound of bones cracking as they smashed against the tomb floor. There was a slight movement and moaning from below and then all was quiet.

"Oh my God, what now?" Abdul asked, his voice quivering. "Where is mother, what happened to her?"

"We would only be too lucky if something actually happened to her," Karim answered. "I'm sure we will find her down inside the tomb somewhere." He pulled the rope up, and for the first time, Abdul noticed a shiny film on the rope's surface.

"My god, Karim, *what is that?* What have you done?"

"It's just a small amount of animal fat, that's all, barely noticeable, but very, very, slippery. It's best I clean it off before someone gets hurt," Karim answered smiling, using his tunic sleeve to wipe down the braided surface.

"You're an evil bastard, Karim. I am ashamed you are my brother. You will be cursed for this."

"You and your curses, you'll see. When mother is gone, and we have the money to ourselves, you'll see Abdul. You will thank me for this someday."

"You will be damned to hell and me along with you, Karim. I only hope we will find mother alive down there."

"With a small amount of luck, no one will ever find her, alive or dead." Karim smiled and shook his head. "No Abdul, you will get used to life without our mother. You'll see it is for the best."

"I can't believe you don't care if we find her or not, our own mother...you want her to be dead. All you can think about is the money we can make. That's all you care about."

"Why should I care about her? She's never really been a mother to us. With her gone from our lives, think of the freedom we could have. No more giving money away to mother. We can keep all that we make. She's no good to us Abdul."

"You will want to get rid of *me* next, you bastard," Abdul cursed. He stared at his brother. *I've never really seen you before. What is that look on your face; is it greed, or something else, something evil?*

"I would not imagine ever hurting my little brother," Karim said, putting his hand on Abdul's shoulder. To Abdul, it felt like being gripped in the talons of a vulture.

Karim wrapped the rope around his waist, controlling the length of rope with one hand. He grinned broadly. "I'll see you soon, brother," he said, as he dropped out of sight.

Abdul stared at the black hole where he saw his brother's face disappear. He thought for a moment how he should just turn around and go back to Gourna. He should just leave his brother and mother together down in the tomb.

He could easily just untie the rope and throw it down into the hole. They would be trapped in the earth and eventually die; they would join the mummies, and become their own part of history.

He shook his head in disgust. "Time with my brother has turned me into a murderer too." he said out loud. Abdul cringed at the word "murderer." *What has happened to me that I am thinking of leaving them to die?*

Abdul looked at the rope. It was still tight. Karim must not be at the bottom yet. "My God, the tomb must be very deep," he said to himself, thinking that his mother must surely be laying at the bottom, far below, in the dark, a huddled mass of broken flesh. He looked at the rope again. It was slack now.

Abdul grabbed the rope. There was no delaying the inevitable. He was powerless to leave the two of them down in the tomb alone. His mother and brother were all that he had.

Suddenly, he envied his brother's associations, with prostitutes, with gambling friends. As bad as he was, Karim still had people he could call friends. But, Abdul had no one, no one he could talk to, no one who even knew him.

He felt the rope in his hands, itchy, rough; it smelled like burnt straw. He grasped it tighter, until it began to cut into his weathered palm. He closed his eyes, said a small prayer, and glided down into the darkness.

Ω Ω Ω Ω Ω

Nineteen

Nebamun's knees were beginning to hurt. In the mighty throne room of Tutankhamun, he sat on his heels, as was the custom for showing deference to royalty, for what seemed like hours. He knelt on a hard grey granite floor, grateful for the coolness of the naked stone.

Only a few feet away, the floor was covered by the soft, tan skin of a gazelle, but he was forbidden to move. He would just have to remain there, head down, and suffer a little longer.

The high priest was summoned to cross the desert in midday, when the sun was at its most unpleasant, to the pharoah's magnificent palace, known as Per Hay, the House of Rejoicing.

Built by Tutankhamun's grandfather, Amunhotep III, it was an immense structure, with many apartments, villas and courtyards; it was a city within a city, connected to the Nile by a system of canals and a large ceremonial lake on the grounds.

The boy king sat, regarding him carefully, in all his magnificence a massive golden and turquoise collar of the vulture goddess Nekhbet covering his small chest. Today he wore the double crown of white, symbolizing the Upper Egypt of Waset, and red, for the delta that was Lower Egypt. He was Tutankhamun, Lord of the Two Lands.

"You may rise, Nebamun. Would you enjoy some water, perhaps?" he asked in a soft voice, with a slight lisp. Even the royal physicians could not cure him of it, and they finally pronounced it was due to the incomplete formation of his palate, surely a mark of favor by the gods.

"Yes, my pharaoh," Nebamun replied gratefully, finally able to fully acknowledge the presence of the Divine One, the incarnation of Ra on earth.

A thinly clad female servant appeared immediately and handed Nebamun a beautiful green glass vessel. It was etched with the design of a fish at the bottom, and when the girl poured water into it, Nebamun imagined he could see the fish swimming at the bottom of it. He drank the cool water and swallowed deeply, as if to replenish his soul.

The boy king, now eighteen, looked at him with the face of someone in considerable pain. His face was slender, with protruding cheekbones and eyes sunken into dark hollows. His lips parted slightly, to reveal wide, protruding front teeth, and he wore a false beard, made of gold netting, strapped to his chin.

Nebamun caught a sudden pungent odor of mold and it was then he noticed Tutankhamun's left leg was propped up on a cushion and bandages were wrapped tightly above the left knee. A large piece of bread, gone grey with mold was strapped to his leg as a poultice against infection. He wore only one golden sandal on his right foot, leaving the left foot bare. Nebamun gasped slightly as he looked at the left foot.

It was badly deformed. The foot had fewer than the normal five toes, making it appear clublike and curved. Today, the left foot was also badly swollen. He saw the carved ivory walking cane propped against the wall. *Poor boy,* Nebamun thought. *He is so young to be in so much pain.*

He was not a powerful looking pharaoh, but what he lacked in physical attributes, he made up for in temperament. Nebamun knew him to be a kind ruler, trying desperately to regain peace and unity of religion in Egypt, after the heresies committed by his father Akhenaton.

The policies of the young pharaoh had accomplished much to restore Egypt to its former unified glory. Once again, all of Egypt was free to worship Amun-Ra, Osiris, Isis, and his namesake Anubis, along with an immense pantheon of lesser gods.

To help him in this, and also to help themselves to the riches of Egypt, he was flanked by his two closest advisors. His general Horemheb, a tall, brooding man with dark, scowling eyes, and dark eyebrows which looked like two fuzzy beetles perched on his face, stood to the left of Tutankhamun.

The other man, to the pharoah's right, was his Grand Vizier Ay. The vizier was an elderly man, with a face lined by the years and stress of his position. There were deep wrinkles around his mouth, as if he continuously pursed his lips in disapproval.

Nebamun noticed Ay casting quick, furtive glances at the queen. *Not exactly admiring glances, more of the look a hungry cat gives to a fat gazelle before pouncing on it,* Nebamun thought.

This was his first meeting with the two men, both

rumored to be greedy and aggressive, concerned only with their own rise to power. Nebamun believed the rumors to be true and found no redeeming qualities to these men. He disliked them immediately.

It was obvious to Nebamun that the two men controlled the pharaoh, for he was still just a young man, inexperienced, and could be bent like the young reeds along the Nile. Even now, the two were busy whispering into pharoah's ear. Tutankhamun smiled.

No doubt they are telling vain flatteries to him, Nebamun thought. *Why can he not see that they do not hold him in high esteem, as they should?*

Ankhesenamun, wife of Tutankhamun, was seated next to him. Although she was five years older than pharaoh, she was a reverent and obedient wife. Nebamun heard rumors that they held a deep and genuine love for each other, and that she was nurturing and cared for Tutankhamun's infirmities.

She motioned to a tall, well-muscled Nubian man, who stepped forward. He carried a large fan made of black and white ostrich feathers, which he began to slowly and rhythmically move up and down. Small currents of air slid lightly past Nebamun's cheek.

"That is better. I am able to think much more clearly now that I am cooled by a gentle wind," Tutankhamun said. "I have had an accident you see, while hunting the gazelle you see on the floor before you. My physicians have told me that I have broken my leg."

"It will heal, as surely as you have healed Egypt, my pharaoh," Horemheb said.

"Yes, it is so," Ay chimed in. "Your leg will heal by the divine power of the gods. All will be well."

"Sadly, I do not share your beliefs, my advisors," Tutankhamun said. "For divine power did not spare me from this grievous injury. And just look at my poor wife, my beloved. She who has suffered as no woman should suffer. I am not certain I will be spared. It is possible I should die of this injury."

"My pharaoh, your father was the heretic, not you," Horemheb said. "Akhenaton chose to honor Aten, above all the other gods. For this he was punished by the gods. But you are innocent."

"The gods will judge me. I believe it will be soon," Tutankhamun answered. "For now, let us talk of Nebamun, and for what reason he was summoned to us."

"Yes, we must instruct him on his duty to pharaoh," Horemheb said. "He must do his duty or be punished."

Nebamun's eyes widened. *What are they thinking? What do they want me to do?*

Tutankhamun noticed Nebamun's look of sudden alarm, and said in a soothing voice, "Nebamun, you have come under my eyes, and my advisors tell me I can make use of you,"

"Anything you ask, Divine One, and I shall perform it for you," Nebamun answered.

"My queen and I have suffered greatly these past months, for a calamity has befallen us, and we ask for your help."

"Yes, Nebamun," Ankhesenamun said, "Please help us in our trouble." It was the first time Ankhesenamun had spoken, and Nebamun was charmed by the sound of her voice. It had the lilting cadence of a song, like the delicate notes of a harp. She had dark eyes, rimmed in black mesdemet liner and shadowed with brilliant green ground malachite, and her lips were painted bright red with ochre from ground clay.

Tutankhamun looked at his wife and smiled. The young pharoah's face grew warm and animated. It was obvious to Nebamun that the two rulers cared for each other very deeply.

Tutankhamun snapped his fingers and an adolescent lioness came out from the shadows, her eyes and teeth gleaming, her muscles taught for a sudden pounce.

Nebamun quickly took a step back.

"Do not be afraid, Nebamun," Tutankhamun said reassuringly. "My lion, Sekhmet, is quite tame. She only kills on command. You have nothing to fear from her."

"As you say, Divine One," Nebamun said, slightly embarrassed. *It is not seemly for me to show fear*, he thought. *They will think me weak, and I do not want to show weakness in front of Horemheb and Ay.*

"Now, before I continue, will you have a piece of honey cake?" Tutankhamun asked, reaching his thin hand into a bowl made of gold and amethyst, to grab a piece of the dessert.

Nebamun shook his head and said nothing as Tutankhamun held the cake in front of his pet lion. The lion stayed still for a moment and then with a small nod of the pharoah's head, the lioness grabbed the cake in her slathering jaws and ran away.

"Nebamun, our royal embalmer is old, and I do not trust him to perform his sacred duty at this time. Word has travelled to me of your skill, and my advisors, Horemheb and Ay have heard the same."

"I do not understand, Divine One. What would you have me do for you?"

Tutankhamun leaned forward with great difficulty. Nebamun could see that the pharoah was sweating profusely, and his face was red with fever. *Malaria is visiting itself upon Pharoah once again*, Nebamun thought.

Ankhesenamun grasped her husband's arm in a firm grip. Each of her fingers and her thumbs were encircled with golden rings set with amethyst and turquoise. Her finely braided Nubian wig swayed gracefully with her movements. Nebamun caught a glimpse of her delicate breast beneath the nearly transparent fabric of her dress.

"My wife and my love, my eternal companion in the afterlife, please send for the royal wetnurse," Tutankhamun said, grateful for the support of her strong body.

Before Tutankhamun leaned back again, Nebamun caught a glimpse of the royal throne. Today, the boy pharoah was seated on his ceremonial throne, a magnificent construction of wood covered in gold, inlaid with ebony, ivory and semi-precious stones.

Nebamun just caught a quick glimpse of Horus, the falcon god, carved against the backrest, his brilliant wings of blue extended in protection. A line of cobras, the urei, formed the upper border of the chair.

The lower part of the chair consisted of four legs, each ending in a wonderful duck head, all held together by elegant carvings of wood.

Nebamun's admiration was interrupted suddenly by a scurry of movement in the shadows. A large woman came out her breasts bulging out of her loosely fitting dress, carrying a tiny bundle of fine white cloth.

"You see, Nebamun, as I said, a terrible calamity has befallen us. Our first child, a daughter, did not live outside the womb of their mother. My beloved Ankhesenamun gave birth only a few days ago to our second child. This is our second child, also a daughter." Tutankhamun said, gesturing with both hands to the motionless form in the wetnurse's arms.

Ankhesenamun was openly sobbing now, her tears falling down her cheeks and under her chin. "Our children may not live now, but they will live on in the afterlife, my husband."

"Yes, my beloved, with the help of Nebamun, we will see them again." Tutankhamun clapped his hands and a trio of beautiful girls in long black tightly curled wigs came out. Each had a fresh white lotus blossom attached to her head, and arranged to hang down in front of her forehead. They wore nothing except small bands of red cloth edged in gold, and tied at their waists.

The girls bowed and each began to play an instrument; the first began to caress the strings of her harp gently, the second joined in with melodious notes on her flute, and the third brought forth a long thin double pipe made of ivory, in order to join in a soft program of sound.

"My beloved," Tutankhamun said, "The music will calm you and you shall stop your crying and be at peace."

Ankhesenamun looked at him, her face a mixture of loving adoration and unspeakable sadness, but she said nothing; with just a few tempered words, her king had not requested, but had commanded her to be quiet.

"Divine One, you wish me to perform the mummification rites for your child?" Nebamun asked. "Surely, I am not worthy of such an honor."

"As I said, our royal embalmer is old, far too old for such a delicate task. We wish you to use your skills for our daughter, so that Osiris may prepare a place for her in the afterlife."

"It will be as you command, my pharaoh. May I see your daughter?" Nebamun asked. "I need to understand how best to proceed. I have not mummified one so young."

"Yes, indeed. It will be difficult. She needs delicate hands to help her on her eternal journey," Tutankhamun said. "Are you willing to help us?"

The wetnurse carefully handed the bundle to Nebamun, who was surprised how little weight there was inside. He drew back the small corner of fabric which hid the tiny body. A small form lay on the white fabric, surrounded by crushed white lotus petals.

The tiny royal daughter was stillborn. Her fragile body lay cushioned among the flower petals, having been cleaned and anointed soon after she was born. No evidence remained of her sad birth; there was no blood, no injuries. She merely lay as if in sleep. Small tufts of hair lay curled against her head, and delicate eyelashes caressed her cheeks.

"Can you help us bring her peace?" Tutankhamun asked. "We must be able to see her again when we are all together at the end of time, walking the fields of Iaru, in paradise."

"My pharaoh, it will be the greatest honor of my life to preserve your little girl," Nebamun answered. "I will use all of my skills and those of my priests, to bring your daughter back to you."

"You may go," Tutankhamun said, "with our thanks and prayers."

Nebamun clutched the small, dead girl to his chest and

turned away. As he left the chamber, he took one final look back at the royal couple. Horemheb and Ay had departed so they were alone in their sorrow.

The boy king sat in his divine glory, his face wracked with emotional and physical pain. His beautiful young wife, her crying restrained now by the subtle command of her husband, held his arm tenderly. He looked down at the small bundle which had once held so much promise, so much forthcoming joy.

She is mine now, Nebamun thought, *my daughter that I will never have.*

Ω Ω Ω Ω Ω

Twenty

Abdul squinted, trying to see into the blackness surrounding him. The air was thick with dust, making it difficult to breathe. There was a fragrance, delicate, a mixture of flowers and spices. There was another fragrance too, more musky, old, resin mixing with the odor of old linen…mummies.

He could see a small torch flame glinting in the darkness from a corner of the tomb a few hundred feet away. He moved toward it. He couldn't see; he could only feel as his feet stumbled over the mummies, small and large, lying haphazardly in his path. He heard the sickening crunch of bones breaking underneath his feet. With each step, a cloud of dust billowed up into his face.

"God, I can't breathe," Abdul said, coughing ferociously. "Where are you Karim?"

"Move it brother," Karim yelled from a dark corner several yards away. "We have a lot of work to do today."

"I'm trying, but I can't see. I need your torch."

Karim walked toward him, the torch flickering and dancing with his movements. As Karim got closer, Abdul could see around him now, picking out the detail of the shapes on the floor.

Many of the mummies were just shapeless masses, with no markings or detail to distinguish them from each other. These were common mummies, most likely buried with no possessions, and would only be valuable ground up into powder.

"Where's mother?" Abdul asked, as his brother joined him in the dark. "Is she hurt? I want to see her."

"Don't worry about her," Karim answered. "Did I tell you brother? This is the tomb that will make us rich."

"I don't think so; these are mummies of commoners. We've been taking these all are lives and we still aren't rich Karim."

"Yes, these are commoners, but there is more to this tomb than you can see at first. Come, I'll show you something you haven't seen before Abdul," Karim beckoned.

The eternal quiet was interrupted by a slight fluttering sound. The sound grew in intensity, more fluttering, more flapping.

"God, what is that?" Abdul asked. "Demons of death, we'll be trapped down here!"

"Quiet! Stop being so scared, fool," Karim said, although he had a slight quiver in his voice.

"See, you're scared too. You don't know what it is either."

"I know it's not any demons of death, or whatever. I'm sure it's just bats."

"Bats? We could die down here, with only bats for company," Abdul whined. "The bats could eat us alive.

"Will you shut up about dying brother? And bats don't eat people, idiot. Let's move so we can get out of here. I have something to show you," Karim said, as he began to retrace his steps back to the dark corner he came from.

Abdul heard a loud flapping noise and looked up. The once solid ceiling was moving. It moved slowly at first, like a black, ghostly current swirling around in the air.

He watched, fascinated. It was like a serpent, writhing, twitching and then, quite suddenly, a large black mass descended down on his head.

Abdul felt the leathery wings of what seemed like hundreds of bats beating against his head and his face. He tried to remove a furry body which had become caught in the curls of his hair.

He felt a sharp pain along his temple and then a sticky liquid began pouring down his cheek.

"It bit me!" he screamed. "Karim, where are you? They are eating me alive."

He could barely see his brother's thin, dark figure swatting and slapping at the black mist surrounding him. Abdul smacked viciously at the bat closest to his face, and he watched as the small, furry body slammed against the floor. He caught a glimpse of tiny white teeth as its mouth opened and closed.

The bats seemed to move as a single unit, dark and terrifying. The flapping sound grew in intensity, like a violent storm. Then, just as suddenly as they appeared, the bats elevated their black swarm toward the ceiling and were gone, disappearing further down into the dark recesses of the tomb.

The brothers looked at each other, their faces a mass of scratches and bites. Blood dripped out of the corner of Karim's eye where one scratch was particularly deep. He wiped at it with a corner of his sleeve. Abdul touched his temple and his hand came away covered with sticky blood.

"Karim, let's get out of here. I'm bleeding, and I want to go home. Let's get mother and go."

"It's just a small scratch, brother, you'll be fine," Karim said, twisting a piece of mummy linen around his brother's head. He took another piece of ancient fabric and dabbed his eye with it.

"My head smells like death now. I think I'm going to be sick, Karim."

"Remind me, brother, not to bring you along next time; Too much complaining, not enough working," Karim said. "Now, as I was saying, Abdul, let me show you why we are here, and I will show you our mother."

He led Abdul to a large, crumpled shape lying within one of the few areas of bare ground. It was Satre.

Her neck was broken, twisted at an impossible angle. Her once dark brown eyes were open, the irises clouded over in death. There was no blood, no injuries even, and except for the vicious twist in her neck, she could have been sleeping.

"Just look at what we have done to our poor mother. How could we have let her come with us? Now she is dead," Abdul said. "And you have killed her, Karim."

"We are lucky to be rid of her. Now we can have everything for ourselves. We'll be rich," Karim said.

"How can you say that, you selfish bastard; she was our family."

"You don't seem to mind the money we bring in. Now we are a family, you and me. I say forget about mother."

"We should never have let her come with us down here," Abdul said. "In fact, we shouldn't even be here either. We should have visited the whores instead. At least we might get some fun out of it."

"There is plenty of time for fun, after we are rich. Now let's get to work," Karim said, stepping over the body of his mother, barely looking at her.

"Are we just going to leave her down here?" Abdul asked.

"What else? She is too fat to carry back up. What do you suggest, brother?"

"Let's at least cover her." Abdul gathered a large, flat piece of linen, decorated with the figure of Osiris. "How about with this?" he asked, holding it up for inspection.

"That's a burial shroud. We might be able to sell it," Karim said.

"Does everything have to be for sale? I'm using it no matter what you say." Abdul placed it gently over his mother's twisted form, trying not to look at her face.

Karim decided not to press the issue, relieved that his brother was finally going to stop talking about their mother.

"Abdul, come have a look at this."

Abdul looked down at the small mummy lying in front of his brother. "What's so special about it?"

"Its face is gone," Karim replied. "It looks like it's been eaten away."

Instead of strips of linen carefully placed, this mummy was completely bare, with no wrappings at all. The naked body reflected the light of their torches on its leathery flesh. A faint stench of cooking meat rose up from the skin-covered bones.

"They must have been a little short on supplies for this one. Just look at that," Karim said pointing to the face.

The brothers knelt to get a closer look. The mummy's nostrils were plugged completely with wax, and what once might have been a gracious smile was now sealed shut with resin. Stone eyes glared out at them from cavernous sockets. Much of the remaining face was peeled away in small, jagged strips toward the hairline.

"What happened to it?" Abdul asked.

"It could've been flesh eating beetles, who knows? All I know is, we're not going to find much to sell with this one."

"Good, let's go," Abdul said, eager to leave the presence of the naked mummy. It seemed shameful to further violate the vulnerable corpse.

"Wait just a minute." Karim took out a small knife and gouged out each of the stone eyes from their ancient sockets and threw them into his pocket. "These are alabaster, I think," Karim explained. "Rahmad might like these."

"You told me, brother, that we are going to be rich," Abdul said. "Did our mother die for nothing, or is there something you are not telling me?"

"Come with me, Abdul, and see for yourself."

Karim led the way further into the dark passage, the light of his torch casting ghostly shadows on the tomb walls. The brothers walked past row upon row of canopic jars, containing the ancient organs of the long forgotten dead. There was no way of telling which organs belonged to which mummy; they had been separated long ago.

"This is an unholy place, Karim," Abdul announced. "With our mother dead, and then, the bats, we shouldn't be here."

"Abdul, if I listened to you and your whining, we'd still be at home, making beer with our mother, and with no future. Now, shut up and keep moving. We're almost there."

The brothers continued into the darkness, past more canopic jars, most with their lids still intact, but some were broken, with the mummified organs scattered about like tiny pieces of dried fruit.

There were dusty remnants of furniture; a chair with its straw seat disintegrated almost to dust, an ancient doll made of reeds, with its tiny smile and dots for eyes, drawn in kohl ink. It was all that was left of a people long dead.

"Here we are Abdul. This, my brother, is our future," Karim said grandly, as he stood in front of an ancient sealed doorway.

$$\Omega\ \Omega\ \Omega\ \Omega\ \Omega$$

Twenty One

"The once mighty Zannanza, prince of the Hittites, see where you are now," Iramen said, looking down at the still form curled in a fetal position on the floor of the darkened cave. The man who once was a member of elite royalty now looked like a small dead animal with the sheepskin covering him.

Iramen had found the cave easily enough, as he knew he would. But there were many caves dotting the rock cliffs above Ta Set Maat, the workmens village, and he patiently looked through one after another until he found the one he was looking for.

In one of the caves he was attacked by a swarm of bats, and his face was now bleeding profusely from several tiny, deep puncture wounds. This was a small price to pay for finding the riches of the Hittite.

The caves he entered were full of common mummies, some grouped together in families, and some lying apart from anyone, to spend eternity alone.

It was in one of these caves that he found Zannanza's final resting place. The prince had the cave all to himself, with no one for company. But now, Iramen had come to visit.

After lying in the dry air of the cave for several weeks, the flesh of the Hittite was now almost completely free of any body fluids and his skin had turned brown and looked like tanned goatskin.

His face retained none of its former fullness. The cheeks were sunken in and the skin was stretched tightly across the man's cheekbones. His eye sockets were empty, the gelatinous eyes having become a meal for birds. His lips were stretched tightly across his face in a mirthless grin of death.

"You smell as though you are rotting, my prince," Iramen said to the corpse. "Your sheepskin cloak has become most fragrant. I believe you will be better off without this animal skin covering you. Then I can see what treasures you hold for me, my friend."

He peeled away the cloak, holding his hand to his nose to block the stench. Iramen could feel tiny lice coming off of the cloak and onto his bare arms. He could feel the tiny bodies slowly travelling upward toward his face. He scratched at his arms viciously trying to ward them off, but they had already begun their journey and would not be deterred.

"You are a filthy one," Iramen said. "Yes, quite dirty, and this sheepskin made matters much worse. Now you are impure as well as filthy. But you do have some value, my prince. Well, I must get about my business, and see what you have been hiding from me."

Once free of the sheepskin, the prince wore a fine tunic of woven fabric of the deepest purple. The garment was edged in an iridescent gold thread.

"Dressed in your finest, I see. To impress that wife you never found. What a pity," he said, as he brought out a small, sharp knife. Iramen cut off the golden edge of the tunic and stuffed the shiny metal border into his sack.

Zannanza's tunic was held together by a pair of bronze clasps, intricately shaped in the form of bulls' heads, their long horns curling in a graceful spiral.

"Well, you will not need these anymore, mighty one," he said, as he unceremoniously grabbed the clasps and threw them into his bag. "Let's see what else you have hiding in your clothes."

Iramen stripped the man naked, marveling at the shriveled body. The once taut, sinewy muscles were now brown and thinly stretched across his protruding ribcage. The prince's once stocky, powerful body was now reduced to a slender, fragile, almost childlike form.

The dead man had three golden earrings of graduated sizes piercing each ear. The largest was almost as large as Iramen's fist.

"I think I will have these also," he said, as he pulled the golden earrings from the prince's earlobes. A tiny drop of dried blood clung to one of the large earrings as Iramen ripped the jewelry from Zannanza's body.

He pried the golden crown from the Hittite's head, a piece of dried scalp and hair still clinging to it. He looked at the man's skull, crushed by a blow from an unknown murderer. The fragile bones looked like pieces of broken pottery.

"Someone certainly did not like you prince, that is certain. Pity, we will never know who has done this to you. Only you will know, but you carry your secret in death."

He placed the crushed crown on his own head. He didn't mind that the pieces of the dead man's scalp and hair intertwined with his own. It was a small price to pay to wear the crown of a royal person.

This crown now belongs to me. I am now Iramen, prince of the Hittites," he laughed, as he danced around in a circle. "I command all to do my bidding."

Zannanza's hands were curled under, almost closed, the leathery skin lying flat against the man's knuckles. His bony fingers held many rings and at the end of each finger was a long brown fingernail, meticulously trimmed.

"You have not done a day worth of work in your life, have you my prince? You would never have survived in Egypt. It is good you are dead, instead of living in our country. But, you are strong, even in death," he said as he firmly pried Zannanza's hands open. "Hittite, you are still no match for me, my friend."

Iramen examined each of the rings as he dropped them into his bag. They were all beautifully crafted of various metals and precious stones, and all of priceless value.

One ring was of copper, with a brilliant orange-red carnelian stone and a small sunburst design carved into the center of it. The sunburst design seemed to smile at Iramen, and he smiled back.

Another was of the finest silver, inlaid with a blue-green turquoise stone the color of the Nile. Still another was a type of colored glass molded and layered. Iramen had heard of such a skill, coming from the towns along the Tigris and Euphrates, and it was highly prized among royal families.

"But this one is for me, my foreign friend," he said, as he slid a gold ring set with the deepest black onyx on the small finger of his right hand. He held out his hand admiringly and smiled. The ring had a tiny figure of a bull etched in gold at its center. "I have always enjoyed black."

Iramen looked down into the small linen pouch happily and counted the many rings he had ripped from the dead man's fingers.

I will have a fine feast tonight, he thought, as he mentally figured how much each of the rings might be worth.

He turned Zannanza over, feeling deep underneath his body, burying his hand deep into the sand. "Where is that beautiful dagger of yours my friend? I will find it, if it takes me an eternity."

He felt around for several minutes, and finally felt the hard edge of the dagger, deep underneath the Hittite's body. He pulled it out violently, and the dead man's body rolled over, face down in the dirt.

"You are getting what you deserve, Hittite. You are worthy only of death in this miserable cave," he said, as he held up the bronze dagger. He ran his finger along the rounded, sickle shaped blade, admiring its razor sharp edge. He pricked his finger on the blade and a small trickle of blood seeped out.

"That is alright, you beautiful thing," Iramen said to the dagger. "We are just getting to know each other, so you can punish me just a little. But know that now you are mine." He smiled as he looked at the brilliant red stones twinkling in the half light of the cave.

Iramen examined the lance, simply designed, with a long shaft and ending in a dull point. It was formed out of a very hard metal he did not recognize. He remembered hearing about new weapons made from iron, but this is the first he had seen one. He knew it was far too heavy to be thrown in battle, and it was dull.

"You are here to make your prince look powerful," he said to the lance. "So I will leave you here with your master. I do not think I could sell you for much."

He picked up the shield. It was unusually light, made of leather stretched over a wooden framework, not at all like Egyptian shields. It was well made, but not of any valuable metal. Iramen cast it aside.

"Let us see what you might have in your chariot, my prince," Iramen said. "Perhaps you have one last treasure I might possess."

He peered inside the heavy chariot and grabbed a quiver of arrows, each tipped with a sharp point made of bronze. Alongside these was a large bow, made of highly polished animal horn.

"Hittite, you no longer have a need of weapons. I think I will take these also," he said, slinging the bow and quiver over his shoulder. Iramen had never shot with a bow before, but he intended to sell the weapons along with everything else.

He almost did not see the two small clay tablets shoved into the shadows inside the chariot. He picked up one of them, examining the writing on it. It was a strange combination of wedge shapes and thin lines. It looked to have been written using a reed or piece of straw pushed into the clay when it was still wet.

"This message is meant for someone, but pity, no one will ever read it. Hittite, you have taken this message with you to your death."

He smashed the first and then the second of the clay

tablets on a large rock, shattering them into many pieces. He kicked at the pieces with his foot, mixing them in with the dirt on the floor of the cave, until they resembled pieces of broken pottery strewn about.

Iramen hoisted his sack of treasure and took one last look at the Hittite prince, his corpse now robbed and defiled. The prince was still lying face down in the dirt, so Iramen could no longer see the sickening mirthless grin of death or the hollowed out orbits of the dead man.

"You should have stayed in your own country, my friend," he said, as he walked out of the cave. Heavy with his treasure, Iramen set off across the sand.

Ω Ω Ω Ω Ω

Twenty Two

"Do you know what this place is, Abdul?" Karim asked, making an expansive gesture at the doorway.

"Just another hole in the desert, I think," Abdul answered, "only this one has a fancy door." He swished away a determined fly trying to settle on his eye.

"No, this is the place where we will grow rich. I think this is the final resting place of many of the ancient kings of Egypt. It is a royal burial cache, of that I am sure. There were many rumors of this place, said to be one of the richest burial chambers in Egypt," Karim explained. "It is said that in ancient times, royal mummies were brought here to keep them from being robbed or torn to pieces."

"But they didn't plan on us, did they? Now, I suppose it's our job to rob them and tear them to pieces."

"Yes, it is our job, and a good job it is, my brother. We must figure out a way to open this door."

The doorway was sealed in with large stone blocks, fit tightly together. Around the edges of the doorway were hieroglyphs, deeply inscribed into the walls.

"What do you think these mean?" Abdul asked. "Could this be a curse?"

"Now of all the places we have been, this is the most likely place to find a curse, Abdul. But after all we have seen, you still don't believe in curses, do you?"

"Now, more than ever, and I don't see how we are going to get this door open. Karim, maybe we shouldn't open it. It could bring us bad luck."

"Fool," Karim said. "We can't have much worse luck than we've had already. Don't even think about not going in there. This is what we came here for, to be rich."

Karim produced a small knife from the pocket of his tunic and shoved it in a tight crack between the uppermost blocks. He pushed the blade in as far as possible and began to move it quickly back and forth, jamming it into a space which was just beginning to form.

"Did you bring your knife with you?"

Abdul nodded, producing his knife in the palm of his hand.

"Good, place it in the crevice on the other side of this block, will you? Between the two of us, we can move it. One block at a time, all we need is a space large enough for us to fit through."

Abdul looked at him dubiously. *I don't want to be trapped down here. Yes, I do believe in curses,* he thought to himself.

The brothers moved their knives back and forth within the crevice, brushing away the sand as they created an ever widening space between the stone blocks. Karim pushed on the block, and felt it give way.

"It's ready, Abdul," he said excitedly. "Come help me, just put your weight into it."

Abdul joined in, pushing hard against the stone. The

ancient limestone slid slowly forward as the brothers pushed more forcefully. Suddenly, the block of limestone which had blocked the doorway for thousands of years came crashing down into the darkness on the other side of the wall amidst a cloud of dust.

Karim peered into the dark opening. "I still can't see anything. Let's remove a couple more blocks, Abdul."

The brothers used their knives to create a space between the next two blocks and pushed against them with all of their strength. The two blocks came crashing down almost at the same moment, creating a large opening into the next room.

"That's it, perfect," Karim said, smiling broadly. He lunged up into the opening and stuck his head through into the darkness.

"What is it, Karim? What do you see?"

"Gold! Gold everywhere! Beautiful things! We must get inside! We have much work to do."

"Let me see, Karim! Move and let me see too!"

Abdul pushed himself up into the opening and looked inside the next room. Even in the murky darkness he could see the glint of gold. He could make out the dim outlines of golden coffins, lying side by side. He caught the glint of precious gems winking at him from their sacred tomb.

"I can't believe what I am seeing!" Abdul exclaimed. "You are right, Karim. We will be rich."

Abdul let out a sudden scream of fear and jumped back down behind the safety of the wall.

"What is it?" Karim asked, shaking his brother. "What did you see? Tell me!"

"*I saw a face, and it was alive!*"

"I swear everything scares you!" Karim exclaimed as he looked into the tomb opening. "That's a face alright, but it's not alive. Look a little more closely, will you?"

"I'm sorry, but it's just seeing the whites of his eyes staring out at me like that," Abdul answered. "The thing scared me to death, brother."

The face of a large bald man stared out at them from inside the tomb, but it was the face of a life size statue, carved out of one solid block of wood from an ancient sycamore tree. The whites of his eyes were alabaster, with pupils made of onyx.

"Let's get inside and I will show you your scary man, idiot," Karim said as he slid down through the opening in the blocks. Abdul followed.

The wooden man's arms were attached at the shoulder, so that they could be moved and positioned independently of the body. In his left hand, he held a stick, and his right hand was clutched and empty as if he once held something, but that was now lost to time.

"He's fat," Karim said, laughing. "Kind of like our mother."

"That's not funny," Abdul answered back. "Our mother lies dead, in another room, and here you are laughing. It's not good to laugh at the dead."

"I suppose you think another curse will be upon me soon," Karim said. "Well, if you call becoming rich a curse, then I'm ready to be cursed Abdul."

The wood surface of the statue was rough, with cracks that resembled wrinkles on the man's worn face.

"Look, he's even got tiny little nipples on his breasts," Karim said, laughing again as he tweaked one of the small indentations on the statue's chest.

"Stop playing with him. It's not right, brother. Besides, shouldn't we be looking for something of value, not this old bald, wood man?" Abdul asked.

"For once, you are right. I was just having some fun," Karim answered as he headed back into the back recesses of the tomb. He turned back around again, and with a few quick movements, Karim gouged out the eyes of the statue and dropped them in his pocket.

"Let's go," Karim commanded.

The brothers headed into the blackness, lit only by their single torch. The walls glistened with the sheen of smooth plaster, interrupted by hieroglyphs and two thousand year old figures of domestic life. There were figures of bare breasted women, bending over and kneading bread.

"Looks like our mother," Abdul said.

"Yes, but thank God our mother had the sense to wear clothes to cover that huge body of hers. I do not think she would look quite as firm and beautiful as these women," Karim said.

The women were drawn gracefully bending their long sinewy arms and legs, their wigs perched elegantly upon their heads. They were painted wearing only simple white skirts, with each fold of fabric rendered in painstaking detail.

There were figures of brown and white spotted cattle with immense horns being led by men in white loincloths.

Even children were depicted carrying offerings of wine and bread in homage to the Gods.

"Karim, I can almost smell the bread and wine can't you?"

"You are a poetic idiot, Abdul," Karim said with a sneer.

"Now, let's get going. No more stopping to admire anything. Just take whatever you can, alright?"

"Fine, I was thinking of what it must have been like, living back then."

"Well, if you delay any longer, I might kill you and then you can live in the afterlife right along with them," Karim threatened. "You will find out what it was like."

After seeing Karim murder their mother, Abdul knew his brother was fully capable of killing him, without even thinking about it.

They headed further into the passage. It was much darker, even with the torch. There were fewer figures of people on the walls now, and many more hieroglyphic inscriptions.

"These inscriptions look different," Abdul commented. "They are not carved as deeply, or in as much detail, almost as if someone was in a hurry to finish them."

"Yes, and do you see what I see? Those are cartouches," Karim said excitedly, pointing to several oval shapes on the walls.

"So what's so special about cartouches?"

"Do you not know anything? A cartouche surrounds a royal name. Inside each of these ovals is a royal name in hieroglyphs, could be a pharaoh, his queen, or a royal family member," Karim explained.

"But how do you know who it is if you can't read the inscriptions, Karim?"

"I don't need to know who these people are to know that they are royals, and buried with treasure beyond our imagining."

The brothers stepped through another doorway, and a small amount of plaster fell from the ceiling onto Abdul's head.

"I don't think we are safe here. What if the walls of this tomb cave in on us? No one would ever know. We would be down here forever. I don't want to die in here with you, Karim."

"Fool. Do you think I want to die here with only you for company? That's why we need to get in and out quickly. Now, follow me."

Karim held his torch high to see down the next inner passageway. Beyond the light of the torch he could see ancient sarcophagi, lying one after another, on the cold and dusty floor.

"After all of our years of stealing, we finally have found something that will secure our futures forever," Karim said with a broad smile. "Do you know what this place is?"

"No, what do you think it is?" Abdul asked.

"This, my brother, is the royal cache of Deir el Bahari. I've told you about the rumors that the ancient priests moved some royal mummies out of the Valley of the Kings. They were afraid of looting. Word was that they were moved into a secret chamber, but no one knew where to look."

"You think this is it?" Abdul asked.

"I know this is it. Look at how everything is, how quickly the cartouches were carved on the walls, and how the coffins look like they were just dropped in here. Whoever was last here got in and out in a hurry."

The brothers moved further into the inner chamber, moving carefully beside the sarcophagi, until they were in the center of the room. All around them lay the dead kings of Egypt, their mummified bodies encased in coffins of gold.

Ω Ω Ω Ω Ω

Twenty Three

"What is it?" Padi asked, staring at the tiny linen bundle in Nebamun's arms.

"This, my friend, this is a little girl," Nebamun answered softly. "She is second daughter of pharaoh, and was stillborn. Pharoah has asked us to use our best skills for her."

"Why does he need us? What about his royal embalmer? Are you not frightened, Great One?" Padi asked, nervously shifting from one foot to another. "What happens to us if something goes wrong, as it sometimes does when we embalm someone?"

"Our most divine pharaoh believes the royal embalmer is too old," Nebamun answered. "Padi, this is a great honor for us, indeed. You should not be frightened, for we will help this fragile royal daughter in her eternal journey, and that has always been our purpose. We do as our pharaoh commands. If something does go wrong, we are in the hands of the gods, as always."

"Yes, you are right, Great One. You will guide, and I will follow," Padi said. "I only wish I could be of a calm mind as you are, but I fear I place too much value on my life."

"Padi, my friend, I too value my life, but of what purpose

is my life if I cannot serve pharaoh and the gods. Now, please let us remove her wrappings and see what needs to be done," Nebamun commanded. "Because of her small size, I do not think we need follow our usual procedures, but we will see."

Nebamun gently removed the royal wrappings and lightly brushed aside the lotus blossoms to reveal the tiny body within.

"I can understand why she might not have been born alive," Nebamun said. "Look at her spine, how it curves and bulges out at the bottom, as if not completely formed. And her right shoulder, you see how much higher than the left it is?"

"Yes, indeed," Padi agreed. "This child did not form correctly while inside Ankhesenamun. That much is certain. This little girl looks more like a bird than a royal child."

"Our poor queen, her first child born dead, and now this second daughter also," Nebamun said sadly. "Our rulers may never have an heir. I fear for Egypt if there is no one to rule and protect her."

"Yes, that may be so, Great One, but there is certainly no shortage of suitors to the throne," Padi said. "There are many corrupt men surrounding our pharaoh, many who want him dead. There are many who would look down on his corpse and smile."

"How do you know this, Padi?" Nebamun asked. "How did you come by this information? Who have you been listening to?"

"Everyone knows, from the priests to the lowliest pig farmer. It is common knowledge that Ay and Horemheb are chief among those wishing the removal of our pharaoh by any means. You know in your heart, what I say is true," Padi answered.

"What you say is very dangerous. You must not speak of it again, or you could well lose your life over such talk. We must not concern ourselves with gossip, my friend. It is best we return to our task." Nebamun commanded.

"Yes, quite right, Great One. I am sorry, and I will not speak of such things again."

Padi began with a tiny, narrow piece of metal. The girl was so small there were no chisels or tools to accommodate her. Using the sharp metal, it was an easy task to pierce the delicate bones of her nose.

Next, he hollowed out the end of a tiny piece of wood to resemble a spoon, which he used to scoop out the contents of the little girl's skull. Three scoops with the spoon were enough to empty all the contents of her brain and place them in a small bowl.

Padi poured cleansing palm wine through the nostrils and moved the small skull forwards and backwards, so that the palm wine could do its work, cleaning out any remaining pieces of brain.

"Padi, because the body is so small, I believe it is best to pack the child's body immediately." Nebamun commanded. "If we wait the forty days, the body will shrivel and there will be nothing to pack. We want her to look as she did in life."

"Yes, my friend," Padi agreed. "Now that I have washed out her skull, I can pack it with linen soaked with natron salt. This should be enough to keep the skull looking full and lifelike, while still keeping it from rotting."

He packed the tiny princess's skull carefully, pushing the

small pieces of salted linen up through her nostrils and into her skull cavity.

"This will preserve her," Padi said, as he sealed the nostrils with wax. "Great One, shall we shave her head? I can make a small wig for her from plant fibers, if you would like."

Nebamun ran his hand across the soft, downy hair clinging to the girl's head. "No, we shall have nothing of a false nature on this most perfect child. We shall leave her hair in place."

"What shall be done with her eyes, Nebamun? Do you want stones placed in front of her eyes?"

Nebamun marveled at the stillborn girl's long dark, curling eyelashes and small eyebrows, so perfectly formed. He placed a finger underneath one closed eyelid and lifted it up to expose a tiny, unseeing brown eye.

"We shall open her eyes, so that she may see in the afterlife," Nebamun commanded. He lifted the other eyelid, and the dead girl's eyes peeked out at them. "She will be almost as we found her, Padi, as if she is our own daughter."

"It shall be so," Padi answered solemnly. "I will make a tiny incision next to the remains of the umbilical cord, here," he said, pointing to the small cord of tissue, already beginning to dry out. "I can remove the viscera myself, and then we can pack her small body with linen and animal fat to give it shape."

"I want this to be special, just the two of us, Padi, working on this little child's body," Nebamun answered. "It seems fitting for one who was not given the breath of life should go into eternity with as few hands upon her as possible."

"Yes, certainly; if you say it, it shall be done, Great One,"

Padi answered. "With one so small, it will be an easy task; just the two of us, then."

Nebamun and Padi handled the small body very carefully, removing the girl's organs, which were no larger than a finger, with delicate precision and care. Padi washed out the abdominal cavity with palm wine until it was clean of any remaining organ tissue.

They stuffed the body cavity with linen soaked in animal fat, giving her body the lifelike plumpness it would have had, if she had lived. Padi stitched the incision closed with a small fiber thread.

"Does she have a wedjat to be placed over the incision, Great One?" Padi asked.

"No, I have not been given anything to place over her, Padi. She will be entombed as she is, without the sacred eye of Horus."

"Does she have any amulets at least?" Padi asked.

"No, we are to bury her without any adornments," Nebamun said. "Her coffin is to be her only jewelry."

"Very well," Padi said. "It is sad for a royal one to be buried so. Do you not agree?"

"Yes, indeed," Nebamun agreed. "But things are as they are, Padi, and we must still do our duty as we are told."

Padi nodded. He gently wrapped the body in linens, and placed her in Nebamun's arms.

"Let us take her to the Per Nefer for her drying out, where she can lay in peace, and the gods will look at her and smile," Nebamun commanded. "Because she is so small, she need only take ten days before we can wrap her, so we shall tend to her again soon.

The high priest cradled the girl in his arms, absently rocking her back and forth as if she were alive. He opened the corner of the linens one more time to look at her face. She lay peacefully, as if in sleep, awaiting her journey into the afterlife.

"Most curious, Padi," Nebamun said as he looked down upon the face of dead princess.

"What is curious, my friend?"

"I do not even know her name."

Ω Ω Ω Ω Ω

Twenty Four

Karim and Abdul stood in a small sliver of space, the dead of Egypt lying all around them. There were many coffins, some decorated in priceless gold, lapis and turquoise. Others were simple coffins of cypress wood without decoration. This was a tomb of royals, but also of their common servants, buried with them.

There were household items scattered everywhere; a simple table and chair made of braided straw, tall drinking vessels made of alabaster, and yards of linen, mostly white, but some dyed a rich red color from crocus flowers.

There were also countless baskets which held bread, eggs, and even grapes, all now mummified by the centuries of laying within the dark tomb.

"Look at this!" Abdul exclaimed, as he held up a wide pleated linen dress, once white, but now yellowed with age. "This must have been for a large woman, servant maybe? It's kind of ugly."

"It would have looked nice on our mother," Karim said with a laugh. "It might have fit her perfectly, don't you think?"

"Yes, if you hadn't killed her," Abdul replied quietly.

"What's that you said, brother? Well, you know you

are just as guilty as I am, so you can't exactly turn me in. Whatever punishment I receive, you will receive also. I will see to that."

Abdul said nothing. He was thinking about what punishment would await the two of them if they were ever caught. There were laws against robbing tombs and selling antiquities, but in the past they were never enforced. The tombs were theirs for the taking.

Things were different now though. There were many foreigners in Egypt, exporting ancient curiosities to museums and private homes in their own countries. The sale of Egypt had to stop, and Abdul knew it. But that meant they had to stop too, and he didn't think Karim would ever stop.

His thoughts were interrupted by a thunderous yell from the opposite end of the tomb. He could only see the outline of Karim holding up a pair of objects in one hand, and the flickering torch in the other.

"It's a pair of sandals, Abdul, and they are solid gold! These alone will make us rich beyond our dreams. They are worth a fortune! Luck is with us."

Abdul made his way over to Karim, carefully picking his way through the darkness. The floor was covered with coffins, mummies, and their belongings, and none of it had been touched.

"We are the first to find this tomb," Karim said. "I am sure this is where the pharaohs were moved to by the ancient priests. We have found the Deir el Bahari treasure, Abdul."

Abdul turned one of the sandals in his hands. The design was simple, a flat sheet of gold, drawn up at the tip by a thin golden strap, and secured by golden straps on the sides.

"Karim, what are these?" Abdul asked, pointing to the array of marching male figures, each with a lance and shield, engraved on the underside of the sandal."

"Hah, those are probably the pharoah's enemies. With each step, he could crush them over and over again; made him feel he had power over them. Smart. Maybe I should draw a picture of you underneath my sandal," Karim said, laughing.

"Not funny," Abdul said. He turned away and began looking through the items laying all around him. He did not want his brother to see him wipe the beginnings of tears from his eyes.

Bronze and copper mirrors were piled into one corner, as if thrown there in a hurry. Most had a simple wooden handle but others had handles molded of bronze in small forms of the goddess Isis, or the papyrus plant.

"I do like this," Karim said, holding up a bronze oil lamp. It was shaped like a human foot, with each toe shaped individually, complete with toenails. "I will take it home. We can use it to light our house. What do you think, brother?"

"I think it is ugly; those toes, they look disgusting, that's what I think," Abdul answered simply. "Maybe if it were gold, but the foot just looks ugly shaped out of bronze."

"If it were gold, we would sell it fool," Karim said. "But out of bronze, I can take it home instead. I like it, besides we need more light around the house."

Abdul shrugged. He picked through a pile of ivory hairpins, some with dark wig hair still clinging to them. Alongside these were ivory haircombs, still intact, as if they had just been used to comb through the black tresses of their mistress.

Alabaster cosmetic jars lay next to the ivory hair accessories. Abdul opened them, hoping to find something interesting inside. Some had remnants of ground green malachite and the black kohl powder known as mesdemet, still in them, once used to accentuate the eyes of the beautiful men and women of Egypt.

"I like this. I think I'll save this for myself," Abdul said, holding up a dainty makeup container, carved in the shape of a duck, with a female swimmer holding on to its tail feathers. "I can use it for something."

"That's just like you, brother. Your fascination with useless objects always amazes me. You know it's worth nothing," Karim said with a sneer.

"Well, it's worth something to me. I'm going to keep it."

"What could you possibly do with that?" Karim asked. "It's just a piece of junk, brother."

"I don't know what I will do with it yet," Abdul answered. "But I'm sure I will figure something out. Our mother would have loved this, Karim."

"Yes, but we will never know now will we? Now, get busy and take only the finest objects you can find," Karim said, stuffing the golden sandals into his sack. "It will take many trips to steal everything, but it is all ours. We will be rich beyond imagining, brother. You soon won't have time for little makeup containers or time to think about our mother."

Abdul placed one of the bronze mirrors into his sack.

"Idiot, I said only the finest objects," Karim said with contempt. "That means only gold. Don't trouble yourself with any other metal, especially bronze. Bronze is far too common for us. I am going to keep the oil lamp I found, but nothing else of cheap metal, understand?"

"Whatever you say, brother," Abdul answered wearily. *I have grown so tired of my brother. I will never be able to do as I like*, he thought.

"Look here," Karim said, pointing down to a mummy without a coffin. "Abdul, this is a royal mummy. Pay your attention to these. They are the only ones worth your time now."

"I can't tell if it's royal or not when I don't have a coffin to look at." Abdul said. "I don't think you can tell either. You are just saying things to make yourself look smart."

"I am smart, idiot, smarter than you will ever be," Karim said. "Now, telling the difference between a royal and a common mummy is simple. Rahmad told me about it once."

"What did he say?"

"Rahmad said to look at the arms. He said look for arms that are crossed and hands that look as if they once held something," Karim explained. "When a royal was buried, the arms were crossed, and one hand held a crook, and the other hand held a flail, ancient symbols of kingship. These royal mummies are where we will find gold."

As if to illustrate his point, Karim pulled the linen wrappings away from the fingers of one hand, exposing five perfectly formed golden finger stalls. In antiquity, a stall had been placed over each fingernail to keep it from falling off as the centuries passed.

The golden fingernails were molded in perfect detail and fit the tips of the fingers exactly. The fit was so tight that Karim had some difficulty prying them off. In the end, he simply took out his small knife and severed each of the fingers with the stalls still clinging to them. He dropped them unceremoniously into his bag.

"Did you have to cut off the man's fingers?" Abdul asked. "There must have been a better way."

"Well there wasn't a better way. We are in too much of a hurry to find a better way," Karim answered. "Now, check that other hand and see what is under the wrappings."

Abdul gently pulled away the wrappings on the other hand, determined not to have to cut the man's remaining fingers off, but he did not need to worry; there were only the long, blackened, naked fingernails clutching away at the darkness.

"Those crafty bastards," Karim said, smiling. "I bet the ancient priests kept a little gold for themselves, figuring no one would ever find out. I guess you will just have to be content with your bronze mirrors brother."

"Oh, I've found a few other things, Karim," he said as he picked up a dozen necklaces made of turquoise and onyx beads and tossed them into his sack. "I like the jewelry. For one thing, it's much lighter to carry."

"It may be lighter to carry, but not so valuable. Stick with the gold, Abdul. You will be much happier, and richer."

Abdul shrugged and tossed in a small copper ring inlaid with the orange-red color of carnelian with a sunburst design etched in the middle of it.

Ω Ω Ω Ω Ω

Twenty Five

Iramen was running, running for his life. He could feel his feet dancing over the hot sand and gravel, creating a cloud of dust behind him. He felt the sweat pouring down his forehead and running down the bridge of his nose.

His arms pumped rhythmically at his sides, his legs carried him forward with huge strides. He didn't know where his arms and legs were taking him, only that they were taking him far from his home.

He only vaguely remembered why he was running; something about stealing jewelry from a dead woman and her dead daughter. He didn't even remember what he had done with the jewelry. He just knew he didn't have it anymore.

All he knew was that his beloved brother, Nebamun, had enlisted an entire force of Medjay, Egypt's policemen, to look for him. He knew, even in his dream, that they would kill him with ruthless expediency if he were caught.

Iramen awoke in a drunken haze, his body covered in sweat, to find a naked arm slung over his throat, not in a menacing way, but with comforting, protective warmth. He liked this feeling. He could get used to this feeling. It was a feeling he had been waiting for all of his life.

He gently caressed the soft pliant skin of the arm, running his fingers down the length of it. He gently touched the warm, relaxed fingers and closed his fingers around them. He remembered suddenly as instead of cozy, supple flesh, his fingers encountered hard, cold unyielding metal.

He held the hand up and tried to focus his blurred vision on the shiny object on one of the fingers. It was one of the dead Hittite's rings, this one of copper inlaid with the orange-red color of carnelian. He lightly touched the sunburst design etched in the middle of the stone. He pulled on the ring, and the woman slowly opened her eyes.

She rolled over next to him, her large round breasts warming his skin. She was naked except for the ring and several necklaces of turquoise and onyx beads which draped against her dark nipples. She smiled, still half dozing, and her long curls of black hair tickled his chest.

"What are you doing with my ring, woman?" he asked, his head pounding. "And where is this place, who are you? How long have I been here?"

"One question at a time please," the woman said. "First, you gave me the ring, remember? You had no money, so you gave me this ring. It is mine."

He drew his hand back and slapped her, the sharp sound cracking the early morning air. "I would not have given it to you. I do not even know who you are."

"And second," she said, rubbing her red cheek, I am Matia, and you are in my tent. And last, you have been sleeping for an entire day. Other customers came, and I serviced them, and they went away again. And you, you did not even wake up until now."

"That is not possible," Iramen said. "As I said, I don't even know you."

"Well, that is gratitude. You certainly knew me very well last night." She grabbed between her legs and smiled. "I am still sore this morning. You are a young lion."

I like this woman, he thought. *And she thinks I am a young lion.* "I am sorry I slapped you," he said aloud. "Forgive me, please. I thought you had robbed me in the night."

"I have grown accustomed to being struck. You men seem to like it," Matia said, shrugging. "But, the ring is mine, because you gave it to me, and if you try to take it back, I can have you killed, as quick as this," she said, snapping her fingers. "I have many friends here."

"Yes, I can imagine that you do have many friends, Matia. You gave me good service last night, and because of that, you can keep the ring."

Iramen felt the small bag inside his tunic; with relief he knew the fabric with the golden thread, earrings and the Hittite's remaining rings were still there. The onyx ring was still on the small finger of his right hand. *At least the whore did not rob me in the night,* he thought.

He thought about the dead Hittite, lying alone in the cave, and how easily he stole the man's last few belongings. He sold the dagger, clasps and crown easily enough, and provided himself with some excellent deben to trade.

The money was meant to last awhile, maybe even set him up with his own shop. He had imagined having the shop of a skilled carpenter, or maybe selling fish or bread. He could even own a brothel, and get women to lie with him and not have to pay them.

But it was not to be. A few games of dice, drink, and evenings with the local whores and much of what he had was gone. It was true he did not have anything to pay for Matia so he must have given her the ring.

He thought better of trying to get the ring back from her, after all, he still had a few rings left in his bag to sell, and Matia had serviced him so well the night before. He decided to be nice to her; she may indeed have dangerous friends.

He knew he could not return to his work, serving under his brother Nebamun, working himself to death. He was the lowliest among them, cutting the entrails out of the dead, only to be shunned by everyone after doing his duty.

He suddenly remembered, he could not go back. It was no longer a choice he could make, even if he wanted to. He would be killed if he went back. Stealing from the dead was a very serious crime, and there was only one punishment, to be executed.

Iramen remembered the last few days just after barely escaping from Ipet Isut with his life. He feared the Medjay, and their relentless pursuit of anyone deemed to be a criminal. Now, they were in relentless pursuit of him.

He could not let himself be captured. He would die an agonizing death, unless his brother would speak for him. But that was unlikely. Nebamun had denounced him to the Medjay in the first place.

I must plan for my future, he thought, his head finally beginning to clear. *If I do not, I will run out of possessions entirely, and end up lying in the street; a sad ending indeed for a man who used to be a priest of Ipet Isut.*

"Matia, what work is there for me here?" he asked as he

sat up on the thin mat of reeds that served as a bed. He squashed a tiny red ant trying to make its way up his leg. "I am willing to do anything."

"What can you do? Perhaps you can be a stonecutter or maybe a fisherman?" Matia asked. She opened a small, round straw basket and pulled out a crusty piece of bread. Iramen marveled at her perfectly shaped white teeth as she tore into it.

"I would like some of your bread," Iramen said. "Being with you has made me a hungry man, Matia."

"First you want sex, and then you want food? What else can I possibly do for you? Surely, you do look as though you have not eaten in awhile. You are a skinny man, Iramen," she replied, as she pinched his bony arm and smiled.

He recalled vainly trying to capture ducks to ease his empty stomach, relying on a trick his uncle had taught him. Iramen put a gourd on his head, with two holes cut for his eyes, so that he could see in front of him. It was thus that he entered the water, in an attempt to grab the ducks by their legs and hold them fast underwater.

He remembered his uncle, able to gather a great many ducks in this way, without the nearby ducks becoming alarmed and flying away. But, it did not work so for Iramen. Instead he remained hungry.

After his failure in hunting ducks, he had to content himself with swallowing the juice of the papyrus plant. This kept him somewhat nourished, but did nothing to quiet his rumbling stomach. Every day, the rumbling grew a little more insistent, and then he met Matia.

"Yes, it is true, what you say. I have not eaten for a few

days," Iramen answered. "Will you spare some bread, Matia, or will you just sit and eat in front of me? I am starving, but it is a pleasure for me to sit and watch you eat."

"Fine, here you are," she said as she handed him a tiny crust of the bread. "Now back to my question. What can you do to support yourself? I cannot feed you and take you to my bed unless I am paid. Do you understand?"

He nodded slowly, his head still hurting from the night before. He knew enough not to tell her of his past work as an eviscerator, or she would have charged him double, even triple for her services; he would be missing two rings instead of one. The cold reality was, he spent so much of his life tending to the dead he did not know much else.

"I know what you can do," she said suddenly. "Go to the market. The butcher, his name is Merkha; he is looking for an apprentice. Are you skilled with knives?"

"Yes, yes, I am highly skilled with knives," Iramen said, smiling slightly.

"Go then, and tell him that you know Matia. As I said, I have many friends here. I am certain he will help you if he thinks you are a friend of mine."

"I will, and thank you, Matia. I will return and find a way to repay your kindness to me," Iramen said as he grabbed his crotch and smiled.

He left the shade of the brothel and stepped out into the harsh sunlight. Before meeting Matia and receiving an offer of a new occupation, he had thought of going to Ta Set Maat, the town of the tomb builders. He had heard that they were paid well, and that each man had a surplus of bread and beer.

He had also heard that after an eight day workweek, men were given two days off from work. They were even given time off if they were fighting with their wives, or if they had drunk too much the night before. *A nice arrangement*, he thought.

Many were using the time off to construct their own tombs. *It must be comforting to know where you are going after you die. I will die out in the desert, alone, my eyes picked out by the vultures, my flesh eaten away by an army of beetles,* he thought grimly. *My brother will never know what happened to me.*

With the heat already bearing down on him, he thought of Merkha, and the possibility of learning a new trade. He must find this man, and take him up on an offer of new employment. For the first time in many days, Iramen was happy and excited about his good fortune.

But, even well outside the priesthood, working as a butcher's apprentice, it was still very dangerous to stay in Waset. He was a thief, being hunted by the skillful Medjay, who seemed to always find what they were seeking. They would execute him if they found him. He knew all of this, but where else could he go?

$$\Omega \; \Omega \; \Omega \; \Omega \; \Omega$$

Twenty Six

Rahmad's shop was already busy as the brothers entered early in the morning. There was a tall, thin, well-dressed man who turned and looked at them as they entered. His eyes, framed in dark, bushy eyebrows, gazed curiously at them. He twirled his stiff mustache as if to twist it off of his face.

"Well, Belzacchi, surely there must be something here which you are interested in," Rahmad said impatiently. "But make your mind up soon. I haven't all day for you to decide. Perhaps I can interest you in these ostraca?" he asked, pointing to pieces of broken pottery lying on the countertop. Some contained hieroglyphs written in black ink. Others had small pictures of animals painted on their surfaces.

"Why would I be interested in those?" Belzacchi asked. "Surely that is just garbage, thrown away in ancient times, but garbage even so."

"Ah, but you are wrong," Rahmad answered. "These are of tremendous historical value. They tell about the lives of the common people, but you probably care nothing for the common people. Of that, I have no doubt. You and your kind care only about wealth."

"What do the messages read?" Belzacchi asked, unperturbed by the shopkeeper's insult. "Perhaps I might purchase one of the more interesting ones for a collector I know. The man is half blind and does not know what he buys most of the time."

"You mean you *cheat* him?" Rahmad asked sarcastically. "Surely not, you who are the most honest man I know."

"Just read me the inscription and be done with it," Belzacchi answered. "I want to leave your shop sometime soon, and not spend my entire day here."

"Very well. This one here, for example, details voting on the banishment of a member of Egyptian society. It speaks of an eviscerator, banished from ancient Waset, we know it as Thebes, for stealing from a corpse," Rahmad explained, holding up a large piece of red pottery. "Did you know this is where the term *to be ostracized* comes from? It means to be voted out."

"I know what it means," Belzacchi said. "I am looking for something more intact, not some small piece of garbage. Find me something a bit more opulent if you please."

"Perhaps you might enjoy this papyrus scroll. It is filled with the most wonderful hieroglyphs; really very interesting."

The shopkeeper held out a well-worn ancient scroll, filled with hieroglyph symbols written in a stark, black ink.

"What is it?" Belzacchi asked. "It's looks to be in bad condition to me. See there? The ends are already frayed."

"I can assure you, sir, the papyrus is made that way. It is as fresh now as in ancient times," Rahmad answered with a slight note of cleverly disguised contempt. "You know Signor that the word hieroglyph means *sacred carved letter?*"

"No, I did not know that. I am grateful to you sir, for your vast amount of knowledge," Belzacchi said sarcastically. "So what does the message read? Anything my patrons might be interested in, or just another one of your worthless copies? I will know the difference, my friend."

"This papyrus is a record of an ancient tomb robbery, recorded in the time of the new kingdom, about 1500 BC," Rahmad said. "It details the robbers' confession, most interesting."

"Well, read it please, if you can Rahmad," Belzacchi said.

Rahmad cleared his throat and began:

"We broke into the tomb of King Sebekemsaf and searched it. We opened the outer coffins, then the inner ones. We found the noble mummy of the king dressed as a warrior; it had numerous amulets and gold ornaments around its neck, and its gold headdress was in place. We took the gold from on top of the mummy, as well as the amulets and ornaments from around its neck. We stole all the goods that we could find-gold, silver, and bronze objects-and we shared out everything between us, in eight lots."

"But why would they admit to such a thing?" Belzacchi asked incredulously. "And put it to paper?"

"Because, in ancient times, they swore an oath to tell all," Rahmad answered. "They deemed it better to tell the truth than suffer the consequences of remaining silent."

"What consequences?"

"They would have their noses and ears cut off, or quite possibly they would be executed."

"So what happened to the robbers after they told their story?" Belzacchi asked.

"Ah, that my friend, I'm afraid that is lost to time,"

Rahmad answered. "We will never know whether they made the right decision or not."

"It is good that such punishments are not permitted in our times, Rahmad, for surely we would all be executed," Belzacchi said with a smile. "I think I shall pass on the papyrus document. It is a bit too grim for my patrons, I think."

"Yes, yes, of course," Rahmad said. "You buy for people of more artistic tastes. Your people prefer beautiful artistic reliefs chiseled from the walls of the sacred temples, rather than a piece of historical value, correct? They would rather have a piece to be hung on their walls, or placed in a glass case, to be admired and envied by their neighbors."

"Signor Rahmad, I take offense to your comments, and although you have many things of interest to me, your price is far more than I am willing to pay. I am not an idiot, you know. I do know a little something about antiquities, and what's more, I do not like the way you speak to me. You, sir, should be begging for my patronage."

"Yes, well, I know of your reputation, Belzacchi. I know you are a collector, and I know also that you purchase items for some of the most famous houses in Italy. But, my Italian friend, that doesn't mean that you can come to my shop and think that I will let you cheat me. And sir, you will never in your life see me beg for anything, let alone your patronage. I am an Egyptian, and I do not need the paltry services of the Italians or anyone else."

"Signor Rahmad, I am not your friend. I am merely a servant of the houses I represent. I am bound by their wishes, and their wishes are to purchase the most exquisite items I can find, at the cheapest price possible," Belzacchi explained.

"So you see why it is that I can pay only a set price. It is a matter of honor."

"Hah, honor, you say," Rahmad said with a sneer. "I spit on your set price, now, get out of my shop and don't come back. If I see you in here again, I will call the town police and denounce you for what you are, a thief."

"I will leave, gladly. But your time is coming, Signor Rahmad. Soon you will no longer be able to sell your wares, to me or anyone else. The antiquities laws are coming, and you will suffer as the beggar and scoundrel that you are," Belzacchi said, his face a brilliant red.

"What do you mean, antiquities laws?" Karim asked suddenly. "What do you know about what is going to happen? Tell us."

"He doesn't know anything," Rahmad said. "How can an Italian know what is going to happen in Egypt? The man can't possibly know what he is talking about."

"I know all about it," Belzacchi explained. "Your government is about to stop the export of your ancient history to other countries. Soon, access to your ancient sites will be forbidden even to Egyptians. Why do you think I am here?"

"To cheat me, that is why you are here," Rahmad said drily.

"No, Signor Rahmad. I am here to give you one last chance to sell me what you have, before the door of fortune closes for good. That is why I am here."

"Well, I told you to get out. You can say that my door of fortune has closed for you, Belzacchi. I never want to see or speak to you again."

"Perhaps your two young friends have something they

might want to sell me," Belzacchi said, looking from Abdul to Karim. 'I will give you a good price if you have something I want."

Karim opened his sack. He wanted a chance to show this Italian the beautiful golden sandals he carried, and the golden finger stalls. He knew such items would be in high demand. The Italians loved gold and the more ornate the item, the more highly prized it was.

"Karim, do not dare to sell to this man!" Rahmad exclaimed, crushing the sack closed with his sweaty hand. "You sell only to me, understand? If I catch you two selling to this Italian swine, I will buy no more from you, ever."

Karim shrugged and looked at Belzacchi. "Sorry, but I do what he tells me. I cannot do business with you, as much as I would like to."

"That is a pity. Well, I imagine you Egyptians must stick together," Belzacchi said.

"Yes, that is it exactly," Rahmad said triumphantly. "We don't trust foreigners, and I especially don't like Italians. You are all unscrupulous thieves, stealing all of our treasures for your collections in Turin and the Vatican. I know all about your dealings."

"Just know this," Belzacchi said smiling implacably, "Ever since one of the obelisks was removed from the Luxor temple forty years ago and transported to France, we collectors have been under investigation by your government. Your people were outraged when the obelisk was erected in the Place de la Concorde in Paris. Now, we Italian collectors, and the English, and the French have been informed by your government that changes are coming in the next few weeks."

"What changes?" Karim asked, frowning slightly.

"New laws are being drawn up as we speak; laws which will make it impossible for us to buy antiquities and bring them home to our countries. It will be very bad for us," Belzacchi said, looking intently at Rahmad as he spoke, "and as a result, bad for you and your tomb robbing friends, Rahmad."

"Get out!" Rahmad screamed as he pushed open the door. "And do not ever come back, do you understand? I will have you arrested, and if we are lucky, the police will shoot you."

"Good day to you Rahmad and good luck. You will need it," Belzacchi replied calmly. He stepped out into the early morning air, his eyes squinting, barely visible under his thick, bushy eyebrows.

Ω Ω Ω Ω Ω

Twenty Seven

Iramen still held to certain practices familiar to priests, even as an eviscerator. Every day he wore the customary black mesdemet powder eyeliner to protect his eyes from the sun and also from various biting insects that were commonplace in Waset. Today his eyes were bare, and the mosquitoes were busy.

He swatted at his face, but it was already too late. A large welt was forming next to his right eye, and it threatened to eventually swallow up part of his vision.

As a priest, he was also accustomed to cleansing himself with purified water every day. His brother, Nebamun, often purified himself three times each day, and shaved himself all over daily.

Iramen scratched the fast growing stubble on his chin; he was not accustomed to the fierce itching it produced. He felt the top of his head, which had developed a thin fuzzy film of hair. He could feel the droplets of sweat immersed in the hair, threatening to run down the side of his face.

I must find a barber, he thought as he looked up the street. *I need to look my best today, for my new boss, the butcher.*

He was close to the Nile, the busiest part of Waset and

the best place to find services. All around him were townspeople bustling about on their way to and from a busy life of work, family, and leisure. He felt a momentary pang of envy as he watched them move about.

If only I had not been born a priest, always within sight of my brother, he thought. *I might have had a happy simple life, I might not have been drunk all of the time. I could have had a family perhaps, people who loved me.*

He shook his head, determined to clear his brain of bad thoughts, and think only of the future. He walked faster toward the river.

His nostrils flinched as he caught the putrid smell of the egg ovens. This was the curious place where unhatched eggs were brought to ripen and hatch under the care of a baking oven, set at low temperature.

The eggs would remain for six days, at which point they would be examined carefully. If there were any signs of a form inside, they would be kept for further hatching. But, if the egg was clear inside, it would be determined to have failed, and would be destroyed.

The surviving chicks would never know their mother, but instead would become the offspring of an uncaring overseer, the bake oven. In this way, mass production of hatchlings could occur with minimal effort and time.

He passed the huge dome shaped granaries that housed the corn to be released as payment of services to the many workmen in Waset. He watched the men pour sacks of corn through a trapdoor at the top, to be taken out when necessary out of a trapdoor at the bottom.

There were storehouses for all of the wealth of Egypt,

copper and precious metals, even cattle. All was carefully housed in a walled complex, guarded by dogs and men. This was the bounty from the taxation of ordinary citizens, to be spread among the populace as payment for services rendered; but nothing for Iramen.

Near to the river, he passed many busy shops on his path to find a barber. In one shop, a man sat, holding one end of a long strap of leather between his toes, and the other end in his hand. The craftsman cut the strap cleanly and added it to his burgeoning pile, in preparation to make sandals.

I could have been so much better than an eviscerator, Iramen thought. *I could have been a craftsman, I could have made shoes.*

He passed another shop where the shopkeeper was sitting on a high wooden stool, eating a mixture of cooked barley and figs, and drinking beer from a pigskin bag. The man belched gratefully and wiped the food and beer from his face with a deeply soiled cloth.

Iramen was most fascinated by a large shop next to the river. This shop stood out from the throng of stores all along the busy street. This was the shop of carpenters, each with their one special task to perform, the task to which each man excelled.

Six men moved about inside, and Iramen watched awestruck as they created beautiful boxes out of exotic woods like ebony, and inlaid them with ivory painted in brilliant colors. These were boxes prized all over the ancient world.

One man held out a beautifully made spoon in the shape of a large fish. Another man compared the makeup container he had made, shaped like a duck, with a swimmer holding on to its tail feathers.

I could have had such a talent, Iramen thought. *I am good with knives. I could have created beautiful things and been honored and revered for my skill; If only I would have been given another chance.*

Next to the carpenters' shop was another large annex building. Iramen stopped just outside the door to watch the coffin makers constructing their containers for the dead called the neb ankh, possessors of life.

Several groups of men were at work. One group was making a coffin for a poor person, of very simple design, out of sycamore wood, held together with a series of wooden pins. The men were bent over, planing the wood down to a smooth finish, their backs drenched in sweat.

Another group made coffins of thick, molded paper, some men forming the thick paper into the smooth shape of a body. Other men were tasked with using black ink to outline, and red, blue and green paint to render beautiful designs which would cover the container's entire surface.

A smaller group was busy building a canopic box, which would hold the four canopic jars containing the mummified entrails of the deceased. Iramen smiled as he noticed the lid of the box, topped with a reclining figure of a jackal, which would serve as a handle.

Reminds me of my brother in the Anubis mask, Iramen thought. *Seems I cannot escape him. It must be destiny for him to follow me forever.*

His thoughts suddenly returned to Nebamun, and he thought of what his brother might be doing at that very moment. *He could be enjoying sitting on the edge of the Sacred Lake, talking with Padi. He could be eating a nice meal of figs and honey cakes along with the other priests. Nebamun could be doing many things,* Iramen thought. *But one thing I am certain he is not doing, is thinking of me. I am certain he does not know or care what has happened to his older brother.*

Iramen quickly wiped a tear from the corner of his swollen eye and set his gaze upon the path ahead. It would not do to dwell on a past which he could no longer return to. He must force himself to think of the future, and forget his old life.

He recognized a man who came up to him as Hesy, a barber he had used only a few times before. Hesy was expensive, but today Iramen felt generous. *I am worth a good shave,* he thought. *I must look prosperous or I will never be prosperous.*

"Iramen, how are you my friend, would you care for a shave today?" Hesy asked. "I have not had many customers this morning, so I will make a good deal for you. You will look much better with a good shave that only I can give."

"Yes, I would like a shave Hesy, but tell me, do you have any black mesdemet powder with you?" Iramen asked. "I must have a liner around my eyes. The insects are thick today, and they have already visited my face."

"Oh yes, they are especially thick around here by the river, and yes, I do have some black mesdemet. I can see you do need some help, my friend, and I am just the man to help you today."

"Very well then, do your profession barber, and make me look good. I am seeing a man about a job today. I must look my best."

Hesy smiled and nodded. He placed his small wooden stool down in front of Iramen and motioned for him to sit. Hesy opened a small box containing a bronze razor, and pulled it out. The sharp blade glinted in the sunlight and blinded Iramen for a moment.

"That is a fine razor you have there, Hesy, no wonder you are more expensive than most of your friends," Iramen said. "But I know you will convince me that you are worth it."

"The bronze is worth the money, trust me, my friend. Those flint razors used by others are not as sharp, and do not shave as closely as I can," Hesy said. "You want to look your best, yes?"

"Yes, especially today. As I said, I am looking for work, and I cannot afford to miss this opportunity, you understand?"

"Yes, of course. It will be my pleasure to help you today, just give me a few moments," Hesy said as he splashed Iramen's bare skull and face with fragrant oil. Iramen winced as the oil hit his swollen eye. "That eye of yours might cost you a job, my friend. I will see what I can do for you."

Hesy deftly swung the razor blade out and aligned it carefully with Iramen's round skull. The barber began humming in a regular cadence of sound. It was not a song, but more of a rhythmic, regimented sound.

"Hesy, do you have to make that noise?" Iramen asked. "Or can you at least make it a song I recognize?"

"I am sorry, my friend. It is something I always do when I am working," Hesy said as he brought the blade down, scraping the irregular surface of Iramen's skin. "The sound helps my concentration otherwise I might make a mistake and cut a gash in your head or perhaps slit your throat."

"I see. Well I would hate for you to slit my throat by mistake," Iramen said, smiling. "In that case, I see the necessity of it. It is just such a toneless, unpleasant noise."

"For that, I am most sorry," Hesy said. "I will try to make my sounds more pleasant to your ears."

The barber began to hum a soft tune, used mostly by mothers for their babies, as he moved across and downward with the blade. He continued in strong, even strokes, removing more of the fuzzy hair on Iramen's head with each stroke. When Iramen's skull was shiny and bald once again, Hesy began on Iramen's face.

"Carefully now, and watch out for my eye," Iramen warned. "I do not want it to bleed."

Hesy nodded and his soft humming was soon replaced once again by the toneless, rhythmic noises he had made before. Iramen did not notice the change in music. He was too concerned about the barber cutting around his swollen eye.

Hesy moved down Iramen's cheek and across his chin in quick, sure movements, finishing up with long strokes on Iramen's throat.

After a few minutes, Hesy was finished and patted Iramen's skin free of the oil. The barber opened a small, round tube shaped container of alabaster and dipped a reed brush into it.

"This is nice," Iramen said, as he held up the container to get a better look at it. It was carved with the figure of a small baboon clinging to the side of it.

"Yes, yes, my wife traded a piece of her jewelry for it, now, hold still my friend," he said, as he artfully spread the black liner along the rims of Iramen's eyes. "I will put a little more black liner next to your swollen eye. It will help to hide it."

It must be a nice feeling to have a wife trade something dear to her in order to purchase a present for her husband, Iramen thought absently. *I think love is a feeling I will never experience.*

Hesy used all of his artistic talent on the swollen eye, taking great pains to camouflage the damage done by the biting insect, and when he was finished, he handed Iramen a shiny bronze mirror to admire his work.

"Well done, Hesy," Iramen said, looking at his reflection with a satisfied expression on his face. "You are worthy of a bit extra today, my friend. I will remember you and what a fine job you did for me."

Hesy bowed as Iramen placed a one of the smallest of the golden earrings in his hands. The barber smiled in appreciation, and without another word, he picked up his simple stool, gathered his shaving tools and resumed his walk along the Nile.

He would work into the night, looking for men like Iramen, men who wanted to look their best in pursuit of their dreams.

$$\Omega\,\Omega\,\Omega\,\Omega\,\Omega$$

Twenty Eight

"What is that?" Abdul asked. "Is that a head?"

Rahmad held an elegantly shaped stone head up to the light of the window, to see it more clearly.

"Yes, indeed, it is," Rahmad answered. "It was found at Giza, in one of the fourth dynasty mastaba tombs and it is over four thousand years old. I bought it from another antiquities dealer in Cairo. He gave me a good deal on it."

"Another antiquities dealer; don't you mean one of your thieving friends?" Karim asked.

"I was just about to tell you about it," Rahmad said. "But now, I don't think I will. You are such a rude person. All you want to do is insult me. I thought we were friends Karim."

"I am your friend Rahmad, and I want to hear about it. Can you tell me?" Abdul asked. "I have not been rude to you."

"That is true. You are not like Karim, are you Abdul?" Rahmad asked. "Try to remain that way; true to yourself. Very well, since you asked so nicely, I will tell you."

He handed the life sized head expertly carved out of limestone and polished to perfection, into Abdul's outstretched hands. Rahmad had begun to like this young man.

"It is what is called a 'reserve head' and as I said, it is from the fourth dynasty, which makes it over four thousand years old."

Abdul whistled. "What's it for? It looks so like a person, it could almost speak to us."

"How much is it worth?" Karim asked, suddenly interested.

"Money, money, money, that's all it is with you Karim. Now be quiet and listen. I was trying to explain to Abdul here, what it was used for."

Abdul smiled appreciatively. *For once, someone is listening to me instead of my brother,* he thought. *I think I am starting to like Rahmad.*

"Now, as I was saying, in case something happened to the dead person's body, the reserve head would serve as a receptacle for the person's wandering soul," Rahmad explained. "Each head has unique characteristics. My friend told me that there is even a family resemblance in some of the heads."

"Do you know who it is?" Karim asked. "Is it a royal person?"

"You only care if the dead are rich or royal. More gold for you," Rahmad said. "I know only that it is the reserve head of a man. But since it was found near an early royal tomb, I suppose it is most likely a royal person. But know this Karim, you can't go anywhere near the site, even if you wanted to go as far north as Giza."

"Why can't I go? Who is going to stop me?"

"The site is crawling with officials and policemen, exactly what Belzacchi said would happen," Rahmad explained.

"Is it true what the Italian said," Abdul asked. "Are we

really going to have to stop robbing the tombs?" He had a hopeful look in his eyes.

"No, I do not believe it," Rahmad answered. "Even if they do enact new laws, it will take them some time to catch up to us. As long as we keep quiet, we should be fine."

"Do you here that, brother?" Karim looked intently at Abdul. "You must keep your mouth shut and your eyes open. No talking about any of our business with Rahmad, understand?"

Abdul nodded. "But what about your people, Rahmad, the people you sell to, your customers? Do you trust them not to say anything?"

"Don't worry about them," Rahmad answered calmly. "I have only foreign customers now, like the English couple, and they will not give themselves away. They are doing something just as illegal as we are, even if they do not know it."

"We may have to work more quickly now," Karim said. "Every night we will go out and find treasure to bring back to you Rahmad. How fast can you sell what we bring you?"

"I can sell your thievery just as fast as you can get it for me," Rahmad answered with a smile. "I have my shop here, and I also sell to private buyers. Make no mistake, I sell to all sorts of people, from all over the world," Rahmad said. "But I am most worried about your mother, Satre. I am afraid she will not be able to keep her mouth shut and say nothing. She seems a most boastful woman; not a good person to be in business with."

"You need not worry about her," Karim said warily, giving a sideways glance at Abdul. "She will say nothing I can assure you of that."

"That is good. I know she is your mother, but she is a most difficult woman," Rahmad said. "I am happy and relieved she will not interfere with us."

"Yes, she has seen the error of her ways. Trust me, when I say you have seen the last of our mother," Karim said. "She will be quiet as the dead."

Abdul said nothing. Tears were forming on his lower eyelids, but no one noticed as he brushed them away with his dirty sleeve.

"So, back to business," Rahmad said, rubbing his hands together. "What have you brought for me today?"

"We have found a new tomb," Karim said, "One that will make us all rich men."

Rahmad looked at them with renewed interest. "A new tomb, you say? Where is it?"

"Hah, if we told you, it would no longer be a secret, true?" Karim asked. "I am smarter than that Rahmad."

"I only meant generally," Rahmad said calmly. "Just tell me, is it on the east bank or west bank of the Nile? Perhaps you can tell me that at least."

"The west bank," Abdul blurted out, excited to finally be able to take part in the conversation. "It is on the west bank, across the river."

Karim looked at his brother with disgust. "Can't keep your mouth shut, can you Abdul? You are always speaking out of turn, like the fool that you are."

Rahmad laughed. "It doesn't matter. I am far too old to go snooping around in tombs. It is much easier for me to let you young men do it for me. Now, show me what you have."

Karim opened his sack and brought out the golden

sandals, turning them over to expose the marching figures, their lances and shields poised for battle, engraved on the bottom of the sandals.

"These are magnificent, truly magnificent!" Rahmad said, rubbing his hands together. "May I handle them and get a closer look?"

Karim handed the sandals to him, and Rahmad examined the marching figures closely. "These look like Hittites. Just look at their pointed beards and their lances and shields. Yes, they are most definitely Hittites."

"Never mind that," Karim said impatiently. "Just tell me what they are worth."

"Oh but I must purchase everything as a package deal," Rahmad replied. "That is how I do things. Now, what else do you have for me?"

"These," Karim replied, holding out the five golden finger stalls. "Now, can you tell me, how much is everything worth Rahmad?"

"Oh I do like these very much! Such workmanship," Rahmad said with a broad smile. "Why, you can even see the form of fingernails, carved into the gold. Wonderful."

"So, how much are they worth?" Karim asked again. "Stop delaying and just tell me how much you will give me for them."

"Not yet, not yet. What do you have for me in your sack, Abdul? You've been very quiet."

"That's because he doesn't have much of any value," Karim spoke for his brother. "He doesn't know what is valuable and what is not, because he is a fool, my brother, the fool."

Abdul opened his sack and produced the turquoise and onyx bead necklaces. He looked at Rahmad hopefully.

"Those may be beautiful, but not of much value," Rahmad said. "I fear Karim may be right about you, Abdul. You may not know what is valuable and what is not. What else do you have?"

Abdul brought out the small copper ring, inlaid with an orange-red carnelian stone, with a sunburst design etched in the middle the stone.

"Now, that is wonderful," Rahmad said as his sweaty hand engulfed the small piece of jewelry. "I might be able to offer you something for the ring."

"Abdul, show him everything," Karim said. "And that includes what you wanted to keep for yourself. Now is no time to be keeping things from him. Rahmad is our partner."

"Yes, yes, I am your partner," Rahmad said, eyeing the open sack with greedy eyes. "Show me everything."

Abdul brought the duck shaped makeup bowl out into the light. He held it out gingerly in front of Rahmad.

"Exquisite." Rahmad said, grabbing the bowl and placing it on the counter behind him. "Well, now that I have seen everything, I can give you a very fair price for it all."

Abdul said nothing, but his mind was full of thoughts. *Why must my brother take everything from me? When I am no longer convenient, is he going to kill me too, like he did our mother?*

His thoughts were interrupted by Rahmad handing his brother a thick stack of Egyptian pound notes, which his brother quickly put in a pocket of his tunic. Karim smiled broadly.

"Oh, I almost forgot," Rahmad said. "I have a special request for you. Something which I think you will enjoy."

"And what might that be?" Karim asked, still smiling.

"Next time you and Abdul go into your new tomb, bring me back the nicest mummy you can find. The whole mummy, you understand? Not those pieces you brought me earlier, but the whole thing. It is for that English couple. They want to bring it back to England with them."

"The new tomb is far away. Can we not bring them one from the common tomb, near our house in Gourna?" Karim asked. "That way, it will be much easier to carry, and a much shorter trip. I doubt our English friends will know the difference."

"Yes, you are right. There is no sense in wasting the richer tombs on foreigners," Rahmad said. "Give them a common mummy of your choosing, whichever you like, it doesn't matter. As you said, they will not know the difference."

Karim smiled. "I will choose a mummy for them; only the best for the English."

Ω Ω Ω Ω Ω

Twenty Nine

"It is time to wrap the dead princess," Nebamun said, as he looked down upon the small form. "Padi let us do our best today."

"If you say it, it will be so, Great One," Padi said. "I believe we do our best every day. Is it not so?"

"Yes, my friend. We are blessed with the task of helping the dead into the better world of the afterlife, and as you say, we do our best every day," Nebamun said. "But, there is something about this little girl, she moves my spirit, like none of the others we have ever worked on."

"Can you explain, my friend?" Padi asked. "There have been so many over the years we have worked together. What is so different about this little girl?"

"I am not certain; perhaps I have come to view her as if she were my own daughter. The daughter I will never have," Nebamun answered.

"You are becoming sentimental Great One. You know what happens when priests become too emotional about the dead?" Padi said.

"Yes, I remember one such priest. The man fell in love with a woman, and when she died, he had to embalm her,"

Nebamun said. "Just after he concluded her ceremony, the priest shoved a sword into his breast and killed himself."

"I am certain you would not do such a thing, my friend," Padi said. "As you well know, if you did kill yourself, you would not be admitted into the afterlife, but your soul would be damned forever."

"Yes, have no fear of me causing my own death," Nebamun said. "I only meant that this little girl was special to me, unlike the many dead we have prepared, Padi."

"Well, if it is any comfort, you will see her again in the afterlife my friend," Padi said. "And that world will be beautiful beyond all understanding."

"Yes, I must not think on her death," Nebamun said. "I must think on her life after this moment, where she will live on in peace. Shall we get started Padi?"

"Yes, indeed. I am at your service, Great One."

It had only been ten days since removing the little girl's organs, but because of her small size, she had dried out quickly. Her flesh was now tight against her small bones.

"Yes, Great One, but what are we to call her, so that she may be recognized in the afterlife?" Padi asked. "It is unfortunate that our pharaoh and queen did not at least provide her with a name."

"Yes, I believe that in their grief, they could not think about what to call this little one, who died before she was allowed to live," Nebamun answered. "Padi, my friend, I have given much thought to this. It is an important question, for to name her wrongly is perform sacrilege against her, and against her father, Tutankhamun. I have decided we shall call her "the Osiris" as both a tribute to her royal birth, and to the god from whom we request protection for her."

"That is excellent, Great One. Certainly, no one can object to such reasoning and consideration," Padi said. "Pharoah himself could not have decided on a more perfect salutation."

Nebamun nodded and placed the Anubis mask over his face. *It seems lighter somehow, less constricting,* he thought. *It is going to be a great day. Our little princess is casting her divine light over us all.*

He carried a small papyrus document with him today, known as the Hymn to Osiris. He unrolled the document carefully, caressing the deep creases in the paper; they became deeper with each passing year. *I must have a scribe recopy this soon, before it falls into dust,* he thought absently.

Nebamun began the wrapping process by touching her forehead gently, anointing it with frankincense. He began to read in a commanding voice:

"Homage to thee, O my divine father Osiris; I come to embalm her. Do thou embalm these, her members, for she would not perish and come to an end; Come then, strengthen her breath, O Lord of the winds, who dost magnify these divine beings who are like unto thyself. Grant thou that she may enter into the land of everlastingness."

"I will remove the stuffing and replace it with new materials. What would you like me to put inside her, Great One?" Padi asked.

"I believe just some myrrh packages will be enough," Nebamun answered. "I want her to have a sweet smell in the afterlife, just as she would as a little girl."

Padi opened the incision and removed the soaked bundles

of brown linen. He placed several small packages of myrrh inside her abdomen and stitched it back up again with thin thread. Nebamun handed him a golden plate, inscribed with the eye of Horus, the wedjat, which he placed over the incision.

Nebamun placed the little girl's arms next to her sides, her palms facing toward her body. Padi placed a delicate full sheet of linen over her small form as the first of three burial shrouds.

"Can we make her body appear more fully shaped somehow?" Nebamun asked. "She just looks so, so much like a small animal, and not a small girl."

"Yes, I understand. I will take care of that, Great One." Padi began to stuff round lumps of linen padding around the body, around the legs, chest, and abdomen. He secured these with strips of linen which he wrapped transversely around the body.

"That is much better," Nebamun nodded approvingly. "You do know your craft, my friend. It is always a great pleasure to work with you."

Padi smiled appreciatively as he placed a second, and then a third shroud over the body. He secured each of the shrouds with strips wrapped horizontally and then longitudinally along the length of the body.

"She is ready, Great One," Padi said solemnly.

"This mask is far too large, but we will have to use it," Nebamun said, picking up an exquisite golden face mask. "There is no time to make another. All has been done with such haste, it is a pity."

Nebamun placed the mask over the small form. Although it covered almost the entire upper half of the girl's body, it was still very finely made, as befitted a royal daughter of the pharaoh. It was fashioned in cartonnage, similar to paper, which could be molded almost exactly like the facial features of its owner.

"The eyes are quite interesting, are they not Padi?" Nebamun asked, pointing to the alert eyes, so carefully outlined in black ink.

"Yes, indeed, Great One. If only she had lived, she might have been quite beautiful, like her mother."

Nebamun nodded. He picked up the girl's small wrapped body and placed it inside the inner coffin. This inner coffin was gilded entirely in gold foil and imprinted as if it was the delicate fabric of a small dress. On the chest was an imprint of an ornate breastplate with designs of tiny birds.

"Is it not my task to handle her body, Great One?" Padi asked, with a curious look on his face.

"Yes, my friend, but I need to be the one to hold the little girl, just this once."

"It is always as you wish, Nebamun. I am certain the gods would approve of your care of the little girl," Padi said.

Nebamun and Padi carefully placed the golden lid on top of the lower half of the coffin, and gently pushed it into place.

They listened for the small clicking sound, indicating a perfect fit by means of interlocking joints on the top half, fitting into perfectly carved holes on the bottom half. The dead princess was now sealed inside.

The final outer coffin was made of cypress wood, painted with black resin. Parts of this coffin were gilded with gold foil containing hieroglyphic inscriptions, to which Nebamun added her simple name "The Osiris."

Padi tied a length of linen around the chin, the waist, and the ankle sections of the outer coffin. He applied wet clay to each of the linens and Nebamun applied the seal imprint of a jackal and nine captive prisoners, the great seal of the royal necropolis.

The two priests stood over the tiny embalmed body, beautifully encased within the diminutive, magnificent coffins. There were no words to describe the abrupt ending of one so young, and with great difficulty, Nebamun finally found an appropriate passage; with his voice choking with emotion, he began to read:

"Osiris, you come to protect her. You bind together her head and the members of her body. You smite down enemies under her. You give unto her a head for ever and for ever, O Osiris, whose word is truth, whose word is truth in peace."

"May you find joy and happiness in the afterlife, and may we meet again in a better place. Farewell, little princess," Nebamun said quietly under his breath.

Ω Ω Ω Ω Ω

Thirty

The brothers wandered through mummies piled high to the ceiling. They were back in the tomb they had found in the beginning, close to their home in Gourna. Today they were looking for a mummy for Rahmad, and they didn't want to have to carry it very far.

They arrived at the tomb early to find and retrieve their special prize. Rahmad had made special arrangements to be open for them in the still darkness of early morning, so no one would see as they carried their large burden into his shop to be inspected and sold.

"Let's go further back, let's move further back, where the older mummies are," Karim said.

"Why can't we just take what we can easily get, and get out of here?" Abdul asked. "Let's take one close to the front and be done with it."

"Don't worry. We will take a mummy close to the entrance when we leave. But first, I want to check for anything valuable we might find," Karim said. "And the older mummies are likely to be more valuable. Now stop complaining and do what I tell you."

The two brothers moved further back into the chamber,

stepping carefully across the wrapped shapes in the dim light. Dust hung motionless in the stale air. In the furthest part of the tomb, a large piece of plaster had fallen from the ceiling, creating a large, hulking, ghost-like shape in front of them.

"Look there," Abdul whispered. "What is that? It looks like it will reach up and grab us."

"It's not a mummy. It's a body," Karim said callously. "Let's have a look. The man looks familiar. I think I might know him."

The brothers moved closer to the still form curled up in the dark. It was a man with most of his body laying smashed underneath the piece of plaster. Only his chest and head were visible, and they could see one arm draped across the lid of a wooden coffin next to the body.

"It's Ahmed. I thought so," Karim announced with a triumphant look on his face. "You remember Ahmed, don't you?"

"Yes, the man with eight children and the always pregnant wife," Abdul answered. "Yes, I remember. Our mother hated him and his family."

"Well, our mother hated everyone," Karim said, but them especially. She was jealous of the woman, mostly."

"Why?" Abdul asked. "What did the woman do to make mother hate her so much?"

"She hated the way Ahmed took care of his wife and their children. She was jealous because our father left us to fend for ourselves, that's why," Karim answered.

"That makes sense. I have known jealousy also, when I see others who can go to school and make a better life, and here we are, always scraping for our next meal. So how, if their lives were so great, how come Ahmed is lying dead down here?"

"The man started out as a butcher, but times became tough, and they had too many mouths to feed. I'm not surprised Ahmed had to turn to tomb robbing to feed his family," Karim said. "Unlike us, the man wasn't very smart, so I'm also not surprised he is dead."

"What is the family going to do now?" Abdul asked sadly. "Perhaps we could help them somehow. We could bring them food, or some money?"

"Not if you want to not get caught yourself, brother. We can not tell anyone we have found Ahmed; otherwise they will ask how we came to know he was down here. We cannot give ourselves away, fool."

"I was only thinking of all those children, with no one to help them put food on the table. I feel sad for them."

"The wife can always turn to whoring," Karim suggested. "She was a pretty woman, as I remember. But enough of Ahmed, start looking for anything of value, so we can get out of here while it is still dark outside. Rahmad will be waiting for us."

The brothers could find only small amulets of clay and some made of green faience. This was a common tomb, with nothing of any particular value, except the mummies themselves, to be ground up into powder.

"Let us find ourselves a mummy and be out of here, brother," Karim said. "After the riches of Deir el Bahari, this is nothing more than a dust pit."

"What about this one?" Abdul asked, pointing down to a round, bundled shape close to his feet.

"That's a good looking mummy, I must say," Karim answered with a laugh. "Wrappings still look tight. There is a good amount of resin on this one. He should last awhile, at least until he gets to England."

"Let's get it to Rahmad, while it's still dark. I'm getting nervous. Let's get out of here, Karim."

"You worry too much, brother. But, yes, I suppose we should get moving. There is probably nothing else down here worth taking."

Karim wrapped the upper section of the mummy in a large linen sack, and Abdul wrapped the lower section in a second linen sack. Karim tied it off neatly with a length of coarse rope.

"There, looks just like we might be carrying a rug, or something." Karim announced proudly. "No one will ever know by looking at us that we are carrying a mummy, brother."

The brothers Abd el Amun each took one end of the mummy and lifted it up, carrying it on their thin shoulders.

"Not too heavy at least," Abdul said, shifting the feet of the mummy to get a better grip. "I'm glad I've got the feet, Karim. Holding onto the head like you are doing seems wrong, almost like you have killed him yourself."

"It doesn't bother me a bit. "You are too sensitive, my brother. You'll be fine once we get this thing to Rahmad's shop."

"It isn't a *thing*. It was once a living person," Abdul said, frowning, "and now we are treating him as if he never existed at all. It is almost as bad as taking him to be ground up by Rahmad."

"Oh shut up, Abdul. You will never be happy," Karim yelled, his voice echoing against the smooth plaster walls of the tomb. "I am just trying to make a better life for us, and you can never think of the good life we could have, only the bad things we are doing. So, since you cannot be happy, just be quiet. Let's get going. It is getting late."

Abdul said nothing, just lapsed into sullen silence. He resigned himself to carrying the wrapped remains of someone long dead. *I will never know who this person was, or what his story might have been,* he thought. *At least he won't be ground up into powder, like the others. At least he will make one final journey, and then hopefully be left in peace.*

$$\Omega\ \Omega\ \Omega\ \Omega\ \Omega$$

Thirty One

"I am told you are looking for an apprentice," Iramen said to the fat man known as Merkha, the butcher. "My name is Iramen, and I would like to find work."

"Really, and who told you I needed any help?" Merkha asked. "I have had many men come to me, looking for work, and I have yet to find a suitable man to serve as my apprentice. Why should you be any different Iramen?"

"Matia, the prostitute told me to come and ask you for work. She recommends me."

"Ah yes, Matia. She is a fine woman, Matia, very beautiful. I would marry her, if she was not a whore. You know Matia then?" Merkha asked, his eyes narrowing.

"Yes, as I said, she recommends me," Iramen answered. "Are you looking for an apprentice or not?"

"Do not be in such a hurry, my friend. Yes, I am looking for an apprentice, but I cannot pay much to a new man. I have to see how skilled you are with a knife first. Then, we will see."

"When can I start?" Iramen asked. "I am in need of employment just as soon as I can find it."

"You have not eaten in awhile have you? Very well, I shall

start you out right now, why not?" Merkha answered handing him a cage with a loudly quacking duck tethered inside. "Kill this and cut it up in pieces for me. It is my dinner for tonight."

Iramen grabbed the duck and pushed its head down onto the bloody butchering table. With ruthless efficiency, he grabbed a large bronze cleaver and severed the head from the body, throwing the head into a basket. The bird was still moving as he swiftly plucked its feathers. Once plucked and bald, he cut the bird up in to cooking pieces, thighs, wings, and a breast.

"Good and fast, I will hire you," Merkha said, laughing. "Now perhaps you will eat this duck with me. As I said, you look as though you have not eaten in many days."

In truth, Iramen was very hungry. The only food he had eaten was the small piece of bread Matia had given him. Before that, he could not remember his last meal. He was drunk through most of the last few days; his appetite for drink was much more pressing than his appetite for food.

Now that he was sober, however, he realized he would like nothing more than to eat roasted duck, especially if it did not cost him anything.

"Yes, thank you. I will join you. You can tell me what it is like to be a butcher," Iramen said.

"Yes, and you can tell me what you did to find yourself in such a desperate situation. I am certain it was not your life's ambition to become a butcher. Do you have anything to trade to help support yourself?" Merkha asked.

"Not much, only a few small things," Iramen answered. "Perhaps you know of someone who might be interested in trading for them."

"I might. After dinner, Iramen, I will take you to meet some friends of mine. You can join in our dice game, perhaps be lucky, or perhaps not." He smiled. "You look as though you could use some luck, my friend. Perhaps fortune will smile upon you."

Merkha served up the roasted duck, cooked with onions and wheat, which Iramen ate greedily, wiping any stray juices from his chin.

"Here, drink. You must be thirsty," Merkha said, offering him a brimming glass of barley beer.

It was not Iramen's intention to get drunk, after all, this was a man he did not know; it was best to be careful. But the beer was delicious, thirst quenching, too good to stop.

Soon he was drunk again. It was a good feeling to be drunk. Not caring about the world around him. He felt an increased sense of happiness, secure in himself. For the moment, it no longer mattered that he was an outcast, no longer mattered that he would never see his brother again.

Iramen was barely aware of Merkha leading him out into the still blackness of night. He could only stagger as Merkha turned him off of one darkened street and into another. They slowly wound their way through the maze of streets in Waset, until they came to a narrow alley, almost obscured in the darkness.

A few more steps and they were in front of a small mud brick house, connected to other houses by a thin wall. The two men had to stoop very low to enter the humble doorway. Iramen struck his head smartly against the hard mud ceiling as he entered.

"Watch your head my friend," Merkha said, laughing.

"Or you will have an even greater pain in your head than from drink."

Inside the small room, three men sat cross-legged on the floor, illuminated by the light of a small candle. It flickered and danced suddenly from a slight breath of air as Iramen and Merkha sat down.

"Iramen, these are my friends I told you about," Merkha said. "It is perhaps better for you that you do not know their names. It seems we are interrupting their dice game."

The three men looked at Iramen intently, their bleary eyes red from drinking barley beer and playing dice for hours. The men were covered in dirt and sweat, and smelled of decay and rot. At this moment, Iramen was glad enough not to know their names. He did not like these men.

"What did you say your name was, Iramen? Was that it? Do you want to join us, my friend?" one of the men asked, pulling at a piece of half decayed food between his teeth.

"I will join you, but be warned, I am a lucky dice player," Iramen boasted, grinning broadly. "I will take your possessions from you this night."

"We shall see, we shall see," the man said as he retrieved the piece of food and swallowed it. "Have a drink, my friend. Then we shall see who is the luckiest of us."

He grabbed the clay vessel and drank deeply of its contents. He was still drunk from dinner, but he could always drink more, and this was such a delicious brew, foamy and full of flavor. He wiped his face happily. It was going to be a good night for him, he could tell.

Iramen pulled out his small pouch and dropped its contents onto the floor. The fabric with gold thread fell out, and the dead Hittite's jewelry, the metals shining brightly even in the dim light of the candle.

"Where did you get those rings?" Merkha asked, looking at Iramen with renewed interest. "They are very finely made, too finely made for a person such as you to be carrying around."

"I took them from a man who did not need them anymore. And I took this one for myself," Iramen announced proudly, displaying his onyx ring with the bull design for them all to see.

"Would you happen to know where this man is now? I mean would you be able to find him again?" Merkha asked. "We might want to speak with him."

Iramen nodded. "Oh yes, I can find him again, and you can talk to him, but he will not answer you, for he is dead. The man's name was Zannanza, and he was a Hittite prince."

"So, you robbed a dead man?" Merkha asked suspiciously. "It is no wonder then that you came upon my shop, starving and looking for work. You are a runaway and a thief. Who is chasing you, my friend, perhaps we can help to hide you from them."

"The medjay are searching for me," Iramen said. "They will kill me if they find me, and they will kill you also for helping me."

"We have no fear of the medjay," Merkha said calmly. "They cannot touch us; we are far too smart, Iramen. We will help you."

Iramen was relieved and happy. Not only was he drunk, but he had found some new friends who would help him out of his trouble. He had found work with the butcher Merkha that would see him through for a few months at least. Best of all, he could win their possessions from them and be that much richer tonight.

"I am indebted to you Merkha, and your friends. I will do all I can for you in return."

"So, how have you come to know all about this Hittite prince and where he is buried?" Merkha asked. "I am certain that is not common knowledge."

"No, it is not. I know of him because I helped to put him there," Iramen answered. "I used to be a priest, and my brother is a high priest. His name is Nebamun."

"*You are a priest?*" Merkha asked, "Then how come you wanted a job with me as butcher's apprentice? Surely, you would have been better served staying a priest."

"I grew tired of being a priest, always in the shadow of my brother. I made a mistake of robbing from the dead, and my brother denounced me to the medjay, so here I find myself," Iramen answered. "But, I do not wish to say any more about my past life, do you want me to show you where he is buried, or not?"

"Did you leave any treasure remaining with him, or did you steal it all," one of the men asked. "What is left for us?"

"There is not much remaining, only the man's lance, shield and his chariot, and some worthless clay tablets I found," Iramen replied. "Zannanza lies on the ground in a cave."

"I am interested in this dead Hittite, and also any other tombs we might steal from," Merkha said. "Perhaps we can all work together to our mutual benefit."

"Why should I tell you anything?" Iramen asked, suddenly wary. "What do I get in return for letting you share in my knowledge of the tombs?" Iramen asked. "What can you possibly give me that I would want?"

"I will let you keep your freedom, and possibly your life, my friend. I will not tell anyone you are still here in Waset," Merkha promised. "You already know what happens to those who steal from the dead. If the medjay finds out you are here, you will be executed."

"My life is of little consequence, Merkha. Tell me, what else do I get for helping you? It seems you are getting the best end of this deal."

"And in addition," Merkha added hastily, "We will share the treasure with you in equal measure. You need our help to retrieve the treasure, and we can help you sell whatever we find. We will all be rich, my friend."

Iramen nodded. "Yes, I could use your help. We can move more treasure out of the caves and into our pockets. I will show you the cave of the dead Hittite, but that is like sand in the desert compared to the riches of other tombs."

"Fine, let us leave tomorrow at midnight then," Merkha said. "But for right now, let us do what we came here for. Let us play some dice. I want to see how lucky you are, Iramen."

Ω Ω Ω Ω Ω

Thirty Two

It was well before dawn when Iramen and his four companions arrived at the cave. Iramen could see the body of the Hittite prince, still lying face down in the dirt, just as he had left it.

"Here is the mighty Zannanza, just as I promised," Iramen announced proudly.

The body lay there naked, the flickering flames of the men's torches casting obscene shadows on the brown flesh. His muscles and tendons were stretched out as if to break apart. Zannanza's skull was now clearly visible beneath its light covering of leathery skin.

"Help me turn him over Iramen," Merkha said. "I want to get a good look at his face."

"What do you want to do that for? The man is covered with lice," Iramen said with disgust. "I remember that from before. I washed many times to free myself from the itch."

"Just do it," Merkha said. Something in Merkha's tone made Iramen uneasy. He grabbed the thin, leathery corpse at the hip and Merkha grabbed him at the shoulder. They turned him as one.

Merkha gasped. "Where is his face? It is completely gone."

The once handsome, powerful face was missing. In its place was a teeming mass of blue-black scarab beetles, busily chewing at the small bulb that used to be Zannanza's chin.

"May the gods curse whoever did this to him!" Merkha said, putting his hand in front of his nose to block the stench. "No one deserves to be left to the scarabs. Surely, he should have not been left like this."

"What? The man is a Hittite, enemy of Egypt. I say, he got what he deserved," Iramen said.

Merkha said nothing. He picked up the man's sheepskin cloak from a heaping pile of clothing nearby. He carefully covered Zannanza's body with it, holding it loosely to keep the lice from moving onto his own clothing.

"What are you doing?" Iramen asked suspiciously. "We had best get moving if you want to go to the richer tombs before it gets light."

Merkha had stopped talking to him. Iramen noticed he wasn't even looking at him anymore. Instead, Merkha had moved to the shield and the lance, and was examining them closely. He gave a small nod.

"What is it?" Iramen asked. "Do you want me to show you the other tombs, or do you want to spend more time with the man with no face?"

"Be silent, fool!" Merkha shouted, making a small hand gesture to his three friends.

The men moved slowly, deliberately, forming a circle around Iramen.

Merkha examined the chariot, noting the faceplate on the front of it, running his fingers gently over the royal seal. He stooped over and retrieved one of the broken clay pieces containing the odd, wedge shaped writing. He turned the clay piece over in his hand.

"Do you know what this is, *former* priest?" Merkha asked, holding up the piece of clay writing.

"I have no idea, and I really do not care what it is," Iramen answered. "I smashed the tablets. They were of no value to me."

"No value, the man says," Merkha said, sneering. "Do you hear that, my friends; as if this man knows anything at all about value."

"Well, tell me what it is then," Iramen mumbled. He was staring intently at the ground now, avoiding looking into Merkha's eyes.

"It is a peace proposal from the Hittite lands, meant for the eyes of your pharaoh, Tutankhamun. Would you like to know its contents?" Merkha asked, his eyes narrowing to tiny slits.

"I know you want to tell me, Merkha."

"It is a proposal of marriage between prince Zannanza and one of Pharoah's royal half sisters, chosen by Pharaoh himself. Whomever Pharaoh chose was to become a Hittite princess, securing peace and prosperity for the good of all. Is it not a pity his message was never delivered?" Merkha asked, dropping the piece of clay to the ground.

"Egypt should never be at peace with the Hittites," Iramen countered. "Egypt should always rule the world, including the Hittites."

"We will never know now," Merkha said sadly. "The message is lost, and Zannanza is dead. I believe the vizier Ay may have had something to do with the murder of our prince. Like you, Iramen, he wants no part of peace with us."

"What? You said *our prince*, and *us*. For an Egyptian butcher, you seem to have a lot of information," Iramen said.

"Now you understand," Merkha said, nodding. "We are not Egyptian, we are Hittites, sent into Egypt to discover what became of our prince. Now we know, and we can take the appropriate revenge on those involved in this most vile act."

"You are Hittites, all of you?" Iramen asked, a look of fear spreading across his face.

"Yes, all of us, even Matia. She knew you had some connection to our prince when you gave her the carnelian ring. She gave the ring to Zannanza as a present. They were very close, some say they were lovers."

"I do not believe what you say," Iramen said. "She is Egyptian, you are lying to me."

"I swear I am not. Her real name is Pudukhepa, and she was the first of us to arrive in your country. What better disguise than that of a whore," Merkha said, laughing. "You would have never guessed at who she really is. One consolation, priest, is that you slept with the same woman as a Hittite prince. You are a lucky man."

"So, what are your real names, then," Iramen asked, trying to control the trembling in his voice.

"My name is Hattusilis," Merkha said pointing to himself. He introduced his three friends with a commanding sweep of his arm. "And this is Muwatalis, Tudkhalias and Esarhaddon. We are all in service to the army of our king, Suppiluliuma." The three men bowed slightly, their arms fixed to their sides.

"Believe me when I tell you that I had nothing to do

with the death of your prince," Iramen said, no longer able to contain the trembling or the whine in his voice.

"I know you did not kill him. Zannanza was a resourceful man," Hattusilis answered. "And you are not nearly clever enough to have killed him. No, no, this was the work of someone devious, and someone with access. No, I believe it was the vizier Ay, although I can never prove it."

"Thank you, Merkha...I...I mean Hattusilis," Iramen said gratefully, falling to his knees.

"You did not kill his mortal flesh," Hattusilis continued. "What you did was far worse, especially for a priest."

"How can I have done something *worse*? Iramen asked, his fear returning. "What can be worse than killing a man?"

"You have killed his soul," Hattusilis answered. "You left him, naked, face down in the dirt, food for the scarabs. Now, with no face, he cannot be recognized in the afterlife. He is truly dead."

"What happened to his face is not my fault. How was I to know that the scarabs would soon have him?" Iramen asked in an increasingly shrill voice.

"You robbed him of all that he could have taken with him on his eternal journey, and you stripped him of his clothing for your own pleasure, leaving his bare flesh unprotected," Hattusilis continued. "As a priest, you should have protected his immortal soul, but you did nothing."

Hattusilis motioned to the three men, who dragged Iramen outside the cave, into the scorching desert heat. He kneeled in the hot sand, trying to control the trembling in his legs.

"What can I do to make amends for this insult to you

and your prince?" Iramen pleaded. "I am not myself when I drink, but I swear to make this right with you and your people."

Hattusilis looked at his men, and then looked down on the still kneeling Iramen. "You swear you will do anything I ask of you?"

"Yes, I swear," Iramen said with relief. "Anything you ask. Just tell me what I can do to make amends."

"Then, you must die priest. You must die and be left in the same fashion as our beloved prince; he who was so ill treated at your hands," Hattusilis pronounced.

"What?"

Iramen moved as if in slow motion, struggling to get up from the ground, but he was pushed down again. He felt two strong hands holding down each of his shoulders.

"You shall have each of your eyes plucked out, as if by birds," Hattusilis continued. "We shall slit your throat and cast you face down upon the ground. You will bleed quickly, and the scarabs will find you.

They will feed upon your face, perhaps the same scarabs which fed upon our prince. No one will speak for you in the afterlife, and no one will know you there. Iramen, you will die, and your soul will die with you."

Iramen closed his eyes and thought suddenly of his brother, Nebamun. *What would Nebamun be doing now, probably washing and shaving, preparing himself for the Anubis mask. He, Iramen, should be wearing the Anubis mask. He was the older brother. If he was high priest, his life would have been good. He would never have robbed the Hittite, never desecrated the dead, never…*

Perhaps it was good that his last thoughts were selfish ones. When he thought only of himself, Iramen became totally unaware of anything else.

So it was that he was unaware of the Hittite, the one called Muwatalis, taking out a small knife tucked into his belt. Iramen had closed his eyes, which was just as well, for he did not see the blade as it plunged into his right eye. With another quick thrust, Iramen's left eye was now gone as well.

Iramen screamed in agony and fruitlessly dabbed at the bleeding holes where his eyes had once been. It was just as well that he could no longer see; just as well that his mind was occupied only with his recent excruciating torment.

So it was that he was unaware of the man named Esarhaddon, who reached into his tunic and pulled out the recently purchased sickle shaped dagger he had concealed there.

It was just as well he could not see how brilliantly the dagger's bronze edge gleamed and how the red stones sparkled as the sun cast its rays upon them.

"Ask for forgiveness from your Gods, priest," Hattusilis said grimly.

"I do not have any Gods to ask," Iramen cried out, as the curved blade came swiftly toward his soft throat.

$$\Omega \ \Omega \ \Omega \ \Omega \ \Omega$$

Thirty Three

"Whom shall he be called?" Nebamun asked, looking down at the dead man on the stone slab. The man was somewhat short, with skin that hung loosely around his neck and arms. It was impossible to tell what the man's face looked like. Where his face should have been, there was only a hollowed out cavity.

"We do not know the man's name. The men who found him brought him to us just as you see him," Padi answered. "They said he was lying in the desert face down in the sand, and when they turned him over, they discovered only flesh eating scarab beetles where his face should have been."

"What happened to this man?" Nebamun asked. "Surely, he did not die of natural causes then."

"We have no idea of who he is or how he came to be dead in the desert," Padi answered. "We can find no one who knows anything."

"I do not need to tell you, Padi, without knowing who he is, we have a problem. The man's soul, his Ba, will not be able to recognize him and return to him. You know what that means."

"Yes, yes I know, Great One," Padi replied. "He will not be known in the afterlife. He will die the eternal death."

"Yes, he will not live on," Nebamun said solemnly. "Your work is simplified today, my friend."

"How is my work made simpler, Great One?" Padi asked. "I will always do my best, no matter how long it takes."

"I know I can always count on you to do what is necessary, Padi, but the man has no nose remaining, from which to draw out the brains. Indeed, he has very little brain left. You may merely scoop it out with your spoon."

"Yes, indeed. But I would wish it were not so," Padi said. "I would gladly trade my time for this man to be able to enter the afterlife."

"You are a good man, Padi," Nebamun said, smiling. "But let us talk not of what we are unable to do for him. Let us talk of what can be done. So, you believe he is Egyptian then."

"It is believed so, yes," Padi answered.

"Very well then, we shall proceed to give him the rites of Osiris," Nebamun said. "It is the least we can do for him."

He placed the heavy mask of Anubis over his shaved head and began: *"Let Ra grant to you a view of the Sun Disk and a sight of the Moon unfailingly each day. Let your Ba come forth to walk about whithersoever it pleases. Let your name be called out, let it be found inscribed on the tablet which recordeth the names of those who are to receive offerings."*

"Padi, please begin," Nebamun said. "Let us try to make him presentable to the gods. Perhaps they will take pity upon him and restore his face in the afterlife."

As Nebamun had said, Padi's work was simple today. He picked up only one instrument, his long, delicate spiral shaped rod ending in a small spoon. He plunged it into the open cavity containing what was left of the dead man's brain.

The beetles had left only a small amount of gelatinous material, and it was quickly scraped away. Padi poured palm wine into the gaping hole and washed out the cavity thoroughly. He packed the opening with linens soaked in resin.

"It is finished," Padi announced. "I have a suggestion, Great One."

"Yes?" Nebamun asked. "What do you propose, my friend?"

"We can restore some of the shape to this man's face when we wrap him. We can place some linen bundles where his cheeks and nose should be. We can create some features for him; features that were taken away by the beetles."

"Let us do that for him now, so that we do not forget later, Nebamun said. "That is a very good idea, my friend."

Padi smiled, appreciating the compliment. He dipped linen bundles in hot resin and shaped them into smooth mounds of cloth. He gently placed the pliable linen over the open crevice of the dead man's face.

Nebamun joined in, and together the two priests molded cheekbones, a nose, and other facial curvatures so that the man once again resembled a man.

"That is the best we can hope for, Great One," Padi said. "Given the circumstances, I think he looks quite well, although his face is a bit misshapen."

"Yes, I agree. We have done what we can for him. As I said, perhaps the gods will pity him and allow his people to recognize him. Please call for the eviscerator," Nebamun commanded.

Padi stepped outside the tent and motioned to a young, very dark skinned man to come with him. He lifted the tent opening just enough to admit the man into Nebamun's presence.

"Nebamun, this is Sebni, sent here to replace Iramen. He has come to us from Memphis." Padi said. "He has a reputation as a good priest."

"Welcome, Sebni. Do your work well. The man who came before you was highly skilled at his work, and we miss him greatly." Nebamun said, looking quickly at Padi.

"Yes, indeed," Padi answered quickly, "highly skilled, and we miss him greatly."

"I can only hope you will find my skills satisfactory," Sebni said. "I have been an eviscerator for only a short while. Before I begin, might I ask where your previous eviscerator is now? What has happened that caused him to leave your service?"

"I have no idea where he is, and as for why he left, that is of no concern to you. Do not ask any questions or your short employment here will be terminated," Nebamun warned. "Do you understand?"

Sebni nodded a look of fearful respect on his face. Padi was surprised to hear his high priest talk to a subordinate in such a manner. Nebamun was usually kind and patient. This Nebamun was another man entirely.

Nebamun grunted. This man might perform his task well, no doubt better than Iramen but he wanted his brother to return. He wanted to see the brother he remembered from his youth, the happy smiling brother.

He wanted to see the young Iramen, before he became an eviscerator; before he was shunned by those around him, having only drink and whores for company.

Nebamun opened the Book of Coming Forth by Day

quickly and began to read. *"Let this man have possession of his Ba and his soul, let his word be truth with the Ba in every place wherein it may be. Observe then, O ye guardians of heaven, this soul. Even if it would tarry, cause you to see his body."*

Padi turned the dead man, exposing his left side and Nebamun drew a long, thin line down the man's torso.

"Begin please, Sebni," Nebamun said, wondering if the young man he saw before him would also go the way of his brother.

Sebni poised his razor sharp knife, ready to cut the outlined tissue and make his way into the man's body. He was anxious to prove to this high priest that he could do his job well.

"One moment," Nebamun said, examining the dead man's right hand, which now dangled off the edge of the table.

"What is it, Nebamun?" Padi asked.

"Curious," Nebamun answered.

"What is curious?" Padi asked, anxious to get started.

"How such a man, lying faceless and still in the desert, could come by such a beautiful ring. He is probably one of many tomb robbers who got what he deserved," Nebamun said, lifting the hand to get a better look at the ring on the dead man's smallest finger.

It was pure gold, with an onyx stone. Etched on its surface was the tiny figure of a golden bull gleaming out at them in the half light of the embalming tent.

"Begin please, Sebni," Nebamun said. "And do your best work."

$$\Omega\ \Omega\ \Omega\ \Omega\ \Omega$$

Thirty Four

"So, my English friends, I have something very special for you today," Rahmad said, his eyes gleaming.

"You are just in time Rahmad," Edward replied. "We are headed to England tomorrow. I must confess that I will miss Egypt very much."

"And Egypt will miss you, Mr. Dunthorpe. Egypt has shown you her treasures, and now you will take something back to remember us."

"Well, I certainly *will not* miss Egypt," Mary interrupted. "I found it nothing but a hot dusty place, full of unscrupulous men." She looked pointedly at Rahmad.

"I am truly sorry you feel that way, Madam. Perhaps I can make it up to you," Rahmad said. "I would like to give you a small present to make you feel better about me."

"Don't try to give me one of your dusty trinkets that you have not been able to sell, Rahmad," Mary warned. "I would rather go back to England with nothing than with one of your pieces of worthless trash."

"Well, perhaps you will take this, madam, as a special present for a special English lady." Rahmad held out a small copper ring, inlaid with an orange-red carnelian stone with a sunburst design etched in the middle of the stone.

"Oh it *is* lovely, and a perfect fit," Mary said with a delighted squeal as she placed the ring on her finger. "The color is wonderful, and the design, why, it almost looks as if it is smiling at me. Edward, what do you think?"

"Mary, anything that makes you happy, makes me happy," Edward said. "Perhaps you would like to stay a little longer in Egypt now?"

"No thank you husband," Mary said. "This ring is beautiful, but it does not make up for the weeks we have spent in this parched, desolate country. I still dislike it here."

"I'm happy you at least like the ring, Madam," Rahmad said with a small bow, anxious to interrupt the couple in the midst of their argument. "Now to the business at hand; I have what you asked for, Mr. Dunthorpe."

"*Really*, I was only half-joking. You actually found me a complete mummy?" Edward asked. "It's all mine and I am free to take it with me?"

"Yes, indeed. You can take it home to England, but you must be quick about it," Rahmad replied. "It is good you are going home tomorrow."

"Why? It's not illegal, is it?" Mary asked suspiciously. "We are not doing anything wrong, are we? Edward, I do not want to get into trouble over your dealings."

"Now, calm down Mary," Edward said soothingly. "I am sure we will be fine. Isn't that right Rahmad? It is not illegal, surely not."

"Not yet, but I am afraid it soon will be. I have been told that laws forbidding the transfer of antiquities are being enacted soon. So, you must be quick and silent about this, do you understand?" Rahmad asked in a near whisper.

"I don't like it, Edward. Not one tiny bit," Mary said. "We could go to jail."

"We won't my dear, we will leave quickly and quietly, as Rahmad suggests. Now Rahmad let me see what I am buying."

Rahmad smiled and ushered them through a dingy blue curtain and into his back room. His brilliant blue shabti figures were still there, and next to them a long, thin figure wrapped in two sacks lay on the table in front of them.

"My God in heaven, is that it?" Mary asked with a disgusted look on her face. "I don't want any part of taking this creature home with us."

"One moment, my dear; let's unwrap it before you make any judgements," Edward said. "In spite of what you think now, you might grow to like having a bit of history around the house."

"Yes, yes, by all means," Rahmad said. "Come sir and madam, let's unwrap your prize."

Rahmad carefully untied the rope and removed the two sacks, one for upper section, one for the lower section, until the entire body was exposed.

The Dunthorpes found themselves looking down at the full figure of a mummy, heavily encased in resin.

"Why does it look so brown?" Mary asked. "I thought it would be a bit whiter, and not look quite so dried out."

"That's the resin used for mummification. It's a type of varnish, made from the sap of myrrh trees, I believe." Rahmad explained. "It is good that the mummy is so thickly covered with the resin; it will travel better, without unraveling."

"But what's wrong with its face?" Mary asked. "His face looks misshapen, rounded and lumpy, looks like."

"The face was damaged in antiquity. That may have been the cause of death. Who knows?" Rahmad asked with a shrug. "The ancient embalmers did the best they could, putting pads of linen where his face once was, to make him look as he did in life."

"You ask too many questions, Mary." Edward said. "I think it's marvelous. Now, how can we get it down the street and onto our boat?"

"Easily done, sir," Rahmad assured him. "I can wrap it as you would a long carpet, and two of my associates will carry it on board for you. No one will ever suspect what it really is. But, don't unwrap it until you reach your home in England, understand?"

"Yes, I understand. Well then, you have a deal, Rahmad. I and my friends at home are going to enjoy our new family addition," Edward said, smiling.

"It has been a pleasure doing business with you, Mr. Dunthorpe," Rahmad said, extending his hand. "I hope you come back to Egypt again someday."

Edward shook his hand, and then quickly used the sleeve of his coat to wipe off the blackened film of grime clinging to his palm.

"That will be five hundred Egyptian pounds for the mummy," Rahmad said calmly.

"What? Surely you are joking?" Edward asked. "Is this your last opportunity to try and cheat me, before I leave for home?"

"It is a fine mummy, and worth every penny," Rahmad said defensively. "If you don't want it, I can sell it to someone else. It took a great deal of trouble to haul it out of the tombs."

"Yes, I suppose," Edward conceded. "Very well, I simply must have it." He produced a stack of pound notes, placing it in front of the shopkeeper.

Rahmad counted the money out carefully and placed the notes in his pocket. He stopped and looked at Mary.

"Only pay me a small amount for the ring," Rahmad said.

"I thought you said you were giving it to my wife."

"I am just about giving it away, sir. I will only charge you a small amount for it. Again, it took a great deal of trouble to find this ring."

"Oh, Edward, pay the man and let's get out of here," Mary said. "Besides, I do love this ring. I wonder who it belonged to."

Mary looked at the carnelian ring, glinting in the light. The sunburst looked as though it was smiling at Mary, and she smiled back.

"We'll never know," Edward said, "but now it belongs to you, my dear."

Ω Ω Ω Ω Ω

Thirty Five

"Where is the princess to be buried, Great One?" Padi asked.

"I have not been told. I asked Pharoah if he would like her to be buried with Maia, in her tomb at Saqqara."

"Maia? Who is this Maia?"

"The mother of our pharaoh died giving birth to the Divine One, Tutankhamun, and he was raised by his wetnurse, a woman named Maia," Nebamun explained. "She was greatly admired, and when she died a few years ago, a large tomb was built to honor her. That tomb is in Saqqara."

"How do you know of this, my friend? I have not heard of this Maia."

"It was I who presided over her mummification and burial. I still remember the inscriptions on the tomb walls. She was known as the One Who Fed the Body of a God. A lion was killed and placed in the tomb with her as an offering to Bast."

"Does Pharoah want the princess entombed with this wetnurse?" Padi asked. "She would no doubt be protected by Bast."

"Pharoah said no to this," Nebamun said. "The Divine

One told me that he had another location for her, a secret place within the royal necropolis tombs, deep in the sacred valley. He would not tell me where, and he also requested it be just the two of us."

"That is strange, Nebamun, why only two priests for one as valuable as a royal princess?" Padi asked. "And how are we to know where to take her mortal form?"

"You and I are to take a boat from Waset across the Nile and meet the royal party on the other side. From there, we shall all travel up the sacred valley to the final resting place of the princess," Nebamun answered. "We must leave now, Padi, if we are to meet them in time for burial."

The two priests put the small form of the princess on a wooden litter embossed with gold. They picked her up with ease and walked out of the shade of the Per Nefer and into the sunlight. It was a peaceful journey at first, as they made their way around the Sacred Lake. In the stillness of early morning, the surface of the water was glassy smooth, reflecting the shapes of the graceful date palm trees as they swayed in the mild wind.

"The geese are quiet today, Great One," Padi said. "It seems it may be too early for them to be about."

"I am thankful for the silence, my friend," Nebamun answered. "I have never understood why they are so beloved of Amun. To me, they are loud, quarrelsome birds. We are fortunate not to be the priests who take care of them."

"As you say." He had never heard his friend the high priest ever question the choices of the Gods. Nebamun was not himself today.

Nebamun and Padi walked through a side entrance,

carrying their precious cargo. They continued on through a sequence of three large gateways, opening and closing each of the massive wooden doors gilded in sheaths of gold. Nebamun and Padi made their way into the court of Thutmosis, with its four beautiful obelisks carved with all the majesty of Thutmosis' name.

They walked through the hall of columns, each column topped with the design of a papyrus flower in full bloom. The entire surface of each column was carved with scenes of the lives of the pharaohs, including Tutankhamun, and the everlasting glory of the Gods. The remarkable carvings were painted in bright jewel tones of yellow, red and turquoise and stood out in a riot of color.

They walked on into the gardens at the entrance to Ipet Isut. They continued past pomegranate trees weighed down heavily with ripe red fruit. The center of the gardens was filled with many small ponds, perfect for the growth of graceful water plants.

Once outside the walls of Ipet Isut, Nebamun and Padi placed the small girl in the shade of an unfinished column and stopped to rest before continuing on to the landing dock.

They saw a group of ever-present workmen in the midst of carving the cartouche of King Tutankhamun on the temple's outer stone walls. The stonecutters' faces were drenched with sweat and dirt, so much so that only the whites of their eyes and jagged teeth shown out.

One of the men was sitting cross-legged on the blistering hot sand, squinting as he attempted to sketch an outline of a figure on the temple walls. He used red ink, sketching quickly and carefully. Although his arm was outstretched and unsupported, it was still strong, and showed no signs of fatigue.

This man was only a fledgling artist, who still painted small dots to outline the height of shoulders, knees, hands, and other body parts. These dots would later be outlined completely after the dimensions and perspective were approved by his superior.

This superior was the master artist, a scribe, who stood by to examine the work, his reed pen and red ink palette at the ready to correct any defect in the work. All had to be perfect, and when the work was without flaw, it would be outlined in black ink, for all time.

Nebamun and Padi carried their burden down through the main city of Waset, past the two storied houses of the affluent, with their backyard ponds, upon which floated fragrant white lotus blossoms. Children played games of dog and jackal, moving their ivory gaming pieces and shouting with delight, while their happy parents looked on with pride.

They passed orchards of fig trees, where the trained monkeys swung from branch to branch, gathering the crop of figs for their owner's pleasure. Not all of the figs reached the owner's kitchen, as Nebamun noticed the greedy creatures often pop a piece of fruit into their mouths.

This was a world in which the priests would never live, a world of family, of children, of comfortable houses. They were chosen instead for the world of duty to the pharaoh and to the gods. This was the only world they knew.

They were close to the docks now. They could smell the pungent odor of Nile perch. They passed by houses of the common people, single story houses, with no ponds, no flowers, only the occasional emaciated dog lying listlessly under a small sliver of shade. These were most of the houses in Waset, most of the lives in Waset. They were the simple lives of routine, repeated day after day, all in service to their pharaoh and their gods.

Nebamun and Padi reached the edge of the Nile, where a boat was waiting for them. It was the same boat they had taken to bury Nasra and Amunet months before. But it was not the same. Today the boat was decked with flowered garlands, and twisted papyrus blossoms.

The weepers were already waiting on the deck, impatient for the day to be over, and for them to collect their earnings for crying on behalf of someone they did not know. Today they would cry and scream, beat their breasts, and claw at their hair, all for the sake of the little stillborn girl Nebamun and Padi carried.

"Great One, once again you are quiet," Padi said, as the ship left the dock. "Are you not happy to be entrusted with this important burial?"

"Oh yes, my friend," Nebamun answered. "I am sorry, I was thinking about Iramen. He has been gone for so long I believe I will never see him again, not in this life."

"It is possible," Padi conceded. "But surely, Great One you will see him in the afterlife, where all things continue forever. Surely, this is the better world."

Nebamun only nodded and stared out into the black waters of the Nile. He noticed a small school of fish just under the water, their scaled bodies shining like silver arrows as they cut through the mild current.

He turned to look at Padi, who in turn was gazing upon

one of the women mourners, her sheath dress torn and her breast exposed. Padi had that look of a man tormented by thoughts he could not fulfill. *At least Padi can think of something besides death,* Nebamun thought.

It seemed only moments before that the ship had left the Waset dock on the east bank, but now it suddenly bumped into the wooden pilings of the dock on the western shore.

Nebamun looked out and was surprised at how few people waited on the shore for them. There were no more than thirty people who waited there, some of whom were mourners; others were servants carrying small amounts of food for the dead princess to consume in the afterlife, and a few soldiers accompanying the small procession.

Among the small group there was only one person of any importance, high above the crowd in a golden carrying chair, held aloft by four men. The chair's occupant was obscured by the fine red and gold fabric enclosure. Nebamun could see the dim figure of a man sitting inside, his white eyes peering out at the high priest.

$$\Omega\ \Omega\ \Omega\ \Omega\ \Omega$$

Thirty Six

"Did you not think there would be more people, Great One?" Padi asked. "I am surprised by such a small group."

"Yes, indeed I thought that a great many people would turn out for such a funeral," Nebamun answered, his eyes squinting. "It is sad how few there are to say farewell to this little girl who never felt the sun on her face, never new the joy of being held by her parents. It is almost too painful to behold."

The procession began to stretch out in a single line, like a small serpent. There were random splashes of color amidst the drab group, deep, vivid greens, like the Nile, and brilliant hues of blue, like turquoise and lapis stones.

"Great One," Padi said, pointing to the carrying chair, bobbing up and down near the front of the line. "It is pharaoh and the queen, I am certain of it."

"Yes, I am sure you are right. Only pharaoh has such a fine carrying chair," Nebamun answered. *We cannot see him. In truth, it could be anyone in that chair,* he thought.

"Yes, surely pharaoh and the queen are inside," Padi continued, as if reading Nebamun's thoughts. "It is such an elegant chair, for an elegant royal couple."

"We will be graced by their presence very soon," Nebamun answered. He wanted to believe his own words, but he was uneasy. It unnerved him how few people were in attendance, and the extreme secrecy of the burial. *I need to make the best of this,* he thought. *It is our moment to serve our pharaoh.*

He placed the Anubis mask over his head. Once again, it felt heavy as it settled like a metal weight upon the bridge of his nose. It was stifling again inside the mask, and the black color of it did not help. The black of Anubis wrestled all of the heat of midday down inside the mask and the heat cloud surrounded Nebamun as he tried to move.

He could barely see; the eye slits of Anubis seemed much narrower today, such that they were cramping down his view of the world.

Nebamun and Padi gently lifted the gilded wooden pallet holding the small coffin of the Osiris, the stillborn daughter with no name. They climbed down from the boat, down the steep, creaking plank and onto the dock.

The two priests transferred the stillborn girl's remains onto a much larger golden carrying table, which was supported on all sides by coffin bearers. They easily lifted the table and held it aloft on their shoulders.

Nebamun and Padi fell in behind the bearers and the small procession turned to make its way up into the valley. They wound their way through the tortuous passage and stopped at the entrance to the royal necropolis.

Four men, powerfully built soldiers of pharaoh's private guard, stepped forward to lead the funeral procession.

"Do you know where we are going Great One?" Padi asked. "I would feel better knowing the destination."

"No, Padi, I know as little as you about where our Osiris is to be buried. The location has been kept secret, even from me."

"Strange is it not? One would think we would be told first, before all others, except pharaoh, of course."

"Yes, indeed it is strange, but I am certain pharaoh has good reasons for keeping the location a secret, even from us," Nebamun answered. "Padi, we must keep our mind on our task."

"Yes, Great One. It is not every day a royal is buried, and we are an important part of it," Padi said, smiling.

The movement of the funeral procession shattered the stillness of the valley, as the clattering of sandals dislodged small rocks in the narrow path.

This was the home of many dead kings of Egypt, ever since the pyramid tombs had become too visible of a target, too tempting for tomb robbers. Now, the pharaohs built large tombs underground, with many rooms to house their belongings for the afterlife.

The soldiers stopped suddenly, almost too suddenly, as the bearers nearly walked into them. The soldiers talked among themselves, in voices too low to be heard by those around them.

They were standing in front of a doorway cut into the white limestone, with steps leading down a passage into the murky darkness.

"Is this it?" Padi asked quietly. "Is this the tomb for the royal daughter? Surely this cannot be."

"It must be so," Nebamun replied. "I have heard of the pharaohs disguising their tombs to look as those of the common people, in order not to be robbed. But, this is far too ordinary for a royal, even a small stillborn princess."

Nebamun turned around to view the faces of others in the procession, to see if they were as surprised as he was.

"Padi, my friend, we have even fewer people with us now. It seems many have turned and gone back to Waset."

Padi turned to take in the few remaining people in the funeral party. All of the mourners were gone. In addition to Nebamun and Padi, all that remained of the tiny procession were the servants carrying food offerings for the girl, a few soldiers, and pharaoh and his queen inside the carrying chair.

"Perhaps Tutankhamun and Ankhesenamun prefer a more intimate burial, Nebamun," Padi said. "I am certain they are still grief stricken and may not want to be seen by everyone in the city."

"Yes, I am sure you are right, Padi. In any case, it will be far easier with fewer people inside that small tomb."

The bearers lowered the carrying chair, and the curtains parted, revealing the passenger.

"Ay," Nebamun said. "Padi, it is not our pharaoh, but only his representative, and a poor one at that."

"Great One, do not speak so loudly. He will hear. He hears everything, I am told," Padi said.

"Do not worry yourself, my friend. He is only concerned with himself at the moment," Nebamun answered.

One of the vizier's unfortunate litter bearers lay down, prostrate upon the ground, to be a human stepping stone as Ay moved down from the litter.

"So Ay, where is your companion, the good general Horemheb?" Nebamun asked. "This trick is not complete without the both of you present. I am certain he would not want to miss the ceremony, and what comes after."

"What do you mean, my friend?" Padi asked. "What trick is this?"

"Nothing, Padi," Nebamun said. "You must be a little disappointed at not seeing your beloved pharaoh and his queen."

"Yes, in truth, I am," Padi answered. "But I am certain they have their reasons for not attending the funeral of their daughter."

Ay came toward the two priests. The vizier wore his finest white linen kilt today, and his naked chest was draped in a gold collar, lined with black onyx. The collar did little to hide his aged breasts which hung flaccid and lifeless underneath it.

Ay smiled at the priests, but there was no friendliness in his expression, only a grim determination.

"Horemheb is in Asia, with his army. He knows nothing of what transpires today," Ay said. "So now, high priest Nebamun, let us talk, for once again, I have an important task for you."

Ω Ω Ω Ω Ω

Thirty Seven

"Where is our pharaoh, Tutankhamun, and Ankhesenamun, the queen," Nebamun asked. "Surely, they must desire to send their daughter into the afterlife with their blessing in person, yes?"

"You have seen Tutankhamun," Ay replied. "You have seen how ill he is, far too ill to make the journey into the royal necropolis, at least not yet."

"What do you mean, not yet?" Nebamun asked. "What is it you are keeping to yourself, Ay?"

"Only that I fear our pharaoh does not have long for this world," Ay answered.

"But what of the queen; how is she and why is she not here for her daughter?" Padi asked. "There must be some member of the family present."

Ay looked irritated, but disguised it quickly. "The queen remained with pharaoh, since his health is so perilous. She felt there was no more she could do for her daughter, but much more could be done for her husband, so she stayed behind. As for a family member, consider me family."

"You mentioned you have an important task for us," Nebamun said, changing the subject. "What more can we do to be of service to our pharaoh?"

"Come, let us bury the small one, and then we can talk," Ay said, commanding the soldiers, with a quick forward movement of his hand.

The soldiers lit their torches and a brilliant flame illuminated the stairway down into the tomb. The procession started walking again, each person carefully stooping down to access the small opening.

They proceeded down sixteen narrow steps, touching the irregular rock wall for support.

"This looks as though it was built in a hurry," Nebamun whispered to Padi. "The walls are still uneven in some places, with the plaster just thrown on, as if the men were suddenly interrupted in their work. There is no decoration at all. I do not like this, my friend; this is hardly fitting for a royal person, even a baby."

"Yes, I am certain the royals were surprised by the sudden death of their daughter," Padi said. "They must not have had sufficient time to complete it. Fortunate for us, we at least had a beautiful coffin to contain her remains. I am certain all will be fine, for we have done our best."

"Yes, indeed, we have Padi. You and I always do our best, and I am certain we will be rewarded by Tutankhamun if not in this life, certainly in the next."

They continued down a long corridor and into a rectangular antechamber connected to a much smaller room behind it. The food bearers stopped. Each of the servants placed their food offerings near a standing figure of Osiris.

There were bundles of bread, figs, and small honey cakes; whatever the small princess would want to consume in the afterlife.

After depositing their offerings, the servants turned all in one motion, moving as a unit back up the stairway the way they had come. They stepped out of the darkened tomb and into the brilliant sunlight.

The four soldiers turned and began their ascent up the stairway soon afterwards, leaving only the three men and the litter bearers alone in the tomb. It was a small tomb and even with so few people, it was still very crowded, such that the men stood very close together.

"Now, let us proceed, Nebamun," Ay said, motioning him into the next room. "Now that we are alone with the princess, we can get this over with quickly."

"Your haste is unseemly, Vizier Ay," Nebamun said. "If I did not know better, I would think you did not want to be here at all."

Ay only smiled as they moved into the burial chamber. Most of the tomb so far was unremarkable, plain white plastered walls, some not even smoothed by workmen.

This room was different. Nebamun was struck by the elegantly decorated walls. The walls contained figures rendered in exquisite detail. On one wall, a body lay on a sledge, being pulled by courtiers. On another, twelve baboons crouched, symbolic of the hours of night and day. On still another, a priest clad in panther skin performed the opening of the mouth ritual on a kingly figure.

"This must be our lord, Tutankhamun?" Nebamun said, pointing to the figure. "It is such an excellent likeness, quite unmistakable."

"Yes, it is," Ay responded. "As you say, it is an excellent likeness. I know the artist, and I plan to have him decorate my tomb as well."

"But who is the priest, surely that is not me?" Nebamun asked. "The likeness does not resemble me in the least."

"No indeed, it is not," Ay answered with a slight smile. "Come, the small one is to be buried in this next room. Move quickly and be careful of Anubis" he said, pointing to the single crouched figure of the jackal god, carved in wood and decorated in black plaster, bordered with gold.

They entered a last room, just off of the burial chamber. This room was undecorated and empty, except for a small coffin lying on the ground in a dark corner. The room was so still, the sounds of their footsteps echoed out, a violation in the stillness.

"Just there, place the small one there, next to her sister," Ay commanded, pointing to the furthest dark corner of the chamber.

The litter bearers moved with solemnity and placed the tiny coffin into the corner, on the hard ground.

"*Her sister?*" Nebamun asked incredulously. "This is the first child of Pharoah? This is where she lies, all alone in an unfinished tomb? What a sad ending for a royal daughter."

"Yes, it may be a poorly made tomb, but she will live on in glory in the afterlife. Is this not what we believe? Ay asked.

"Yes, it is as you say," Nebamun answered. "She will live on with all the wealth and happiness she deserves."

"I personally believe we achieve the glory in the afterlife in equal measure to what we had in this life. And that is why these children of pharaoh, who were never given the breath of life, will not live on in the afterlife. This is what I believe."

"That is blasphemy!" Padi shouted. "Sacrilege, how can you say this? You should be punished as a heretic."

"Be silent priest! You do not need to tell me what I should believe. Begin please, Nebamun," Ay commanded.

Nebamun, as Anubis, looked through the papyrus pages of the Book of Coming Forth by Day, and came upon a passage. He began to read:

"Come then, strengthen her breath, O Lord of the winds, who magnifies these divine beings who are like unto thyself; O Lord of the funeral chest. Grant thou that she may enter into the land of everlastingness, according to that which was done for thee."

"A nice passage Nebamun," Ay said. "It seems you are indeed very good at your work."

Nebamun said nothing. It was becoming far too hot in the Anubis mask, stifling almost, but it was not possible for him to take it off. *If it were only Padi and I, I would most certainly give up the Anubis mask,* he thought.

The Vizier headed up the stairway, anxious to leave the confined, dark space of the tomb. Nebamun turned to leave the small room, followed closely by Padi.

"Great One, how dare Ay speak of pharaoh, and how dare he speak to me in this fashion," Padi said. "I cannot understand this."

"Do not try to understand, my friend," Nebamun said. "Think upon the small Osiris, here with her sister, together throughout eternity. Think on the fine work we have done for her today."

As he said this, he turned for a final look at the two small coffins, lying side by side in the dark. *Better they did not live, to see their father die so young,* he thought.

Nebamun stopped close to the tomb entrance and turned to face Padi. The high priest looked at his friend and smiled.

It was a small smile, not of joy and happiness; it was a smile of irony.

"My old friend, it seems we are now to perform our last task for pharaoh," he said. "Our work will soon be complete and we can rest."

"What do you mean, Great One?" Padi asked. "What more is there to be done?"

He moved outside, and motioned for Padi to come out of the tomb and into the sunlight. Nebamun removed the mask of Anubis and set it down on the ground.

"I believe I will not become Anubis again in this life, Padi," Nebamun said, wiping the rivulets of sweat running down from his hairline to his cheeks.

The four soldiers were standing still, their once white kilts now stained a dark crimson. Their knives were poised as if to strike, frozen in the middle of violent action. The men's faces were sweaty from the effort of what they had just performed.

The food bearers were strewn about on the ground, lying in defensive positions in a vain attempt to ward off the showering of the knife wounds which had taken their lives.

Their bodies were covered in blood, a stark contrast to the brilliant sand around them. The perfume cones which once graced the heads of the young women lay crushed and melting, scattering the pungent scent of lotus blossoms into the air.

"What has happened here?" Padi asked the soldiers. "Why have you done this?"

The soldiers remained silent. It was Ay who spoke, his voice toneless and calm.

"Before the sun sets today, Tutankhamun will be dead,"

he said with no emotion in his voice. "It has been agreed, I am to marry his queen, and since our pharaoh is without an heir, I will succeed him as pharaoh."

"Did pharaoh agree to this?" Nebamun asked. "I do not believe it possible."

"Tutankhamun is far too ill to agree to anything," Ay said. "It was the queen, Ankhesenamun who agreed to it. She had to be persuaded, of course."

"*Persuaded? And how exactly did you persuade her, she who is beloved of pharaoh?*" Padi asked.

"I do not have to answer to one of your lesser priests, Nebamun," Ay said. "I do not, in fact, have to answer to you either. I suggest you keep your man silent, lest I cut out his tongue. Now, I must do what is necessary so that history can move on."

"What do you mean, what is necessary?" Nebamun asked. "Was it necessary to murder the food bearers? They were just simple slaves. I do not see the sense in it."

"You believe we have just exited the tomb of the young princesses, do you not?" Ay asked.

"You are going to tell me the tomb is for someone else, are you not, vizier, or should I call you pharaoh?" Nebamun asked.

"No vizier for now is fine, but yes, the tomb is for someone else. I was building the tomb for myself, but now, Tutankhamun will reside there," Ay said. "He has but hours left on this earth. It took some doing to change the decoration on the walls to accommodate him."

"So, the priest figure on the walls is not me, but it is you, Ay," Nebamun said.

"Indeed, you are correct. Who should attend pharaoh, but his closest advisor, and the next pharaoh of Egypt," Ay said triumphantly, placing his fist upon his chest.

"So, vizier, what of us? What happens to Padi and I?" Nebamun asked.

"I believe you know the answer to that, high priest," Ay said. "You and your entire party, foodbearers, litter bearers, and of course your rude friend and yourself must die."

"What, why?" Padi asked. "Why would you kill us? We have done nothing but serve the will of pharaoh and the gods."

"The high priest knows why," Ay answered. "You do know what your final duty is, do you not, Nebamun?"

"Padi, we cannot know the location of the royal tomb of pharaoh and live to tell about it," Nebamun said.

"Yes, that is the truth," Ay said. "It is the last duty for you to perform for your pharaoh. You must think of it as an honor."

Ay motioned to his soldiers, who assembled the litter bearers and instructed them to kneel in the sand. The litter bearers knew there was no escape for them, and so they waited, resigned to a swift death.

The soldiers sliced their throats quickly, and the litter bearers fell to the ground. Their blood seeped onto the scorched earth and became absorbed by the sand and gravel. One man moved slightly, in an effort to hold on to the last few moments of his life, and then he was still.

"Your time has come to die," Ay said to the Nebamun and Padi. "Do you have anything to say?"

Padi shook his head. But Nebamun began to speak from

the Book of Coming Forth by Day, words that he knew without reading, from his heart:

"Hail, ye gods who tow along the boat of the Lord of Millions of Years, who bring it over the sky of the Duat, whose hands hold the steering poles and guide it straight, who grasp tightly your paddles.

Avenge me, destroy ye the enemy and he who would do evil unto me, set him under my feet forever and ever. Thus shall the boat rejoice, and the Great God shall travel on his way in peace.

The place which is closed is opened. The place which is sealed is sealed. Let you gaze upon my earthly body, may it neither perish, nor be destroyed, forever and forever. I have made my name to be remembered. O all you gods, and all you spirits, prepare a path for me."

Ay looked at Nebamun, his eyes showing a small glimmer of respect for the man who would be Anubis, the man who he would now silence forever.

But just as quickly, the glimmer was gone, replaced by a look of greed and power. This greed and power would carry the vizier almost through to the end of the eighteenth dynasty.

Horemheb, as the designated successor to pharaoh, on his return from Asia, would find his position usurped by the aggressive vizier. Ay would be married to Anhesenamun, become pharoah and place himself firmly on the pages of history.

That history would later be rewritten when Horemheb succeeded him as pharaoh and chiseled out Ay's name from the stones it was carved upon, and destroyed the former vizier's monuments in revenge.

For now, this was Ay's moment in history as he motioned for the two priests to kneel.

Nebamun and Padi knelt in the sand, and with one last look at each other, they bowed their heads.

"Farewell my friend," Nebamun said. "I hope that the new embalmers begin with us, and do their work well.

$$\Omega\ \Omega\ \Omega\ \Omega\ \Omega$$

Thirty Eight

"So, how did you come into so much money suddenly?" Chief Hamadi asked. The police chief of Luxor was an extremely fat man, whose body was squeezed into an old uniform much too tight for him. Now, a button had popped off of his shirt, and his flesh squeezed out, released as if from bondage.

Thanks to the sudden ability to purchase goods to improve their lives, the Abd el Amun brothers attracted attention in the poor village of Gourna. They now found themselves sitting in the police station in Luxor.

The brothers said nothing, just stared at the filthy floor. Abdul began to count the brown roaches as they scurried across at his feet.

"We have been working many hours," Karim said. "We are laborers.

"Yes, yes, I'll bet you have been working many hours," Hamadi said. "But I'm quite sure you aren't laborers. You have a chance to help yourselves. Are you going to tell me what you have been doing?"

"I really don't have any idea what you are talking about," Karim said.

"Suit yourself," Hamadi said. "These are my deputies, Fadil and Masud. They will take good care of you while you are here."

He motioned to the two men who looked up, their eyes red from cigar smoke.

"Stop drinking your tea, and take them away. Put the quiet one in the hot box for now. I will handle this one personally. Karim, isn't that what you said your name is?" the chief asked.

Karim nodded, determined not to show fear in his face, as he watched the men lead Abdul away. Karim wasn't afraid for himself; he was afraid Abdul would tell the men the location of Deir el Bahari, the tomb that had made them both rich.

The officers led Abdul outside into the blazing sunlight. There were six large black steel containers sitting on the ground. Their doors were open and they moved slightly in the light breeze. In a few hours, that breeze would be gone, replaced by hot, stale air.

"Go ahead, pick whichever room you like best," Fadil said. "We don't have any tenants at the moment, so you have your choice."

"Sorry about not having a view," Masud said, laughing. "But at least you won't be distracted from coming up with an answer for us."

"Yes, and you better be quick about it, or you will turn into one of those mummies you've been stealing," Fadil added.

Abdul went into the farthest steel container, wanting to stay in the fresh air as long as possible. He resisted the urge to cry; he didn't want to give his captors the satisfaction. The inside walls were dark black, just like the outside, guaranteed to provide maximum heat and sun exposure. Even with the door open, it was already very hot inside the enclosure.

Without a word, the officers slammed the door shut, and Abdul could hear one of them putting a key in the padlock and locking the door. He heard muffled voices as the men walked away.

Now, Abdul was alone in the pitch blackness. The air was stifling, and he began to breathe rapidly. He tried to slow his breathing down, to conserve his oxygen, but he knew that wasn't going to happen. He knew, by the time the officers came back and opened the door, he would either be unconscious, or dead.

Chief Hamadi had taken Karim into a large interrogation room. There were reddish brown stains on the walls and floor, and vicious looking hooks hanging from the ceiling, whether they were there just for effect, or whether they were actually used, Karim did not know.

"Now, will you tell us how you came into the large sum of money you've been spending?" Hamadi asked.

"I am telling you, I don't know what you are talking about," Karim answered.

"Come now, I know that you have been engaging in a little tomb robbing, haven't you, Karim Abd el Amun?"

"No, I swear on my mother, I don't know what you are talking about."

"Then, your mother must be a whore," Chief Hamadi said.

"Go to hell," Karim answered back.

"I believe you will get there long before I do, Karim," Hamadi said. "I gave you a chance, a chance that you chose not to take. Ah, well, we must begin, I'm afraid. Strip him," He ordered to the two junior officers.

Fadil and Masud complied with the order, and ripped Karim's newly purchased clothing from his body. They seemed to take great delight in tearing the rich fabric into as many pieces as possible. Karim looked with dismay at the pile of cloth he had paid so much money for.

"Why so sad?" Fadil asked. "This is just the beginning my friend."

"Yes, indeed Karim," Hamadi agreed. "You will not need such fine clothes where you are going. It seems you have been eating well with your newly acquired wealth. Not spent it all on whores."

Karim was heavier; his once very visible ribs were now covered with a thin layer of fat from the beer and roasted pork he had been eating over many months. He had decided after finding Deir el Bahari that he would no longer deny himself. He would eat, drink and do whatever he wanted.

Chief Hamadi tied Karim's hands together and Fadil and Masud lifted him up and suspended him by his roped hands from one of the hooks in the ceiling. Karim swung slightly, his arms stretched out above him.

"Do you know what I am going to do to you?" the Chief asked.

"No, I have no idea, and I still have no idea what you are talking about," Karim answered defiantly.

"You lie! You know that you have pillaged our ancient dead for your own benefit, and now you must pay the price for what you have done to our ancestors, my friend," Hamadi said.

"Oh, and what price is that? Know that I am not afraid and I can take whatever punishment you decide to give."

"Well, you know Karim," Hamadi began in a conversational tone. "In ancient times, the authorities did not always kill people. Sometimes they put them into community service and made them raise an entire town or build walls around the town where they were from, or where they committed the evil act. The ancient town of Bubastis was raised in such a way."

"Fascinating, can we get on with it?" Karim said with a sneer. "I am tired of your conversation. I would rather die than listen to more of your babble."

"As I was saying," Chief Hamadi began again, "Community service was one form of punishment, but there were many others. I have something more special in mind for you."

"Will you stop talking? You are a punishment to my ears."

"To continue," the Chief started in again. "Back almost seven hundred years ago, there was a great famine, all over Egypt. So bad in fact, people began to eat each other. Children were especially vulnerable."

"What does this have to do with me?" Karim asked. "As I said, I am very tired of your conversation. Why don't you just get on with it?"

"You are in too much of a hurry, Karim," Chief Hamadi answered. "We have all the time in the world. Now, as I was saying, things got so bad, parents would even eat their own children."

"Again, what does this have to do with me?"

"I'm getting to that, you must be patient," the chief said

in a soothing voice. "As the story goes, the streets were full of people selling boiled or roasted children. There is a story of a man seeing five children's heads simmering in a pot filled with spices."

Chief Hamadi stood directly in front of Karim. The chief's face looked puffy and bloated, but his eyes were full of menace.

"Now, if a parent was found guilty of killing his child, he was required to wear the corpse of his dead baby around his neck for three days and three nights, in full view of everyone, including his guard; a gruesome custom, but effective."

The chief shifted a little on the hard floor and grabbed Karim's chin in his hand.

"So my thieving friend, if a parent or anyone else was found eating human flesh, they would be burned alive," Hamadi continued.

Karim did not interrupt this time. He was too interested in how this conversation was going to end. He had suddenly grown fearful as to what the chief of police had in mind for him.

"What? Nothing to say?" the chief said, as if reading Karim's mind. "I have a combination of ancient punishments in store for you, my friend."

"Stop calling me your friend. You are not my friend, Chief whatever-your-name-is," Karim said.

"Bring me the whip," Hamadi said smiling. "You know, the specially made one, made for special people, like Karim here."

The junior officer crossed to a cabinet and opened a drawer. He pulled out a long whip of twisted leather, each one its nine tails ending in a viciously sharpened point made of reeds.

"I see you have noticed my whip," Hamadi said, smiling again. "It is made out of hippopotamus hide, much the same as our ancient ancestors used. I thought it fitting."

"Thank you for the history lesson, Hamadi," Karim said. "Just get on with it, why don't you?"

"Defiant to the end, aren't you, Karim?" Hamadi continued. "If a man was known to have killed his parent, a portion of his punishment was to be whipped with sharpened reeds, like so," Chief Hamadi said as the whip made contact with Karim's bare skin. The chief was an expert at his craft, and made practiced movements with the whip. Each contact resulted in bloody shreds of skin being torn from Karim's body.

Through Karim's agonized screaming, chief Hamadi just kept smiling. He smiled even as his junior officers looked away from the mass of shredded skin swinging wildly now from the hook in the ceiling.

"Now, if a man was known to have robbed a tomb in ancient times, his hands were cut off," Hamadi said, mostly to himself, since Karim had long sinced lapsed into unconsciousness.

"Should we cut him down now, chief?" Fadil asked.

The chief nodded and with one long swipe of a sword, Karim was free from his tether and fell heavily to the floor.

"Wake him," Hamadi commanded. "And then hand me that sword."

Masud grabbed a large clay container filled with a few days worth of the three men's urine. By now, the yellow liquid was cloudy and emitted the stench of ammonia. He dumped the container onto Karim, lying unconscious on the floor.

Karim stirred slightly and opened one eye to stare up at the sword descending down upon his right hand, cutting it off at the wrist. Karim screamed wildly and tried to protect his left hand from the blade, but he was too late as the blade neatly severed his other appendage.

He screamed and screamed, but Hamadi only smiled.

"Now, will you tell me the location of the tomb, or do I have to kill you?" he asked. "This is your last chance, my friend."

"Kill me. I will not tell you, you son of a whore," Karim whispered.

Chief Hamadi went outside for a moment and came back carrying another clay container, but this one was not filled with urine. He dumped the container of oil over Karim's body, and for a few seconds, Karim felt comforted by the slick liquid quenching his skin.

It was only for a few seconds. Chief Hamadi lit a match and tossed it onto Karim's drenched body. Amid the screams of agony of a man on fire, Hamadi merely smiled and went out.

Ω Ω Ω Ω Ω

Thirty Nine

Abdul had no idea how long he had been sitting in the hot steel box, in the dark. He was sure he had spent most of the time unconscious. So now, when he finally heard the key in the lock, and the door finally open, he wasn't sure if he was dreaming. He squinted as the sunlight flooded into his eyes.

"Wake up, Abdul," Hamadi said cheerfully. "It's time to come out now."

Abdul staggered to his feet, his knees aching from being in a crouched position. He was covered in dirt, mixed with sweat. His once fine clothes, bought with his newly found riches, clung to him like a burial shroud.

"You are a dirty one," Hamadi said. "You are almost unrecognizable, just like your brother. Come, I've got something to show you."

Abdul crawled out of the steel box, his legs shaking as he tried to stand up. He fell into a crumpled heap on the ground. The junior officers picked him up roughly and shoved him forward.

He had a sudden feeling of dread as the officers led him into the same interrogation room Karim had entered days before. Abdul noticed the reddish brown stains on the walls and floor and the way they seemed to run together to form one huge block of baked color.

He noticed the hooks hanging from the ceiling and the way they hung there motionless, like the threads of a spider's web. The interrogation room looked humble and unpretentious, designed for one simple purpose, to get information.

Abdul had already resigned himself to give the chief whatever information he wanted. If he did, the chief might be kind to him and let him go, he reasoned.

It was then that he noticed something lying on the floor in a corner, at some distance away, as if it had crawled there to die. He moved closer to try and make out what it was.

It could hardly be seen as a man; it looked more like a large piece of charred meat lying on the floor. Abdul squinted again, not sure if his eyes were playing tricks on him. He knelt down next to it, to get a better look at what was in front of him. He held his sleeve to his nose, the stench was staggering.

It was Karim. His feet were still tied together, but where his hands should have been, there were only two knobs of flesh.

That was not the worst of it. Most of his outer skin was blackened beyond recognition, the skin hanging in long, charred strips off his exposed bone.

There were no recognizable features left on Karim's face. His mouth, nose and ears had long since burnt off, and his eyes had exploded from the heat. Still, Abdul knew it was his brother.

Abdul looked over at the only chair in the room. Hanging

from the back of the chair was a long, braided leather whip ending in nine strands. At the end of each strand was a piece of glass, now covered in his brother's blood and tissue. He knew Karim had been beaten with it, and then set on fire while he was still alive.

Chief Hamadi initially stood at a distance, waiting for Abdul to take it all in. But now, he moved towards Abdul. Hamadi was not menacing, there was no need for that now. Instead, the chief looked sympathetic, almost comforting as he clasped his hand on Abdul's shoulder and leaned in to whisper something in his ear.

"And so, who have you been selling your treasure to?" Hamadi asked. "You can tell me, and things will go easier for you. Just tell me his name."

"Rahmad, his name is Rahmad."

$$\Omega\ \Omega\ \Omega\ \Omega\ \Omega$$

Forty

"I have never seen this man before," Rahmad said, his face a mask of innocence. "I don't know what he has told you, but it is false. I am nothing more than a dealer in souvenirs. I sell copies of ancient keepsakes, to tourists, you know."

"And you swear, you only sell legally, nothing stolen from the tombs," Chief Hamadi asked. "If you are lying to me, I will find out."

"Yes, I swear," Rahmad said. "Please, come in and check my shop if you don't believe me. I have nothing to hide."

Rahmad had heard of the arrest of Abdul and Karim, and he knew it was only a matter of time before the police would be coming to question him; so, he removed every trace bit of evidence linking him to the tomb robbers. He felt magnanimous and generous as he invited them in, knowing they would find nothing.

"There is nothing here," Hamadi said after poking through a few dusty corners. He was far too lazy to do a thorough search, as Rahmad guessed.

"I told you," Rahmad said with a smile. "I am just a poor souvenir dealer."

"And you have never seen this man before? Look closely

at him. He says his name is Abdul Abd el Amun, and he lives in Gourna."

Rahmad moved closer to Abdul and looked him straight in the eyes. The shopkeeper was an expert at deception and gave no indication of recognition. Even to Abdul, it seemed they had never met before.

"No, I tell you, I do not know him," Rahmad said. "But I have heard of tomb robbers from Gourna, and their name came up. There are two of them, I've been told, brothers, yes?"

"Well, yes, however the brother, Karim, has met with an unfortunate accident," Hamadi said.

"*Oh?* What sort of accident?" Rahmad asked, with a smile on his face.

"It doesn't matter," the chief said, suddenly anxious to leave. "Sorry to have troubled you. We won't be back."

"That is quite alright, no problem," Rahmad said. "Always a pleasure to help the authorities any way I can." He shut the door quickly. *God is good*, he thought.

Chief Hamadi, his two officers and Abdul made their way from Rahmad's shop out to Deir el Bahari, sailing in a small felucca across the Nile. Abdul was tired. He had just seen his brother viciously tortured and murdered, and for what?

If only Karim had just told them what they wanted to know, he would still be alive, he thought. After seeing his brother's body, mangled and charred almost beyond recognition, Abdul resolved to tell the police whatever they wanted to know. They would find out eventually anyway.

"So, you are not quite as foolish as your brother, it seems,"

Hamadi said, as if reading Abdul's mind. "We may find a place for someone like you, we will see. There is always employment for a man who helps us."

Abdul felt encouraged, and for the first time in a long while, he smiled.

"I would like to do honorable work," Abdul said. "It was always my brother who wanted to rob the tombs. I knew it was wrong all along, but I went along with him. What else could I do?"

"I understand completely," the chief said, nodding. "Sometimes you get forced into doing what you don't want to do, but that life is over for you now. If you help me, I will help you."

"I want to do what is right, for once," Abdul said. "Now that my brother is dead, I feel free. I guess there is some good to come of his death."

"Yes, indeed. Your brother was a bad man," Hamadi said. "You are well rid of him."

The felucca glided silently next to the dock, and Abdul jumped out. He watched as the obese police chief lunged out of the boat, followed by the two junior officers.

"Now, we must walk for awhile to get to the tomb entrance. This way," Abdul said, pointing to the remnants of a rudimentary path.

The irregular path sloped up and to the right, past large limestone boulders, baking in the sun. Chief Hamadi, accompanied by his two deputies, and Abdul struggled up the slope and continued on for some time before anyone spoke.

"This is it," Abdul announced, pointing down into the large black hole.

"Doesn't look like much of an entrance," Hamadi said. "Good thing you told us we needed rope, Abdul, otherwise it wouldn't be possible to get down in there."

"Yes, that's how Karim and I did it," Abdul said.

"Well, then that's how we will do it," the chief said. "Let's get moving, shall we?"

They expertly secured one end of the long rope around a large boulder, making a firm triple knot and pulling it taught.

"Ready?" Hamadi asked Abdul. "You go first, my friend."

Abdul nodded and grasped the rope. He slid his way down into the now familiar blackness, landing lightly on the ground below.

Fadil and Masud came next, their faces apprehensive as they too slid down into the dark. The chief was last, and with his great bulk, he crashed down onto the ground, the noise shattering the quiet of the tomb.

The three policemen each lit a torch and stared into the large chamber. Dust hung in the air, and danced in the dim light.

"What's that?" Hamadi asked. "That doesn't look very ancient to me."

"That is my mother. She fell from the rope and landed there," Abdul explained. "Her name was Satre."

Satre lay exactly as the brothers had left her, so many months before. Her bones were there, but the fat and flesh were all gone, eaten away by insects.

"We will move her out of here, so she can have a proper burial, if you like," Hamadi said.

"Yes, I would like that very much," Abdul said, wiping a muddy tear from his cheek. "Karim just wanted her body to be left down here."

"As I said, your brother was a bad man. We will take care of her, when we move the royal mummies out to the museum," the chief said.

Abdul decided it was best not to mention that his mother had been murdered by Karim. *Why give the police an excuse for killing him?* He thought. *I want them to feel bad about what they've done to him at least.*

"The mummies to the front are the common ones, less valuable," Abdul explained. "Karim and I didn't take much from here. The more valuable mummies are further back."

"Well, by all means, let's move to the back," Hamadi said. "I would like to see what all the mystery is about."

Abdul led the three policemen further into the tomb, past the common mummies, some interred with their personal items, combs, cosmetic pallets, furniture, but most were lying there with not a single item for company.

"So, do you suppose these mummies are just wandering about in the afterlife, then?" Fadil asked.

"Who knows?" Masud answered. "I don't believe I'm going anywhere when I die. I'll just be dead, that's all. What do you think, chief?"

"I think people get what is coming to them," the chief said. "If they are good, they will have peace, like Abdul here. But if they are bad, like his brother, Karim, they will go to hell. I do believe in hell, not the fire and brimstone kind, but a hell made up of what each person hates most in life."

"What do you mean?" Abdul asked.

"Well, I will give you an example," Hamadi explained. "What did your brother hate most in this world?"

"Two things. He hated being poor, and he hated our mother; he hated her most of all."

"Well then, hell for your brother will be like going to a feast where all are served a bountiful meal, and he is served nothing," Hamadi said. "Oh and he has to sit next to your mother throughout eternity."

Fadil and Masud laughed, but Abdul did not. It was all too real for him to imagine his dead brother and mother spending eternity together. *But who will I spend eternity with?* He thought.

"Look around," Abdul said. "This is what we came here for."

"This is indeed the lost treasure of Egypt," the chief said. "The dead are all over the place, and all royals."

The men were surrounded by mummies, all with their arms crossed over their chests, hands curled, as if holding the crook and the flail, symbols of royalty. Many still had precious amulets peeking out from under their wrappings. Several still had golden finger stalls on the nails of their hands.

"Fantastic!" Hamadi shouted. "Truly fantastic! Abdul, I will bring my wife's uncle down here. He is a caretaker with the Egyptian museum. I will consult with him about moving these royal mummies into the museum. We will also move your mother, as I promised, so that you may bury her."

"What about me?" Abdul asked tentatively.

"Oh yes, well, you my friend, I will find you a job in the museum also. How would you like to be the caretaker of the royal mummies?"

"I can think of nothing I would like better," Abdul said, with a big smile. "I would like to take care of them as if they are my own family."

"I am sure you will do very well, Abdul," Hamadi said.

"This way, you will see your mummies every day, and look after them. You will make sure no more harm comes to them."

"Yes, my family put them through enough already," Abdul said. "Now it is my turn to atone for what Karim did to them."

Abdul looked down at the royal mummies and riches of Egypt scattered at his feet. He felt satisfaction and a sense of peace. *Finally, they will get the care that they deserve, and I get to do something honorable with my life,* he thought.

What Abdul could not know was that among the mummies they would transport in the coming weeks were those of two priests, one a lesser priest, and one a high priest who put on the heavy black mask of Anubis so many centuries ago.

Ω Ω Ω Ω Ω

Forty One

"So, Dunthorpe, how did you find Egypt?" Lord Hampstead asked, as he stabbed at the large, bloody portion of roast beef in front of him. "Tell us all about it."

"Yes, do tell," Lady Hampstead agreed. "We must know all. Charley and I may travel there next year."

Lord Charles Hampstead and Lady Evelyn Hampstead were from one of the oldest and wealthiest families in Sussex. They were now the caretakers of the "old money" left to them by Charles' father, Sir Lawrence Hampstead, and his father before him, Sir Anthony Hampstead. No one really knew where the Hampstead money came from. It was enough for the current Hampsteads to know that the money belonged to them now.

Edward and Mary Dunthorpe felt privileged to be friends with the Hampstead's, and tonight their wealthy friends were staying for dinner. After dinner would come the usual glasses of port and cigars for the men and talk of fashion for the women.

"You know, Charley, it was fantastic, truly," Edward said, helping himself to the limp, overcooked green beans. "Mere words don't do the place justice, how magnificent and ancient everything was. We tend to think England has a rich history, but believe me, we are a pale comparison."

"Speak for yourself, Edward. I couldn't wait to get out of there and back to England. I would prefer our good old English history over those uneducated fools and their scratching around in the dirt. Let us toast to England," Mary said, holding up her glass of red wine.

"My dear, you are far too harsh," Edward answered, ignoring her request for a toast. "They are anything but uneducated. They put us to shame with their knowledge of mathematics and engineering," Edward countered.

"That may be so, husband, but I'm still happy to be home, in our comfortable house, surrounded by our rose garden, instead of surrounded by never ending sand and dirt."

"Be fair, Mary." Edward said, "Did you not find the sun and heat wonderful when compared to our countless days of clouds and rain?"

"No, believe me, our cloudy, rainy skies are a gift from God," Mary said. "Egypt was an inferno, so hot I could feel my brains boiling inside of my skull."

"Well, tell us about your cruise, how was it?" Evelyn asked, anxious to change the subject. "And the shopping, was it all you imagined?"

"The cruise was pleasant, with the cool breezes from the Nile." Mary conceded. "And our stateroom was decent and clean. The food was good, but the service was incredibly slow. I had to chastise the waiter more than once for the poor service."

"But, what about the temples of Luxor; surely you must have enjoyed the temples?" Evelyn asked.

"Oh yes, they were very interesting," Mary agreed grudgingly. "But there were abhorrent tourists everywhere. Evelyn, honestly, I couldn't wait to get back to the ship."

"They probably felt the same about us, my dear," Edward said. "I'm afraid one cannot go to Egypt without encountering hordes of curious foreigners. As for me, I loved everything entirely."

"But what about the shopping; what did you buy?" Evelyn asked. "Did you bring home anything exotic and mysterious?"

"Yes, Edward, old chap, show us something exotic and mysterious," Charley said with a wink at his wife. "I'm finished with dinner. How about you, my dear?" he asked his wife.

"Oh yes, who can eat when there is such excitement!" Evelyn replied. "Yes, by all means show us what you brought back with you."

"As you wish my friends," Edward said, taking Mary's arm. "Prepare yourselves. We brought back some wonderful things."

They proceeded into the study, a space crammed with curiosities from many parts of the globe.

"This is the first thing I bought," Edward said, proudly holding up a rectangular glass case.

"My god, man, what is that; some old ratty arm of a dead Egyptian?" Charley asked. "What on earth are you going to do with it?"

"My point exactly," Mary chimed in. "What *are* you going to do with it, Edward?"

"It's my own piece of history," Edward replied. "You said you wanted to see something exotic and mysterious, well, here you are."

"Never mind about the arm; just look at that beautiful bracelet," Evelyn said. "What is that design, a bird?"

"Rahmad told us it is an ibis," Edward said. "An ibis represents the god Thoth, patron god of the scribes of ancient Egypt."

"Who is Rahmad?" Evelyn asked.

"Oh, yes, Rahmad, the shopkeeper we met in Luxor," Edward explained. "Well, I didn't think he was that bad, but Mary couldn't stand the sight of him. Thought he was some illiterate fool, when in fact, the man was quite smart."

"*Smart?* You think so?" Mary said incredulously.

"Yes, yes, I do. He seemed to know quite a lot about ancient Egyptian history actually, a lot more than you gave him credit for, my dear wife."

"You two, how did you get on in Egypt, when all you can seem to do is argue?" Evelyn interrupted, "I think the bracelet is extraordinary, Mary, and with such beautiful turquoise inlay. What a pity you can't wear it."

"I wouldn't want to wear the disgusting thing. The bracelet is beautiful, I agree, but it reminds me of death. I wouldn't want to touch it," Mary said. "And besides, our dear Rahmad told us the arm would turn to dust if we opened the case."

"Yes, ladies, whatever you do, do not open the case, or there will be nothing left but the bracelet," Edward cautioned.

"Come Evelyn, have a look at this," Charley said, holding up a small linen bundle.

"That is our little kitty cat," Edward said. "Just look at those little slanted eyes, and those whiskers, drawn on him thousands of years ago by god knows who. Best of all, we don't have to feed or look after him."

"What's the story with the cats?" Evelyn asked, still looking intently at the bracelet on the mummy arm.

"Rahmad told us cats were the servants of the goddess Bast, and that there was a cult back in ancient times," Edward explained. "Thousands upon thousands of them were killed, mummified, and taken as presents to a place called Per Bast. We call it Bubastis now."

"Never heard of it," Charley said, suddenly bored. "What else did you bring back, old man?"

"Well, Hampstead, how would you like a taste of some powdered mummy? It's good for all kinds of illnesses," Edward said.

"Oh my heavens, you're joking!" Evelyn exclaimed. "I can't imagine such a thing."

"Oh, yes, it's true, I'm afraid," Mary conceded. "Edward seems to be quite taken with it. He drinks it in his whiskey."

"Well, I certainly will have a go at it, Edward," Charley agreed. "I'll have a taste and maybe rid myself of those old aches and pains."

"Good. I'm glad you're with me. Mary thinks I have lost my mind," Edward said. "Do you think so too, Evelyn?"

"Yes, frankly, I do," Evelyn agreed. "Maybe you men can see some sense in it, but we women can't."

"Well, we know that women are smarter anyway, my dear Evelyn," Mary said. "You wouldn't catch me swallowing any of that horrible death powder."

"Nor I," Evelyn agreed. "I want to watch though. I want to see Charley's face when he swallows two thousand year old mummy dust."

"More like three thousand, my dear," Charley said. "Isn't that so, old man?"

"Yes, indeed. Rahmad told us this batch was from new kingdom mummies, around 1300 BC," Edward explained.

"It could be ground up cow horn for all you know," Mary said sarcastically. "How would you ever know? The same goes for that god awful mummy you bought from him."

"*Mummy? Do you mean to say, old chap, you have an entire mummy, here, in your house?*" Charley looked incredulous. "Are you trying to be another Dr. Peabody?"

"Who is Dr. Peabody?" Edward asked.

"You know, that professor of anatomy," Charley said. "Name of Dr. Peabody, used Charing Cross Hospital for his famous mummy unrollings. You remember."

"Oh yes, that was some time ago. People paid good money to see his mummies unwrapped," Edward replied. "Made quite a tidy sum, audience was packed, as I remember."

"And then there was that showman in New York, a Mr. Gleason," Charley continued.

"Oh yes, I heard about him," Edward said. "Seems he made a big production out of unwrapping what he said was a female mummy. When fully unwrapped, his female mummy had a perfectly erect mummified penis."

"Two fine examples," Charley said. "Perhaps you could do the same, old man, assuming your mummy has an erect penis, that is."

"It's time to end this unseemly conversation, thank you," Mary blurted out. "In addition to the horrible mummy powder, Rahmad sold my husband his precious mummy and Edward paid him a small fortune for it."

"I despair of finding a way to get you two to stop arguing," Evelyn said. "Mary, now didn't Edward buy that ring for you in Egypt?"

"Yes, that's right, I did," Edward agreed proudly. "And from Rahmad too. See he wasn't such a bad man."

"Mary, that is quite a beautiful ring," Evelyn said. "What kind of stone is that?"

"It is a carnelian," Mary said, holding out her hand so all could admire the ring fully. "Do you notice the wonderful sun design at the center? Rahmad said it was very old and once belonged to a Hittite or some such person."

"Back to this mummy of yours, Dunthorpe. Can we see it?" Charley asked impatiently.

"What do you think I invited you here for, Hampstead?" Edward asked. "But first, let me mix you some of that dried mummy powder, and we can drink a toast to our new friend, the mummy. Scotch?"

"Yes, old man. Scotch is perfect for this occasion," Charley answered.

Edward poured his finest single malt. Nothing was too good to impress his friend. He smiled with satisfaction as the amber liquid poured into his finest crystal.

"Now, I warn you, Charley, the mummy powder clouds the scotch. Makes it look a bit nasty."

"Thanks for the warning, but I can take the punishment."

Edward smiled and measured out a small spoonful of beige powder and stirred it in to Charley's glass. Immediately the scotch began to bubble and turn opaque brown.

"You weren't kidding old man," Charley said with a wince. "That looks absolutely disgusting, but, as they say, down the hatch."

Charley gulped it down in one swallow and coughed ferociously, almost coughing it back up again.

"Now, Dunthorpe, your turn."

Edward mixed his concoction and downed it in one swallow, but unlike Charley, he was used to the noxious mixture and had a serene look on his face afterwards.

"See, not so bad," Edward said.

"Where have the ladies gotten themselves off to, do you suppose?" Charley asked, his face still red from coughing.

"What was that?" Edward asked.

"What?"

"Didn't you hear it? That cracking sound; Came from the study," Edward said, with a sinking feeling. "I think I know what it is."

Edward and Charley moved quickly into the study, Edward still holding his crystal glass, the inside of which was now smeared with a brown pasty film.

"Mary! What the devil are you doing?" Edward asked.

His wife loosely held a small hammer in one hand, poised for another strike. But it was unnecessary. The glass case lay in pieces on the table, the mummified arm exposed to air. To Edward it looked like it had already begun to wither away. The arm was bare, the bracelet was gone.

"Evelyn wanted to wear the bracelet, and so I thought, why not?" Mary said. "It does look beautiful, don't you think?"

Evelyn stuck her arm out gracefully, and the beautiful turquoise ibis bracelet clung tightly to her wrist.

"Too bad, old man," Charley said. "Sorry about my wife. She does love her jewelry."

"I just couldn't help myself," Evelyn said, laughing. "Here, you can have it back, it's too tight anyway." She reluctantly twisted the bracelet from her wrist and handed it to Edward.

"I guess no harm done," Edward replied. He had spent so much time and effort trying to impress the Hampsteads; he couldn't spoil it now by getting angry.

He gently placed the bracelet back on the withered arm, grimacing as he heard the small cracking sound of bones and dried flesh. The glass case was unusable now, so he placed the ancient arm in the sideboard, right next to Mary's fine crystal stemware.

"My Lord, Edward, does it have to go in there, with my crystal? What are you thinking?"

"You brought it on yourself, my dear." Edward said. "Now, let's all go see the mummy, shall we?"

"Where do you keep it?" Evelyn asked. "Surely, not in the house?"

"Oh my lord no! The house is no place for that, that *thing!*" Mary replied. "We keep it in the stables."

"Yes," Edward said in a resigned voice. "That was the only way she would let me have it. So now, it keeps company with the horses. This way, please."

Edward led them down the garden and into the stables at the back of the manor. He opened the large wooden doors and ushered them inside.

He walked over to a long, rectangular object, covered by a burgundy velvet shroud. Edward solemnly pulled away the shroud and with a theatrical flourish, cast it aside.

"Here he is," He said triumphantly. "Our newest addition to the family. We've not yet given him a name."

"My god, Dunthorpe. There he is indeed." Charley said. "Are you certain he is a man? How would you ever know?'

"Rahmad told us that it was a man, and I've no reason to doubt him," Edward said.

"Do you know how old he is, or anything about him?" Evelyn asked.

"Rahmad told me that he is from what they call the eighteenth dynasty, somewhere around 1320 BC," Edward replied. "He was found in a tomb on the west bank of the Nile, near a place called Gourna."

They looked down at the glass case in wonder. Inside lay a body, expertly wrapped in linen, and covered with a heavy coating of resin.

"Look how perfectly the wrappings surround his body," Evelyn said. "It is as if great care was taken after this man died."

"Yes, indeed, dear," Charley said. "We should all be so lucky."

"He is lucky he was not ground up into mummy powder by Rahmad, if you ask me," Mary said callously.

"But what happened to his face?" Evelyn asked. "It looks as though there is nothing left of it, no chin, no mouth, not even sockets where the eyes were."

"Yes, I must say, Dunthorpe, looks as though you are missing the most important part of him," Charley said.

"Oh, I wouldn't say that," Edward said. "Take a look at his right hand. I don't think even Rahmad, with those greedy eyes of his saw this. Take a look."

He pointed to the right hand of the mummy, where some of the wrappings had fallen away. Charley could see the dark brown skin, dessicated by the ancient embalmers. They had done their work well.

The dead man's hand was curled under, as if still grasping for life. His fingers clutched into a loose fist, and on the smallest finger of the right hand, Charley could see a hint of gold.

"Dunthorpe, don't you want to see what it is?" Charley asked.

"See what *what* is?" Mary asked. "What are you men talking about?"

Mary pushed her way in between the two men, to get a better view of the mummy. She motioned to Evelyn, who came up beside her.

"Edward, let's see what he has on his finger," Mary pleaded. "He certainly won't need it anymore. Let's find out what it is."

"*No*! It's bad enough that he has to spend his eternal rest in our stables," Edward said. "But now you want to take this man's last possession from him."

"I will make you a deal, husband," Mary said. "If you let us remove the wrappings from his hand, just to take a look, I will let you move him into the study, where he can remain. What do you say?"

"Seems like a fair deal, old man, and do you really want your wife mad at you forever, or, for all eternity, as the Egyptians might say?" Charley asked.

"Yes, Edward, let's do have a look at it, please?" Evelyn entreated.

"Well, I can't fight you all," Edward said with a resigned look on his face. "Let's have a look, but let me do it."

He opened the glass case and a light current of air assailed his nostrils. The smell was pungent, like a syrupy, thick smell of tree sap, mixed with an odor of old, dried fabric.

Edward gently lifted the dead man's right hand and

slowly unwound the remaining thin linen strips to expose the skin completely.

The hand was smooth, with skin stretched tight against the bony framework underneath. Even with the dried state of the skin, Edward could tell it was the hand of a young man, possibly a man his own age.

He held up the man's hand to give them all a good view of the source of the glint of gold. It was a small ring, expertly fashioned from the finest gold, and inlaid with a deep, black onyx stone. The figure of a tiny bull etched in gold winked out at them from the center of the stone.

Mary clasped her hands together and smiled.

"I do so love black," she said.

Edward tried to smile. This ancient dead man, faceless, anonymous, and now about to lose his only possession from a life lived long ago. *I suppose it is a small price to pay,* he thought. *Now at least he can come into our house where he belongs.*

Ω Ω Ω Ω Ω

Epilogue in Archaeology

The Pharoah Tutankhamun's broken leg would never heal, and he would live only a few more months. He would die in the year 1323BC, most likely from his injury, exacerbated by malaria, which he had suffered from most of his life.

His reign would be unremarkable and short. He would be entombed, along with his two stillborn daughters and his possessions in a small, unpretentious tomb.

His wife, Ankhesenamun, laid a small wreath of flowers over her husband's coffin, as possibly a last act of devotion to him. These flowers, although dried out, still retained some of their original color when the tomb was opened over thirty two hundred years later.

After her husband's death, Ankhesenamun, in fear of her life, searched for a new husband. She sent a message to the land of the Hittites, asking for a prince to be her husband. The letter read:

"My husband has died and I have no son. They say about you that you have many sons. You might give me one of your sons to become my husband. I would not wish to take one of my subjects as a husband... I am afraid."

The Hittite prince died or was murdered before he could reach her. She married Ay, the former vizier of Tutankhamun, most likely against her wishes. She is lost to history after that. Evidence of the marriage was found in the 1920's, in the form of a ring with cartouches of Ay and Ankhesenamun next to each other, indicating a royal marriage.

The Pharoah Tutankhamun, as unremarkable as he may have been in life, proved to be quite remarkable after his death. His tomb, known as KV (King's Valley) 62 was found in1922, in the Valley of the Kings, known in ancient times as the royal necropolis, by an Englishman, Howard Carter.

The tomb was small, consisting of four rooms. After proceeding down sixteen steps and a long corridor, Carter first reached the room he called the antechamber.

When Carter first entered the antechamber he found golden funeral beds, one shaped in the form of a lion, and the other a cow, battle chariots, loaves of bread and mummified ducks. He also found the spectacular famous golden throne, with figures of Tutankhamun and Ankhesenamun.

Behind the antechamber was a much smaller room, he called the annex. This room was so filled with treasure, Carter and his men had to hang suspended, for there was not even enough room for them to set their feet down.

In this room, Carter found shabti figures, bottles of wine, baskets of produce, and a wooden ceremonial throne gilded in gold, inlaid with ivory and ebony.

To the right of the antechamber, Carter entered the burial chamber, the only room to be decorated. On one of the walls, the figure of Ay can be seen performing the opening of the mouth ceremony for Tutankhamun.

There are also the figures of twelve baboons, indicating the hours of night and day. The intricately detailed designs are rendered in reds, blues and white, all on a muted background of dusty gold. The burial chamber originally contained four gold gilded shrines nestled together, which are now in the Cairo museum.

The final room Carter discovered he called the treasury. The entrance to this room was guarded by a large, wooden statue of Anubis, covered in black plaster and overlaid with gold.

It was in this room that the archaeologist found the mummified female fetuses of what are believed to be the unborn daughters of Tutankhamun and Ankhesenamun. The princesses were each contained in an inner coffin of gold foil, and an outer coffin of wood covered in painted black resin, on which was inscribed "The Osiris." No other names for them were found.

Items found in the intact tomb give an insight into the life of Tutankhamun. Among the artifacts recovered and now on display in the Egyptian museum in Cairo are numerous senet games, some with pieces still set up, as if to play, and two trumpets. There are also chariots, sets of bows and arrows, and weapons.

After recent radiographic analysis of Tutankhamun's remains, evidence indicates he suffered from malaria, had a club foot, cleft palate, and a bad fracture of his lower left thigh. Several walking canes were found in his tomb as well.

The body of the young pharaoh lies at rest inside a beautifully carved red quartzite sarcophagus, and he can be visited today in the Valley of the Kings.

WV23 is the tomb of Ay, former vizier and immediate successor to Tutankhamun. He became pharaoh after his marriage to Tutankhamun's widow, Ankhesenamun, and reigned from 1323 to 1319 BC.

As the number of this tomb indicates, it is in the West Valley, apart from the other tombs. The tomb has two corridors and stairwells, leading to three chambers. As in Tutankhamun's tomb, only the burial chamber is decorated.

Ay is shown with Hathor, Nut and Osiris. There are scenes of Ay hunting flying ducks, and a representation of twelve baboons, just as in Tutankhamun's tomb. The colors are also similar including the rich reds, blues and white, on the gold background. There is speculation that both the tomb of Tutankhamun and that of Ay were decorated by the same artist.

Much of Ay's tomb was damaged in antiquity, perhaps by Horemheb. It is believed that Horemheb should have succeeded Tutankhamun, but his position was usurped by Ay and the vizier's marriage to Tutankhamun's widow. Ay's remains have never been found.

The tomb known as KV 57 is also in the Valley of the Kings, and it is the tomb of Horemheb, Tutankhamun's general and later pharaoh from 1319 to 1292 BC.

In contrast to the tomb of Tutankhamun, this one is quite large, with multiple corridors and stairwells, four main chambers, and nine side chambers.

It is beautifully decorated, with scenes of Horemheb in the company of Anubis, Hathor and Horus. The colors are striking, rich reds, tans, blues and blacks, all executed onto a background of soft grey-blue.

The beautiful tomb of Horemheb is all that remains of him; his mummy also has never been found.

The character of Nebamun, although portrayed as a High Priest of mummification, was actually an Egyptian scribe and "counter of grain" who lived sometime around 1350 BC. He was wealthy, with an elaborately decorated tomb in Thebes, the location of which has been lost.

Many of the spectacular wall paintings were removed from the walls of the tomb by a zealous British collector, who later sold them to the British Museum in 1821. They can still be seen there today.

Among the wall paintings is one titled "Pond in a Garden" and depicts a pond full of fish, surrounded by trees. It is executed in brilliant blues, greens, reds and browns.

Other paintings depict hunting fowl with sticks, and musicians playing the double pipe and clapping, with dancers dancing to the music.

One of the characters embalmed by Nebamun, Iramen and Padi, was Zannanza the Hittite. He was in reality a Hittite prince, son of King Suppiluliuma, who died mysteriously in Egypt in 1324 BC.

Maatkare, the woman wrapped with her pet monkey, was a figure also taken from history. She lived during the 21st dynasty (1075-945 BC). When she underwent radiographic examination, her pet monkey was discovered mummified and wrapped with her.

The remains of these individuals and others were first found in a cache of royal mummies at Deir el Bahari and they are now in eternal rest in the Egyptian museum in Cairo.

The caches of royal mummies at Deir el Bahari were

moved there sometime in the 21ˢᵗ dynasty (1075-945 BC), in an effort to prevent tomb robbery and the desecration of the mummies. In the end, tomb robbers from Gourna found them anyway.

Ω Ω Ω Ω Ω

CPSIA information can be obtained
at www.ICGtesting.com
Printed in the USA
FSOW01n1559040515
6904FS